Bad Blood

Also by Brian McGilloway

Benedict Devlin series

Borderlands

Gallows Lane

Bleed a River Deep

The Rising

The Nameless Dead

Lucy Black series

Little Girl Lost

Hurt

The Forgotten Ones

Bad Blood

A Lucy Black Thriller

BRIAN McGILLOWAY

WITNESS
IMPULSE
An Imprint of HarperCollinsPublishers

Originally published in Great Britain in 2017 by Corsair, an imprint of Little, Brown Book Group.

Digital Edition JUNE 2017 ISBN: 978-0-06-268455-4

Print Edition ISBN: 978-0-06-268457-8

8 9 10 11 12   LSC   10 9 8 7 6 5 4 3 2 1

For Jenny Hewson and Emily Hickman

&

In Memory of Patricia Hughes

Bad Blood

Prologue

THE HALL WAS already packed by the time Detective Inspector Tom Fleming arrived. The air was sweet with perfume and talc and, beneath that, from the farmers still wearing their work clothes, the scent of sweat and the smell of the earth.

The congregation were on their feet, being led in the opening hymn by Pastor James Nixon. Fleming smiled apologetically at those he squeezed past to get to a free seat in the third row from the back. The hymn finished, the assembly took their seats just as Fleming reached his, and settled to listen to the words of Pastor Nixon.

'My brothers and sisters, it is a great honour to be here with you this evening and to see so many of you have taken the time to come and pray with me.' His voice was strong despite his age, a rich baritone still carrying the inflections of his native Ballymena accent.

'But it is a time of great challenge for us all. Daily, all good people face an assault on their morality with the rampant homosexual agenda that assails us and belittles everything we hold to be true and dear. Men of conscience are tried for refusing to make a cake celebrating homosexuality or print leaflets and posters furthering that agenda. And on the other side of the border, the Irish Republic has voted to allow homosexuals to marry, as if two women playing house is no different to the consummated union of a man and a woman. As if it is not a perversion which shames us all.'

A few voices appended his comment with 'Amen'.

Nixon raised his hands, acknowledging their support. 'There are those who would silence me, silence us. They tell us we must accept homosexuals in our town, our shops, allow homosexual bars and public houses to operate on our streets. We must allow sodomites to teach our children and to corrupt our young. We must stay silent while a new Gomorrah is built next to our homes and farms, our shops and schools. They say I am dangerous. They say I preach hatred. They say I should be silent. But I say this: I say that there is no danger in truth. I say that there is no hatred in goodness. And I say that I will not be silent.'

Another chorus of 'Amens' greeted his proclamation, accompanied by a smattering of applause which began at the front and rippled its way through the hall.

'I will not stand idly by as our families are exposed to sin and depravity. I will not countenance the laws of the land being used to protect profane persons, allowing them to indulge their lustful practices, forcing those of us with consciences to humour this lifestyle. It is an abomination. The people who practise it are abominations and, like those before them, they will end in fire and brimstone.'

Fleming glanced around at the others in the congregation. While one or two shifted uncomfortably in their seats, for the most part the listeners sat intently waiting for Nixon to continue.

'Friends, only last week, I read of an African nation – a heathen nation, a Godless nation – who arrested two men for homosexual acts. One of these men was sixteen. Sixteen! And do you know what they did to the pair of them? They stoned them. They took them out of the town and they threw rocks at them until the pair of them were dead. And do you know what I thought? Shall I tell you?'

An elderly lady in the front row called out 'Yes', to the amusement of those around her. Nixon smiled mildly at her, as if indulging her.

'Stoning was too good for those men. Every rock that struck them was a just reward for their sinfulness, their immorality, their ungodly behaviour. Every drop of their blood that stained the ground was a reminder that they deserved to die. It was the wages of their sin!'

Friday

Chapter One

'ROMAN'S OUT!'

THE WORDS WERE written with red paint, each letter almost a foot high, on the gable wall of the house, large enough certainly that Detective Sergeant Lucy Black could read them clearly in the light of her car's headlamps even as she rounded the corner into the Greenway Estate. A small crowd of neighbours was standing on the pavement outside the house, watching as a uniformed officer, notebook in hand, copied down the content of the graffiti. Considering it only consisted of two words, he was taking a suspiciously long time to do so.

'DS Black,' she offered as she approached him. He was a little taller than her, lithe, wiry, with dark brown hair that had curled with length. She noticed in the glare of the street lamp a patch of shiny skin on his cheek, half hidden beneath the length of his sideburns.

'Lloyd,' he said. 'My partner, Constable Huey, is in with the family.'

'So what's the story?'

Lloyd nodded at the letters, as if Lucy had somehow missed them. 'Someone doesn't like Romanians living in the area.'

'Nor Romans, apparently,' Lucy joked.

'What?'

'It says Romans,' Lucy explained. 'Romans are from Rome, not Romania.'

Lloyd stared at her a moment. 'Well, that's useful, Sergeant,' he said.

'Glad to be of assistance, Constable,' Lucy said. She knocked on the front door, then moved into the house. The small hallway gave onto a kitchen to the rear and, to Lucy's left, a lounge. It was here that the family was sitting.

The mother sat at one end of the sofa, leaving a gap between herself and the uniformed officer, whom Lucy assumed to be Constable Huey. On the only other seat in the room – an oversized armchair – sat the father and, balanced on the armrest next to him, their teenage son.

'Good evening,' Lucy said. 'I'm DS Black with the Public Protection Unit. We deal with any incidents involving vulnerable individuals. I'm sorry to see what's been done to your home.'

Huey stood, her relief at having another officer with her clear, and Lucy began to understand why Lloyd was spending so much time out at the wall. 'I'm Constable Huey. We were the first on scene. My partn—'

'I met him,' Lucy said.

'This is Constanta, Andre and Adrian Lupei,' Huey offered, nodding at each in turn as she named them, though the proximity of the father and son meant Lucy wasn't initially clear which was which. 'Would you like a seat? Shall I make tea?' she added before Lucy could refuse. Constanta Lupei rose to help her but Huey raised her hand. 'No, please, Mrs Lupei, I'll make it. I'm sure DS Black would like to hear what you've told me.'

Lucy smiled encouragingly, taking the vacated space on the sofa. 'So, can you tell me what happened? In your own words?'

Constanta looked to her husband who nodded lightly, as if granting permission for her to speak.

'Andre was at work,' she began. 'Adrian was in his room when I heard him shouting. I was in here, with the TV on,' she explained. 'I'd been cleaning the house and wanted to sit,' she added. Lucy nodded, encouraging her to continue, keen not to interrupt.

'I heard Adrian calling and I went out. "There's someone in the garden," he shouted. "I think it's them." I looked out of the window and they were there. Two of them—'

'Three,' Adrian said. 'There was one waiting by the car. The driver.'

'Three,' Constanta agreed. 'They were finishing when they saw me. One came running over and threw the rest of the paint . . . the pot, at the window. Then they ran. Adrian came down and went out after them, but they were already getting into the car.'

'Did you get a good look at any of them?' Lucy asked. 'The one who came to the window?'

Constanta shook her head. 'They had their faces covered,' she said, 'with scarves. Like football scarves.'

'What about you, Adrian? Did you see anything? The make of the car, maybe? Or the colour.'

'I'm not . . . I can't remember exactly. Dark, I think,' he said.

'You didn't notice anything else?'

'Sorry,' Adrian said, bowing his head a little in a gesture Lucy took to be apologetic.

'I take it this isn't the first incident,' Lucy said. 'You told your mother, "It's them again." What else has happened?'

'We just want to be left in peace.' Andre Lupei spoke for the first time. 'We don't want any trouble.'

'I understand that, sir,' Lucy said. 'And you deserve to live in peace.'

'Do you think they'll leave us in peace if they see us talking to you? That man standing out there at the wall in his uniform, letting everyone in the estate know that we reported them to the police.'

'Where do you work, Mr Lupei?' Lucy asked. 'Your wife mentioned you were at work.'

'The hospital,' the man said, his annoyance at her changing the subject reflected in the curtness of his reply. 'In the kitchens.'

'That must be a tough job, feeding all those patients. And staff. Long hours, too, if you were only getting home now.' She glanced to the clock on the mantelpiece. It was gone 10 p.m.

'I finished at eight. It was almost nine by the time I walked down.'

'I can understand how angry you must be,' Lucy said. 'Someone doing this to your home, your family.'

Andre shook his head. 'I'm not angry. I just want to be left alone.'

'So, *has* anything happened before?'

He stared at her, then shook his head. 'They shout some abuse at me, when I'm on my way home from work, sometimes,' he admitted. '*Gypsy* mostly. They know we are Roma.'

'Tell her about the leaflet,' Constanta said, earning only a glare of disapproval from her husband.

'What leaflet?' Lucy asked.

'It's nothing,' Andre began.

'If you want me to help you, I need to know the whole picture,' Lucy said. 'What leaflet, Mrs Lupei?'

The woman glanced again at her husband, but this time, Lucy could sense that she was no longer seeking his permission. She stood and moved across to the mantelpiece. From behind the clock she withdrew a small folded page which she handed to Lucy. It was an A5 sheet. The headline banner read simply 'Warning', while beneath was a Photoshopped picture of people of various ethnic minority groups. Lucy scanned down through the brief text. It referred to the upcoming Brexit vote and the chance to end immigration, before stating, 'Local housing is for local people only!' In the bottom right-hand corner was a hand raised, like the red hand of Ulster, though in the colours of the Union Jack flag. Beside it, in small print, was the name 'McEwan's Printers' and a telephone number.

'Can I hold onto this?' she asked.

Constanta nodded.

'When did you get it?'

'They were posted into all the houses in the area,' Andre said. 'A week ago.'

'That must have been quite unpleasant,' Lucy said.

'For her,' Andre commented, motioning towards his wife. 'It's just talk. That's all.'

The door opened and Constable Huey came in bearing a mismatched set of mugs of tea on a tray. 'I couldn't find sugar,' she said apologetically.

'Have you anywhere else you could stay in the meantime?' Lucy asked.

Andre shook his head. 'This is our home. We put everything into buying this. We have a right to stay.'

'I understand that,' Lucy said, 'but you have your wife and son to think of as well.'

'I am thinking of them,' he said simply. 'What kind of a father runs from bullies?'

Chapter Two

THE SMELL OF gloss paint caught the back of her throat the moment Lucy opened her front door. The hallway carpet had been lifted and the wooden boards beneath exposed and polished. They were covered now in old sheets on which Grace, Lucy's lodger, knelt as she painted the skirting boards.

'Hi,' she offered, not looking up from her work, careful not to smear the wooden floors with the brush, the tip of her tongue poking out the side of her mouth as she concentrated.

'I thought you were working tonight,' Lucy said, stopping to survey the paint job. 'It looks well. I feel guilty you're doing it mostly yourself.'

'My shift finished at seven,' Grace said. 'I'm happy enough; there's a big Gay Pride bash tonight, so it'll be manic busy. The rent's on the table, by the way.'

Grace had been living on the streets when Lucy first met her while investigating a construction gang that had been exploiting homeless people for free labour. Grace had been surviving

on money she earned as a prostitute, working out of an old abandoned building in the city centre. One of her Johns had beaten
her severely enough to leave her in hospital. On her release, Lucy
had suggested that Grace lodge with her. In the months since, the
young girl had got herself a job in a local pub and had not failed
to pay Lucy the agreed nominal rent of £10 per week. To com-
pensate for the paucity of her financial contribution, Grace did as
much work around the house as she could, including leading the
redecorating that Lucy had long ago planned but never managed
to start.

Lucy moved into the living room and lifted the envelope sitting on the table. The top left-hand corner carried a small set of
angel's wings, the logo of the club, Paradise, where Grace worked.
Inside were five ten-pound notes.

'There's too much in here,' Lucy said.

'It's a five-week month,' Grace muttered.

Lucy knew better than to argue. 'Have you eaten yet?'

'There's nothing in.'

Lucy pulled out two of the tenners from the envelope.

'Pizza?'

Grace poked her head around the corner of the architrave she
was painting.

'Always.'

As THEY PARKED outside the pizzeria on Spencer Road, a group
of men disgorged onto the street from the bar opposite. One of
them wore a pair of false breasts over his shirt and a feather boa
around his neck. The others were cheering him on as he downed
the remains of the pint that the doorman had tried to take from
him to transfer into a plastic cup.

Lucy and Grace ordered a large Chicken and Mushroom, then sat on the windowsill inside, waiting for their order. As they did so, the group of men pushed their way into the takeaway.

'Have youse shitters?' one of the men asked.

The cashier nodded without comment towards a door in the far corner marked with a wheelchair sign. The request, it transpired, was for the benefit of the man who'd downed his beer, for he staggered in through the main door and, with his friend's prompting, made a blundering beeline for the toilet. Now in the light, Lucy could see that the man wore eyeliner and lipstick, while someone had drawn a huge beauty spot on his cheek. The cashier watched wordlessly as he made his way past her, then she glanced at Lucy and Grace and raised her eyebrows.

'Lucy!'

It took Lucy a second to recognise the speaker, seeing him so out of context. DS Mickey Sinclair, a member of CID in the city, stared down at her where she sat, bleary eyed but smiling broadly. He wore jeans and a white shirt. Lucy noticed that on one cheek he bore a lipstick kiss that, she guessed from the size, he'd earned from the stag who was currently trying to operate the handle on the toilet door.

'Mickey. Are you—'

'Stag night. Ian there's getting hitched next weekend.'

'Very good.' Lucy smiled. 'Congratulations. To him, obviously.'

Mickey had transferred his attention to Grace. He leaned over, losing his balance as he offered her his hand, with the result that he had to grip Lucy's knee with his other hand to keep himself upright.

'Sorry,' he said, raising both hands in a pantomime of apology. 'Mickey Sinclair.'

'Grace,' she said, managing a light smile, then glancing at Lucy.

'Are you out for the night?' Mickey asked, straightening, in an attempt to appear more sober.

'Just grabbing dinner,' Lucy said.

'That's you,' the cashier called and Grace stood while Lucy pulled the money from her pocket and gave it to her.

'Are you her sister?' Mickey asked Grace, glancing from one to the other as if searching for familial resemblances.

'No. I just live with her,' Grace said. 'Excuse me.'

Mickey straightened again, as if having trouble balancing on the balls of his feet. 'She lives with you?'

The emergence of the stag from the toilets distracted them. He came out fondling his rubber breasts while one of his mates rushed across and started rubbing his groin against the man's leg as he too groped at the rubber.

'She lodges—' Lucy began to explain.

But Mickey had already made up his mind for he raised a finger to his lips and winked at her conspiratorially.

'Goodnight, Mickey.'

'You too, Lucy.' He looked across at Grace, his expression changing. 'You two girls have a good night.'

He watched them leave and, as Lucy climbed into her car outside, he was still watching them through the window, joined this time by two of his friends. Grace fastened her seat belt, then wound down the window and blew them a kiss.

'Who's he? A friend?'

'A colleague,' Lucy said. 'He's—'

'A bit of an asshole,' Grace said, closing the window.

Mickey was still staring after them as Lucy drove back down the street and on towards home.

Saturday

Chapter Three

'THERE'S NO EXPLICIT threat to this family,' DI Tom Fleming, Lucy's boss, said, laying the leaflet she had given him on the counter. He'd been making tea in the small kitchenette of Block 10, which housed the Public Protection Unit, when Lucy had arrived for work.

'There is an implicit threat,' Lucy said. 'All that stuff about keeping immigrants out? Non locals not being welcome?'

'But made in the context of Brexit,' Fleming said. 'It's hardly the first leaflet to make that connection.' The following Thursday, the country would be voting on whether or not to remain part of the European Union. Much of the debate had focused on the issue of immigration and border control: not all of it had been particularly edifying.

'But now there's graffiti—'

Fleming raised a hand in placation. 'I'm not saying they're not being intimidated, Lucy; I'm saying that this leaflet—'

'They're being specifically targeted,' Lucy said.

'But not in *this*,' Fleming said, holding up the sheet of paper. 'Look, you know if we take this further, that's what we'll be told. There's no specific threat, it doesn't actually name the Lupei family. If you take this to the Assistant Chief Constable, you know she'll say that. Have they anywhere else they can go? Any family?'

Lucy shook her head. 'The father's digging in his heels. He doesn't think he should be forced out of his house.'

'Well, he's right,' Fleming said. 'But that will be little comfort if things escalate. Let's check out the printers who produced this, find out who placed the order. And maybe see what we can dig up on the Greenway Estate; see who's running things there at the moment. I know Jackie Moss was—'

The main office phone rang. Fleming lifted the extension-line receiver. 'Tom Fleming,' he said. Lucy could hear snippets of the other speaker's words as she got the milk from the fridge and sniffed it to ensure it was still fresh.

'We'll be right across,' Fleming said, hanging up.

'No tea?' Lucy said, pausing before pouring in the milk.

'The Chief Super wants us down to Bay Road Park. A body's been found, badly beaten. They think he's in his teens. They want us to check whether we know him.'

THERE WERE ALREADY a number of PSNI vehicles and an ambulance parked at the Bay Road Industrial units when Lucy pulled in. A cordon had been set up at the entrance to the park and a small forensics tent marked the site where the victim lay, just on the green area next to the car park. Lucy could see Chief Superintendent Mark Burns standing outside the tent with several members of CID, among them her friend DS Tara Gallagher and, stepping out of the tent now and pulling down his face mask, DS Mickey

Sinclair, who appeared to be struggling to not be sick where he stood.

Burns turned at their approach and nodded to Fleming. 'Tom, Lucy. Thanks for coming across.'

'What have you got?' Fleming asked as the officer on the cordon handed them both forensics suits.

'Late teen, we think. He has no wallet, no ID, nothing. We were hoping he might have featured on the Public Protection Unit radar at some stage.'

The PPU's remit meant that frequently, Lucy and Fleming would come into contact with youths who would later reappear at some point in the criminal justice system, whether as a perpetrator or, in this case, as a victim.

'What happened to him?'

'Extensive head injuries. We're waiting on the pathologist to get here. SOCOs are working with the victim now.'

Once dressed, Lucy dipped under the cordon and made her way across to the tent. She glanced around her as she did so. Up to her left, at the top of a steep grass embankment, elevated high above the park, were the rears of properties situated in Gleneagles. She could see various occupants standing at their windows looking down at what was happening. Further along to her left, at the far end of the park, she could see the point where the arch of the Foyle Bridge rose beyond the embankment and high above the river running alongside the park. The concrete pillar there was covered with graffiti, though it was impossible to read from this distance.

'We ready?' Fleming asked, stopping alongside her.

They moved in under the flapping canvas of the protective tent. The boy lay prone on the ground, his head turned to one side, facing back towards the houses. Immediately, Lucy could see the series of wounds to the side of his head. The forensics photographer held the camera close to one of the wounds and took a final shot, while another officer inched a blue light slowly up and down the victim's legs, looking for spots of fluids that might not have been instantly visible.

'Do you recognise him?' Burns asked.

'No,' Fleming said, then glanced at Lucy who shook her head as she studied the boy's face.

On closer examination, she could see that the head injuries extended around the rear of his skull and onto the left-hand side of his face where his temple carried an open gash. As the photographer leaned in to take pictures of the injuries, the camera's flash caught something wedged in the open wound.

'What was that?' Fleming asked.

The question prompted Burns who had been standing outside the tent assigning duties to the team to step in beneath the covering.

The SOCO clicked on the menu to the rear of the camera and examined the image in the display screen, zooming in to better see.

'Glass,' she said. 'Pieces of glass.'

She held the camera out to show to Burns, then Fleming and Lucy in turn.

'Sir,' the other SOCO said. He was running the blue light across the legs and trunk of the victim. Splatters were clearly visible on his shirt but the SOCO indicated a second set around the boy's crotch and legs.

'Is that blood too?' Burns asked.

The SOCO pulled away the light and examined the staining on the boy's jeans. He shook his head. 'I'll take samples,' he said. 'I'd guess semen.'

'He has something on his hand,' Fleming said suddenly.

They looked to where the blue light the SOCO had held to one side had illuminated an image on the back of the boy's hand. Moving the blue light away caused the image to vanish.

'Invisible ink,' the SOCO commented. He moved the light over the hand again and the photographer took a shot and pulled the image up on the camera's display.

'Is it a club stamp?' Burns asked. 'An admittance stamp?'

The photographer showed the display to Lucy and Fleming. A pair of wings, blue beneath the forensics light, covered the skin on the back of the boy's hand.

'That's Paradise night club's logo,' Lucy said. 'I know someone who works there.'

'Good work,' Burns said to the SOCO. 'Let's find out if they had anything on last night and, if so, whether our victim was there.'

'They did have something,' Lucy said. 'It was a Gay Pride night.'

Burns stared at her a moment longer than necessary. 'Okay.' He glanced at the boy again, then nodded once. 'Well, that gives us something to work with,' he said. 'We'll bring the team together for an update at noon; hopefully we'll have a name by then.' His phone began ringing and, pulling it from his pocket, he said, 'Thank you, Lucy. Tom.'

Lucy looked across at Fleming, but he was staring at the boy's injuries again, his expression unreadable behind the paper mask he wore.

Chapter Four

THEY DROVE ACROSS to the Waterside, to McEwan's Printers, whose name and number had been on the bottom of the leaflet that had been posted around the Greenway Estate. It was a family-run business, situated in one unit of an industrial estate just past Altnagelvin Hospital. Most of the other units were deserted, the signage above them proclaiming businesses long since closed.

As Lucy approached, two young men who had been standing outside having a smoke stubbed out their cigarettes and stepped back in through the roll-up metal door of the unit. A moment later, an older man stepped out, rubbing his hands on a stained cloth.

'Mr McEwan?' Lucy asked.

The man nodded. 'Is there something wrong?' he asked.

Tom Fleming handed him the leaflet. 'Did you print this?'

McEwan took the leaflet and peered at it. 'Seems we did. That's our name on the bottom.'

'Did you do this of your own volition or did someone place an order for it?' Fleming asked.

McEwan raised his right shoulder slightly. 'I've never printed anything for free,' he said. 'Someone must have paid for it.'

'Would you remember who?'

McEwan stuffed the cloth into his trouser pocket and studied the backs of his hands. 'One of the printers is leaking,' he said. 'The cost of ink, we can't afford to lose a drop. Come in.'

They followed him in beneath the shutter. He led them into his office, which was a small room partitioned off from the rest of the unit by unfinished stud walls. Pulling out his chair, he sat at the desk and opening the large drawer to his left, took out a folder of order documents.

'We done nothing wrong in printing that leaflet,' McEwan said. 'Regardless of what it says.'

'Do you agree with this?' Lucy asked, holding the sheet aloft.

'I just printed it,' McEwan said. 'Work's work.'

'You've no qualms?'

'I can't afford to turn away jobs,' he said. 'Besides, it's not illegal, what it says.'

'So you do agree with it?'

'Did I say I agree? I said it wasn't illegal. I've done nothing wrong.'

He flicked through the last of the sheets in front of him, then closed the folder.

'I can't find the order sheet,' he said. 'I'm not sure where it is.'

'You must remember the order, though,' Lucy said. 'The leaflets were only distributed a week ago. I can't imagine they were printed too long before that.'

'I remember printing them, but I don't remember who placed the order. Sorry.'

'What about the rest of your staff?'

'Staff?' McEwan laughed. 'Those two out there? One's my wee lad and the other's his mate.'

'Can you check with them?'

McEwan sighed and stood, taking the leaflet from Lucy. 'Frankie? Bobby? Did either of you take the order for this?'

They appeared in the doorway of the office and stared dumbly at the leaflet he showed them.

'Nah,' one said.

The other shook his head. 'Never seen it before,' he said.

'Sorry we can't be more help,' McEwan said. 'If I come across the order form I'll call you.'

As they moved back out into the main part of the unit, Fleming handed McEwan his card. 'I've ordered printing for my local church,' he said.

McEwan smiled. 'Well, give us a chance to give you a quote. I'll give a discount for a member of the PSNI.'

Fleming laughed lightly. 'I might just do that. What I meant, though, is that any time I got work done, I was given a mockup to sign off. A proof. Do you do that?'

McEwan glanced across to Bobby and Frankie, then nodded curtly. 'Yeah, we do proofs. So no one can blame us for mistakes.'

'Maybe you'd have the sign-off sheet for this order, then?' Fleming continued. 'Even if the order form is missing.'

McEwan's smile faltered. 'I might.'

'We'll wait,' Lucy said.

A moment later, McEwan reappeared from his office. 'I can't find it either,' he said, then added, before Lucy could speak, 'Let's step out for a breath of air, eh? The fumes in here!'

He did not speak again until they were outside, out of earshot of the two younger men.

'Look, I've no choice but to print this stuff,' he said. 'I'd be out of business in a week if I said no.'

'Do you have the proof sign-off or not?' Lucy asked.

McEwan nodded. 'You can't say I gave you that. Please. I'd be finished.'

He pulled a sheet from his pocket and handed it to her.

'Put it away quickly,' he said, glancing behind him, towards the unit. But the two younger men were standing in the doorway now, looking across to where McEwan, Lucy and Fleming stood.

'I hope you're happy now,' McEwan snapped and turning, stalked back to the unit.

'Get back to work,' he said, passing the two workers, though Lucy noticed one of them was slower to follow the instruction than the other.

She waited until she was in the car before opening the sheet.

The signature scrawled on the sheet was difficult to decipher.

'Charles?' Lucy guessed. 'Charles . . .'

'It looks like Dougan,' Fleming suggested.

'Does that name mean anything to you?' Lucy asked.

Fleming shook his head. 'But I know someone who might be able to help,' he said.

Chapter Five

JACKIE MOSS HAD settled himself onto the leatherette bench behind table 5 in the Bluebell Café when Fleming and Lucy came in. The combination of low ceilings and nicotine-coloured walls made the space seem smaller than it was, accommodating, as it did, twenty tables, many of which were already occupied.

Moss looked up from his breakfast, lifting a forkful to his mouth, angling it to catch an errant thread of yolk from dripping off the toast before shovelling it into his mouth.

'Inspector Fleming,' Moss mumbled through his mouthful of food. 'Table for two?'

'We're not staying, Jackie,' Fleming said. 'Can we sit?'

Moss motioned for them to take the seats opposite him, then shifted his girth on his own seat, getting himself more comfortable. 'I don't think we've met before,' he said to Lucy as he forked a piece of bacon, smearing it through a dollop of ketchup.

'DS Black,' Lucy said.

Moss nodded. 'And what can I do for you both today? Are you sure you won't eat?'

'We're good, Jackie,' Fleming said.

Despite this, Moss glanced across to the counter where two women were serving a queue of customers.

'Bring another pot, Annie,' he shouted. 'And two spare cups.'

If Annie heard, she made no indication of it, yet a moment later she appeared with a fresh pot of tea and two cups and saucers for Lucy and Fleming. No one in the queue seemed to mind Moss being given preferential treatment.

'Perks of being the owner,' Moss said, as if aware of Lucy's thoughts.

Fleming pulled the leaflet from his pocket and set it in front of Moss. Moss cast a quick glance in its direction, then lifted a napkin, wiping the sauce and egg yolk from the corners of his mouth before balling it up and laying it on his plate.

'Can you tell us anything about this, Jackie?'

'It did the rounds of Greenway last week, I believe,' Moss said.

'Did you arrange it?'

Moss glared at Fleming. 'I'm a community activist, Inspector. I don't condone this kind of nonsense. I was told it was a group of young lads trying to make a name for themselves.'

'Threatening immigrants?' Lucy asked incredulously.

'Nothing cements a community like a common enemy. The crowd that are doing this are trying to get a foothold, get some community cachet. The Provos did it targeting drug dealers and joyriders. This crew are targeting immigrants. It's not a new concept.'

'What threat do immigrants pose to the community?' Lucy asked.

Moss considered the question. 'People round here never saw the promised peace dividend, Sergeant Black. There's no jobs, no benefits; their marches are banned, their flags taken down. Now the housing estates, always the one place they felt completely safe among their own, seem to be eroding too. Outsiders coming in and taking over, that kind of thing. I'm not saying I agree with that, by the way; just that that's how things are. These young lads are acting out,' he concluded, tapping the leaflet with a nicotine-stained finger. 'I wouldn't take it too seriously.'

Fleming nodded. 'Maybe they fancy running the place themselves.'

Moss snorted derisively. 'They're letting off steam, is all. I'll ask around, maybe call with the Romas myself and let them know they're welcome here. This type of rubbish is just giving Greenway a bad name.'

Lucy handed him the proofing sheet McEwan had given them. 'Do you know that person?' she asked, pointing at the signature. 'Charles Dougan.'

Moss held her stare a moment, as if weighing up the cost of answering. Finally he nodded. 'Yeah, I know him.'

'Where could we find him?' Lucy asked.

'He runs the taxi firm in Greenway,' Moss said, draining his tea. 'He's harmless.' He stood and tapped the leaflet where it lay on the table before him. 'I'll make sure that family know they're part of the community here, too. This does no one any good.'

With that he lumbered up to the counter with his tray of empty dishes and handed it to Annie. Then he moved across to one of the other tables and began chatting with some of the diners who greeted his arrival with smiles and handshakes. Lucy realised that they'd not had to tell Moss which family was being attacked; clearly the news had already spread through the estate.

'He seems decent,' Lucy said.

Fleming nodded. 'He served four life sentences for murder in the eighties and nineties. He's a real local hero.'

Chapter Six

GREENWAY TAXIS WAS situated at the centre of the estate, just opposite the Green that gave the place its name. When Lucy and Fleming arrived, a number of cars were parked up outside and, stepping into the office, they realised that the drivers were having their mid-morning break, sitting around a low coffee table. On it sat an open tub of margarine and a few butter knives as well as a torn white bakery bag, which spilled scones onto a table surface scarred with cigarette burns.

'Where are you going, love?' one of them asked, winking against the vapour of his e-cig. He was short bodied, with thinning sandy hair, already greying although he looked to be in his mid forties.

'We're looking for Charles Dougan,' Lucy said, holding up her warrant card.

'You've found him, then,' the man said, smiling affably at the others around the table. 'What's wrong?'

'Maybe we should talk outside, Mr Dougan,' Lucy said.

Dougan straightened, worried now. 'Has something happened?'

'We're speaking to people about the attack on the Roma family last night. Your name has come up.'

Dougan pantomimed confusion but stood, swallowing the final piece of his scone and lifting his mug of tea to bring with him. His movements were small but quick, precise, like a bird's. 'Excuse me a minute, lads,' he said to the others.

They stepped out onto the pavement. The sky above was bruised with cloud, the air heavy with the promise of rain before lunch.

Lucy handed Dougan the leaflet. 'We've been told you know something about this?'

Dougan nodded. 'That's right. I collected it from McEwan's Printers as part of a job.'

'You didn't order it?'

He shook his head, blinking mildly against the light.

Fleming sighed audibly. 'Do you know who ordered it?'

A shrug. 'I don't know. I dropped the parcel off here and someone collected it. I don't remember who.'

'And you don't remember who placed the order for you to go and collect this?'

'That's right.'

'Would your boss remember?' Lucy asked.

'I am the boss.' Dougan smiled apologetically.

'You'd no problem being involved in this?'

Another shrug. 'I just collected it, love. It's harmless.'

'It's intimidation,' Lucy snapped.

'Or community protection,' Dougan countered, angling his head a little, feigning discomfort at expressing such a view. 'The people here are proud of their homes, proud of where we come from. Outsiders can bring all sorts of problems.'

'And if a Roma customer called here looking for a cab?'

'I've been stung before with fares doing a runner and not paying,' Dougan said. 'I'd be wary, if I'm honest.'

'Where were you last night between seven and ten?' Lucy asked.

Dougan frowned. 'I was at the bowling alley with the family. It was our youngest's birthday and we had an evening out. I was there from six until eleven.'

'Have you heard anything about the attack on the house?'

Dougan nodded. 'Of course I heard; I drive the estate for a living.'

'And?' Fleming asked, encouraging him.

'And nothing. It was a bit of paint on a wall. No one was hurt. There was worse done to the people of the estate over the past forty years and no one batted an eyelid.'

'No rumours of who was involved?'

'Involved?' Dougan repeated. 'What, like it was orchestrated or something?'

'Exactly like that,' Lucy said. 'A leaflet drop, then abuse on the street, now an attack on the house. It's unlikely these things are a coincidence.'

'Maybe they are,' Dougan said, his expression hardening. 'Maybe people are reacting to the numbers of break-ins there've been here recently. TVs going missing; rent cheques lifted. One woman's purse was taken from her car when she was carrying in the groceries.'

'And this is the fault of the family attacked last night?'

'No. maybe it was just *coincidence* too. They move into the estate and these robberies and such start happening. Drugs, too. Ask them about that!'

LUCY DROVE THROUGH the estate to let Fleming see the extent of the damage in daylight. When they arrived, Andre Lupei was standing in the garden in a pair of overalls, a bucket and scrubbing brush next to him. He was scouring at the paint, having already managed to remove most of the R, O and M, though the shadow of each letter was still visible on the brickwork. Another man knelt on the grass next to him, working at the lower word, OUT. Constanta Lupei stood at the window looking out at them, her fist balled at her mouth as she watched them work. She opened it in a brief wave to acknowledge Lucy's arrival.

Andre turned at the sound of the car doors opening and moved across to the low wall surrounding the garden to greet them.

'Officer,' he said, clearly not remembering Lucy's name.

'Mr Lupei. DS Black. We met last night. This is my colleague, DI Tom Fleming.'

Fleming extended his hand to shake. Andre gestured to do likewise, then stopped, regarding his own hand, before holding it up to show the stains.

'Sorry. My hands are dirty,' he said.

'That's fine.' Fleming smiled. 'I'm sorry for the trouble you've had.' He nodded towards the wall, where the other man still worked.

Lupei shrugged. 'We deal with it. White spirits will take it off. I'll paint over it later. Good as new.'

'Is this one of your neighbours?' Lucy asked, hoping that someone living near the Lupeis had came across to help. Her own house had been targeted once and it had been her neighbour, Dermot, who had cleaned the wall for her. That one act had made her feel more a part of Prehen than all the time she had spent living there.

'No,' Andre said. 'This is my brother, Cezar. He lives on the city side.' He turned and called something to Cezar which Lucy didn't understand, but Cezar stood and wiping his hands on his own overalls, he limped across to them, acknowledging them with a curt nod.

'This is a mess,' Lucy said, struggling for something to say to the man. He was a head taller than his brother and wider too. His face was broad, his features pugnacious, and, perhaps as a result of it receding, he'd shorn his hair into a buzz cut, all of which was in contrast with the softer features of Andre. He pulled a tobacco tin from his pocket and took out a rolled cigarette.

'They are scum,' Cezar said, putting the rollie between his lips and lighting it, the tip flaring briefly with the flame. He took it between his fingers and blew lightly on it to put out the flame, then dragged deeply. From the scarring on his knuckles, Lucy guessed he was a manual labourer. 'I've had the same in Belfast. I had to move three times before I come to Derry. *Because it is a nice place*, they said. Look at this. Nice?' He spat out a stray strand of tobacco from the tip of his tongue, then drew heavily on his smoke again.

'Be careful smoking around the white spirits,' Fleming said. 'We're following up on the attack, Mr Lupei,' he added, turning to Andre. 'But be sensible. Take precautions. Maybe don't be out walking alone too late at night. That sort of thing.'

Cezar sneered. 'He'll be fine, won't you, Andre?'

Andre smiled benignly at his brother, though Lucy could tell that he didn't share the other man's confidence.

'We'll do all we can, Mr Lupei,' she said. 'Call us straight away if anything more happens. Anything at all.'

She handed Andre her number. He took it, wiping his hand on his trouser leg again before doing so, as if afraid to dirty the small card.

Chapter Seven

THE INCIDENT ROOM in the Strand Road station was already almost full when Lucy and Fleming arrived, just shy of noon. A timeline board had been set up at one side of the room and, next to it, a second board with a map of the park and several images of the victim taken in situ, including one of the angel wings stamp.

Glancing around for a free seat, Lucy caught sight of Mickey, nursing his hangover in the corner, an untouched mug of coffee on the desk next to him. Tara smiled across at Lucy, raising her eyebrows lightly as she did so. As she passed Mickey, on the way to her own seat, Tara slapped him on the back of the head and laughed at the snarled expletives she earned for so doing.

Burns arrived a moment later, with Lucy's mother, Assistant Chief Constable Jane Wilson. Wilson had left Lucy and her dad when Lucy was eight and reclaimed her maiden name; the two women had been estranged for many years. As a result, when Lucy joined the PSNI, no one was aware of the relationship between them, with the exception of Tom Fleming who had served with Wilson when she had still been married to Lucy's father. Lucy had worked very hard to keep their connection hidden, but a year previous, Tara Gallagher had guessed at its true nature. She'd promised not to tell anyone else and, in the absence of any evidence to the contrary, Lucy trusted that she had been true to her word.

'Right, folks,' Burns began. 'As you know, our victim was found this morning at seven fifteen. He had been dead for no more than five hours, with time of death placed at some stage between approximately two and five a.m. We do know the victim had attended a gay pride event in Paradise night club last night. Any luck with getting an ID for the vic from the club?'

'No, sir,' Tara said. 'We've contacted the owner who was able to provide us with the CCTV from last night. He doesn't know any of the clientele, though; he suggested we speak with the manager. He's from Armagh apparently and went home after his shift last night. He's due back this afternoon. We think we have a visual of our victim, though, and possibly a friend or partner.'

She passed around printouts she had made of the CCTV footage from the club, the paper still warm from the printer. Lucy took one and shared it with Fleming. There were two men in the image, which had been enlarged enough for their faces to be visible but not so much that they would become pixellated. The boy on the left of the image wore the same blue jeans and slim-fit purple shirt as the victim in the park had been wearing. Next to the boy stood a second youth. He was taller than his friend, with a shock of blond hair styled into a quiff. He wore black trousers and a red checked lumberjack shirt. There was a further picture of the blond-haired youth, clearer this time, standing with his arm around the shoulders of a girl in glasses wearing a white vest top.

'Good. Try to get IDs for all three of them,' Burns said. 'Find out if they left together.'

Tara nodded. 'Perhaps DS Black could help me with this, sir? She has existing contacts in the club, so we might have more success—'

'Lucy?' Burns asked.

'Happy to help, sir,' Lucy said.

'Good. Any luck with CCTV for the area yet, Mickey?'

Mickey straightened himself. 'We're following up on it, sir. The main cameras around the fuel depot at the entrance to the park are of limited value, sir, as they focus on the depot, not the roads outside. We're widening out to include traffic cameras along the Strand Road, too, but at that time of the morning on a weekend, the roads were pretty busy, what with the bars emptying. We need something to narrow the search field a bit.'

Burns nodded. 'Well, hopefully this might help. The Tactical Support Group found what we believe to be the site of the attack.' He leaned across and turned on the small projector set on the table to the head of the room. A few seconds later, an image of broken glass emerged on the whiteboard behind him. He moved across to the map of the park on which a red sticker already marked the spot where the boy had been found. He now added a second sticker, blue this time, to a spot on the map about ten centimetres from the red one.

'There's a small parking bay here. Secluded by bushes on each side. We found the broken glass you see on the screen there this morning. SOCO have examined the area – the glass is part of a shattered car window. They've confirmed the victim's blood was found both on the broken glass and on the ground in the area. Which means, Mickey, that we should be looking for cars with damage to the windows, possibly the front passenger one.'

'Now, as far as motive for the attack goes,' Burns went on, 'we have nothing concrete at the minute. We do, however, suspect that the victim was a gay man. And there is no doubt that he was sexually active before death, based on samples taken from his clothes and body.'

'He was with someone in the car?' Tara asked.

Burns nodded. 'That would seem likely. We believe then that someone attacked him from outside the car, smashing through the passenger window, striking him while doing so; we've found pieces of glass in the impact wound to the left side of his skull. Glass found on his clothes, as well as the scrape marks on his arms and trunk, would suggest he was then pulled out of the car onto the ground where he was subjected to a further attack. The absence of drag marks on the ground suggest he made it to his feet and staggered for around fifty yards before falling where he was eventually found, just inside the green area of the park.'

'How was he assaulted?' Fleming asked suddenly. 'With what?'

'I was coming to that, Tom,' Burns said, pressing the return key on the laptop again. The image this time was a close-up of a rock, badged with blood. 'We found this in the undergrowth near where the broken glass was located. The pathologist's preliminary findings are that our victim was beaten to death with a stone.'

Lucy heard Fleming groan quietly next to her. 'I'm going to need a word, Mark. When you're done,' he said.

FLEMING WAITED UNTIL the last of the CID team had left, then moved across and closed the incident-room door.

'I attended my church last weekend,' he began. Wilson looked to Lucy, as if questioning whether she knew where Fleming was going with his story, but it was obvious she didn't.

'The speaker was Pastor Jim Nixon. He's from Ballymena orig-inally but—'

Wilson nodded, folding her arms and leaning against the desk. 'I'm aware of Pastor Nixon's history. He was quite vocal in his belligerence during the Troubles. I thought he'd retired. I've not heard of him in years.'

'His particular brand of fire and brimstone went out of fash-ion for a while,' Fleming said. 'Look, it could be nothing but the other night he preached about homosexuality and mentioned spe-cifically the stoning of gay men. He called it justified. It was the "wages of their sin", he claimed.'

Burns stopped, took his hand off the door handle, turning towards Fleming. 'Did he actively encourage people to stone gays or was he condoning it being done elsewhere?'

Fleming looked to Wilson as he answered Burns' question. 'Honestly, I can't remember. But if I've made a connection, other people are bound to as well.'

Burns accepted the comment with a nod. 'Should we speak to Nixon about the comments, ma'am?'

Wilson thought for a moment, her gaze fixed on Fleming. 'Is Nixon due to speak again?'

'Tomorrow,' Fleming said.

'And you know him?'

Fleming paused a moment. 'Barely. I've spoken to him a few times through the Church. He organised a collection for the Phil-ippines last year, which I helped on.'

'Perhaps the two of you should go and have a word with him. Quietly explain what's happened. Ask him to tone it down a bit. The last thing we need is word about this to get out.'

Chapter Eight

PARADISE NIGHT CLUB was situated on the Strand Road, one of a number of bars and clubs along the thoroughfare on which the main PSNI station was also located. Tara drove while Lucy sat in the passenger seat, looking out at people shuffling through the grey mizzle of rain that had settled over the city. She found herself absentmindedly hoping that Andre Lupei had had a chance to finish repainting his wall before the rain started.

'I hear you were out at Greenway last night,' Tara said, as if reading her thoughts.

'How did you know that?'

'I overheard one of the uniforms in the canteen this morning. He was chatting with the two from Lisnagelvin station who were the first responders. They were complaining about being out there half the night, questioning neighbours.'

'Did they learn anything?'

'Only that Romans come from Rome, apparently,' Tara laughed. She mimicked the man's deeper tones. 'Some smartarse from the PPU told them Romans are from Rome. Like uniforms are morons.'

Lucy laughed at the impression.

'Which *he* is,' Tara added, in her own voice now. 'Mickey said he saw you last night, too,' she added.

'I can't move for being seen!'

'I'm not gossiping,' Tara said, suddenly defensive.

'I know.' Lucy placed a conciliatory hand on Tara's arm. They had been fairly close until Tara guessed at the real nature of Lucy's connection to ACC Wilson. Her annoyance had not been so much at the fact Wilson was Lucy's mother as that Lucy hadn't trusted Tara enough to tell her. Things had improved considerably in the time since then, but Lucy still felt she was treading on eggshells at times with her colleague.

'Apparently he told the others that you're living with another woman,' Tara continued. 'I'm not judging; I'm just letting you know.'

Lucy nodded. 'Thanks.'

'Is she . . . the girl you live with . . . is she . . .?'

'She's a lodger. She was homeless and I offered her a room. She pays her way.'

Tara nodded, pulling in opposite the cinema and parking up on double yellow lines. 'We'll hardly be that long,' she reasoned.

PARADISE OCCUPIED THE top floor of the building, which housed a bar/restaurant on the ground floor, stretching almost half a block. They asked the cleaner hoovering the stairs where they could find the manager, Alan Porter, though it was unnecessary for they had barely reached the upper floor when he arrived at the entrance to greet them. Lucy recognised him, having collected

Grace from work a few times, and she could tell that while Porter recognised her face, he couldn't place her.

'Officers,' he said. 'Tea? Coffee?'

'Nothing, thank you,' Tara said. 'You were expecting us, I believe.'

'Seamus said you were coming,' Porter said, leading them into the club. Lucy guessed Seamus was the club's owner.

Two life-size statues of the Greek god Hermes guarded the entrance to Paradise, the musculature of his torso sculpted. He bore a spear in his right hand and wore a helmet, painted gold, and gold winged sandals. The statue to Lucy's right was missing its left hand, the plaster of the wrist raw and crumbling.

Inside, the club was dim in daylight, heady with the smell of stale beer. The floor was carpeted as far as the dance floor, the material tacky, pulling at the soles of their feet as they walked. The booths to the far side of the room, black vinyl, were all empty and Lucy could see where the stitching had been ripped in one or two of them and the green foam inside exposed.

They crossed the dance floor, which dominated the centre of the space. The main wall to the rear of it was painted with a mural of Adam and Eve standing in the Garden of Eden, at the centre of the image an apple tree, the serpent coiled round the trunk like a vein.

'Aren't you mixing your religions?' Lucy asked. 'Christian and Ancient Greek.'

Porter laughed. 'As if any of our clients care,' he said. He led them to the booth where he had clearly been sitting, a half-empty mug of tea steaming next to a pile of till receipts.

'Are you sure you won't have tea?' he repeated.

Tara shook her head, sliding into the booth opposite him. Lucy remained standing.

'Do you recognise either of the youths in this image?' Tara asked, handing him the picture taken from the CCTV footage.

Porter studied it carefully. 'I recognise them, yes. I think they were here last night.'

'We *know* they were here last night,' Tara said. 'This is from your own CCTV. We need names. Particularly for this one.' She pointed to the victim.

Porter shrugged. 'I'm sorry,' he said. 'As I say, I think they were here last night, but I don't know the names of the people who come in here. What's happened to him? Seamus said it was an assault?'

'We can't say yet,' Tara said. 'You'll hear about it on the news, no doubt.'

'How did he get in?' Lucy asked.

Porter feigned bewilderment. 'Into the building?' he asked, glancing at the main doors through which they had themselves entered.

'The boy in that picture looks to be in his mid teens. As does his friend. How did they get into the bar last night?'

'They would have been stopped for ID,' Porter said. 'The security staff are very careful about that. We have an over-twenty-one policy.'

'So they were checked for ID?' Lucy asked. 'Definitely?'

Porter stumbled on his words a little. 'I can't guarantee . . . I mean, you . . .' He paused, took a breath. 'No, actually, I think I could guarantee that. Our doormen are very careful. Especially last night. We had a gay disco on in here. The staff knows to ensure the clientele, straight or gay, will behave. We need to make sure everyone feels safe. But the chances of them remembering names of people from last night are tiny.'

Lucy nodded. The boy they had found in Bay Road Park had no ID on him when they had checked this morning.

'Can you think of anyone who might be able to help us identify these youths?' Tara asked. 'Or this girl,' she added, handing Porter the picture of the blond-haired youth with the girl in glasses.

Porter nodded now. 'I know her,' he said. 'Shauna Kelly. She was one of the organisers of last night's event.'

'Would you have contact details for her?' Tara asked.

'I should have her number in the bookings records,' he said, sliding back out of the booth.

'I'm going to nip to the toilet while we're waiting,' Lucy said.

Tara nodded. 'They're over in the far corner, behind the Greek god with the fork.'

Another cleaner was hoovering the carpet outside the toilet areas, in the shadow of Poseidon, when Lucy approached. She smiled as she stepped back. 'I've not got in there yet,' she said, 'so God knows what state it's in.'

'I'm sure I've seen worse,' Lucy laughed.

She hadn't. She picked her way past four cubicles before finding one that wasn't splattered with something. As she closed the door and locked it, she noticed something tucked behind the coat hook on the back of the door. At first she thought it was a condom packet until she realised that the image on the small empty sachet was actually a red cartoon dragon with, beneath it, in bubble letters, the name, *Magic Dragon*, and the warning, *Not Suitable for Human Consumption*.

Lucy pulled off a few sheets of toilet paper and lifted the packet down. She opened it and peered into the package, which was empty, save for a few loose strands of what looked like mixed herb.

She brought the packet out with her when she was finished. Porter was standing with Tara now.

'Ready to go?' Tara asked.

Lucy nodded. 'Do you have much of a drug problem here?' she asked, showing Porter the packet.

He held out his hands impotently. 'We do what we can. If someone wants to take something, we can't stop them. But we do try to keep an eye on things. Where did you find that?'

'The bathroom,' Lucy said.

Porter glanced angrily towards where the cleaner, oblivious over the drone of her vacuum cleaner, was busily working. 'They should have been cleaned by now.'

'That's hardly the point,' Lucy said.

Porter nodded. 'We're doing what we can. Of course, that's a legal high.'

'Not any more,' Tara said. 'Not since last month.'

'We're doing what we can,' he repeated weakly.

He walked them to the top of the stairs where they thanked him for his help. 'Why was the entrance stamp invisible?' Lucy asked. 'The wings? You don't normally do that, do you?'

Porter glanced at Tara, then addressed Lucy. 'Privacy,' he said simply. 'Some of our clients won't want people at home to know they were here. We do our best to respect their right to privacy. Everyone has a right to feel safe.'

Chapter Nine

SHAUNA KELLY OWNED a craft stall in Bedlam Market on Pump Street. The market was housed in what had formerly been a convent for the Sisters of Mercy before the nuns had moved to newer residences. A variety of stalls and shops, including a bookstore which Lucy frequented, had filled the lower levels of the building, though Lucy noticed that many of them had closed up and relocated. Shauna's stall was still in the basement, a space whose walls carried examples of her handiwork. Shauna nestled behind the small counter on which sat a cash register and a hat stand decked with woollen berets. She stood when Lucy and Tara came in, putting down the book she'd been reading. She was shorter than Lucy had expected, perhaps little over five feet, the thinness of her frame accentuated by the skinny jeans and T-shirt she wore.

'You're the ones who phoned?' she asked.

Tara nodded. 'DS Gallagher and DS Black, Miss Kelly.'

'I knit them all myself,' Shauna explained when she saw Lucy surveying the work hanging on the walls.

'They're very nice,' Lucy said.

'If you've kids, I can do nice cardigans,' Shauna offered.

'No kids,' Lucy said and smiled.

Tara opened out the picture of Shauna and the blond-haired youth. 'We're investigating an incident that happened last night. Do you know this person?' she asked, pointing to the youth.

Shauna glanced at the picture, then looked from Tara to Lucy. 'What type of investigation?' she asked.

'An ongoing one,' Tara said. 'Do you know this person?'

Kelly smiled nervously. 'Am I getting someone into trouble?'

Lucy shook her head. 'Maybe take a look at the other image,' she suggested. 'The other youth, not the one with the blond hair, was subject to an assault last night. We need to identify him.'

Shauna took the other image from Tara and looking at it, asked, 'If you know he was assaulted, why do you not know his name?'

'We can't say.'

'Do you know either of these youths? Yes or no?' Tara added, not attempting to hide her frustration.

'Yes,' Shauna said. 'The blond guy is Gareth McGonigle. His friend's Marty Givens.'

'How do you know them?' Tara asked.

'Gareth comes into the shop quite a bit,' Shauna said.

'A knitwear shop?' Lucy asked, incredulous.

'I used to waitress in the café in the village. He came in there a lot. Once I opened up here, he'd call in for a chat and a cuppa. He liked the arty feel of the place; all the history. Thackeray stayed here when it was an inn, you know. And Conan Doyle's grand-daughter was one of the founding—'

'Did Marty ever come in with Gareth?' Tara asked.

Shauna nodded. 'He came with him a few times. Then, when he knew I was gay, he called in once or twice on his own.'

'For advice?'

Shauna nodded. 'More like friendly support. He was pretty clear about his sexuality, said he'd known for ages. It was more about having the courage to come out. He asked me how I had done it, how I'd told my parents and that.'

'And is he out?'

'He's making his way there,' she said. 'He's a good guy. Nice to chat to. Is he okay?'

'We can't say, I'm afraid,' Lucy commented.

'Well, was he badly hurt in the assault?'

'Again . . .' Lucy began, shrugging.

Shauna stared at her, as if in hope that she might let something slip.

'This isn't related to the body they found down at Bay Road, is it?' she asked suddenly.

'We can't say,' Lucy repeated, hoping Shauna would be able to read between the lines.

Shauna's eye widened. 'Jesus, did someone—'

'Miss Kelly,' Tara said, 'we really can't give you any further information, I'm afraid. Would you know where Marty lives?'

Shauna paused, struggling to piece together the fragments of their conversation.

'I don't. The city side, somewhere,' she said. 'Messines Park, I think.'

Tara nodded. 'Thanks for your help, Miss Kelly.'

'Please, just tell me, is Marty . . . is he still . . . okay?'

'We can't say,' Lucy repeated a fourth time. 'I'm sorry we can't be more forthcoming.'

'Are Marty and Gareth McGonigle in a relationship?' Tara asked.

Shauna shook her head. 'It's no one's business if they are,' she said. 'You'd need to ask them that yourself.'

Chapter Ten

THE GIVENS LIVED in a semi-detached in Messines Park, on the outskirts of the town, a small estate of thirty houses not even a mile away from Bay Road Park where Marty Givens had been found. And Lucy had no doubt that the young man whose remains she had seen in the park that morning was Marty Givens. His portrait now smiled down at them from the framed picture on the living-room wall, hanging above the sofa on which his parents sat, their faces streaked with tears.

'We were away last night and Martin said he was staying over with a friend, Gareth.'

'Gareth McGonigle?' Tara asked.

Mrs Givens nodded, looking to her husband for confirmation. But he seemed dazed, his mind somewhere other than the conversation unfolding around him. 'It was a nephew's wedding,' she explained. 'Marty said he'd be all right. Then when he hadn't been home we started to worry. We called his mobile but it just rang out. When we tried again it went straight to voicemail. Robert said I was worrying, but I phoned anyway, to the police. He's only eighteen. They said someone would be out with us. I should have known then that—' She dissolved into tears again.

Robert Givens roused himself enough to look at Lucy. 'Can we see him? In case it's not . . . you know, in case you're wrong?'

'You'll need to, I'm afraid,' Lucy said. 'But I think you should prepare yourself for the worst.'

'Why would someone attack Marty?' Mrs Givens managed, swallowing back her tears again. 'He's the most inoffensive wee man. He's not the type to hang around Bay Road Park like that. He'd never go there.'

Lucy sat forward. 'Did Martin ever mention having a partner that you know of? Gareth McGonigle, perhaps?'

His father shook his head. 'He didn't talk about that stuff with me at all,' he said.

'He would have with me,' his wife countered. 'But he never mentioned anyone. I asked a few times had he met someone, but he said he hadn't. He's too young and good-looking to settle down, he says.' She smiled briefly at the memory, then the smile collapsed under the weight of the situation in which she now found herself.

'He was *out*, though,' Tara said.

'*We* knew,' Mrs Givens said. 'I always knew. Even when he was a boy, I thought I knew. It was nothing he did, like . . . it's just . . . well, when he told me, I wasn't surprised. It was like he was just confirming something for me, you know?'

She looked to her husband for support. He was staring at the coffee table that sat between them and Tara and Lucy, picking at the cracked edge of the Formica with his thumb.

'He was so certain when he told me. I told him he might be confused or something. Maybe he just hadn't met the right girl, but he said he knew himself. He was always brighter than me,' he said simply. 'Like, he'd be explaining things to me and I'd have no idea what the fuck he was talking about. And *he* knew it, too. How shit must that have been for him, knowing that his dad was thick.'

'That's not true,' his wife said, laying her hand on his arm. He continued to pick at the table top, his fingers thick and stubbed, his nails grimy with oil. 'He loved you.'

The comment seemed to catch him by surprise. 'We just stopped talking about all that stuff. I guess I didn't want to think about it. He didn't get any brains from me, that's for sure.'

'Martin pushed himself,' his wife explained to Lucy. 'That's what he means. Robert's a wonder with cars; all those bits and pieces that have to fit together just right, there's a talent in that.'

'Was it because he was gay?' Robert Givens asked suddenly. 'The attack? Was he hit because he was gay?'

'We don't know,' Lucy said, looking to Tara. 'It's one line of inquiry.'

'How would someone even have known he was anyway?' Givens asked. 'You think they followed him from that club, the whole way down through the city?'

Lucy shook her head. 'He was . . .' she began, struggling to articulate her response.

'We believe he was with someone, intimately, before the attack,' Tara said. 'It may be that that's connected in some way to his assault.'

'What did they do to my son?' Mr Givens said suddenly. 'An assault. What does that mean? Did they kick him? Hit him? What did they do to him?'

'I think it's best if you wait until you go to—' Tara started, but the man stood.

'He's my boy!' he snapped. 'What did they do to my son? Tell me!'

'He was beaten,' Tara said.

'With what?'

'It's best—'

'Tell me!'

'With a stone,' Tara said finally. 'I'm so sorry, Mr Givens.'

Chapter Eleven

LUCY HEADED BACK across to the PPU in Maydown, and found Fleming sitting in his office, working at the computer. He spoke without looking up. 'You saw the parents. How was that?'

'Grim,' she said.

Fleming nodded. 'I'm not surprised. Burns has had a team looking for Marty's friend, Gareth McGonigle, but he's in the wind apparently. His flat in Rockmills is being watched in case he shows up.' He continued scrolling through the page he was looking at as he spoke. 'I did a bit of digging on Charlie Dougan from Greenway while you were away,' he said. 'His Facebook page makes for interesting reading.'

Lucy moved in next to Fleming as he scrolled down through Dougan's page. His profile picture showed him standing at a protest of some sort. He wore a white T-shirt emblazoned with a red cross and held aloft a placard that read, *There's no Black in the Union Jack*. Moving down through his newsfeed, most of his postings were political; all were right wing in nature. Many were statements of protest against the opening of mosques and links to newspapers detailing atrocities carried out in the Middle East by Islamic extremists.

'I ran his background,' Fleming said. 'He's ex army. He served for eight years; did two terms in Afghanistan. He was a member of the British National Party but according to his newsfeed he left during one of the splits five years back. His profile picture was taken during a neo-Nazi rally in London in 2011.'

'Charming,' Lucy said. 'He's making no efforts to hide it either, is he?'

Fleming shook his head. 'But he opened that taxi service two years ago with himself and two other drivers. He has forty drivers working for him now. He's being supported in Greenway.'

'What about Jackie Moss? I thought he was the local hero.'

'He is,' Fleming said, 'but he's getting on. Talking about what he did in the 1970s doesn't really do much for people struggling in 2016. Dougan's being backed by the community; the question is whether he's organising the attacks on the Lupei family or he's just creating an environment where that type of racial hatred can thrive.'

'Would it be worth canvassing some of the Lupeis' neighbours?'

Fleming shook his head. 'Not at this stage. Let's just keep an ear to the ground for now. We're on our way back to Greenway anyway,' he added.

'Why?'

'I've managed to get an audience with Pastor Nixon,' he said. 'He's at the Gospel Hall this evening, meeting a prayer group. He's agreed to speak with us for a few minutes.'

THE GOSPEL HALL where Nixon was speaking was a small red-brick building, nestled in the space next to Greenway Estate, though just outside its boundary. When Fleming went in, he was greeted like an old friend by the man who opened the door to them.

'Tom!' the man cried, shaking Fleming's hand firmly, his free hand gripping the bicep of Fleming's other arm. 'Pastor Nixon said you were calling. What did you think of him last week? Powerful, eh? Powerful.'

He turned to Lucy, even as he led Fleming down the narrow corridor towards a kitchen area to the side of the hall.

'Welcome,' he said. 'Norman Friel.' He paused long enough to shake hands.

'DS Lucy Black,' Lucy said.

Friel smiled and wagged a finger playfully. 'I've not seen you in our congregation. Has Tom not managed to convince you to join us some evening?'

'I have my own church,' Lucy said. 'Not my own, like Henry the Eighth obviously, but . . . you know.'

Friel's smiled remained in place, but it didn't extend into his eyes quite so much as it had previously done. 'Well, Pastor Nixon's a terrific speaker,' he said. 'You could do worse than come along tomorrow night.'

'I fully intend to,' Lucy said.

'Good!' The smile was full again, his eyes bright and twinkling. 'The pastor's having a quick bite to eat with his family,' he said. 'I'll tell him you're here.'

A moment later, they were ushered into the dining room which, judging by the partial wall halfway across it, had once been two rooms but had been knocked through to accommodate more guests. Rows of long white tables were spaced out with old plastic school chairs around them. All were empty save for two tables at the far side of the room, next to a set of French doors, at which sat Nixon at the head of a table laden with plates of sandwiches and finger food.

Nixon looked up when he saw them and stood, wiping his hands and then the corners of his mouth with his napkin, before tossing it onto his plate. He was almost six feet tall and, though heavily built, the erectness of his carriage, and the braces he wore attached to his trousers, mitigated his size but did little to make him any less imposing.

'The police have arrived,' he announced. 'Tom, good to see you again. And you are . . .?'

'DS Lucy Black.'

'Lucy,' Nixon said warmly, taking her hand in both of his. 'How lovely to meet you. Please, join us for a bite.'

'We're fine, thank you, Pastor,' Fleming said, though he took a seat at the table.

'So, have I done something wrong?' Nixon asked. Despite directing the question at the two officers, he glanced around at the other members of his own party, encouraging them to share his mirth.

'Would you like to confess anything, sir?' Lucy asked.

Nixon laughed loudly, and patted the softness of his belly with satisfaction. 'I like that,' he said. 'Confession!' He laughed a moment longer than was polite, as if drawing attention to the manner in which he was humouring them.

A woman, whom Lucy assumed to be Nixon's wife, was sitting next to him. She laid her hand on top of his and squeezed it as she watched Lucy with open suspicion.

'I saw you last week, at our prayer service,' Nixon said to Fleming.

'That's why we're here, Pastor,' Fleming said.

'Did I do something wrong?'

'A man was beaten to death last night in the city. With a rock.'

'That's dreadful,' Nixon said, frowning. 'Though I'm at a loss as to why you'd come to me.'

'The young man was gay.'

Nixon nodded now, swallowed whatever he had been preparing to say as he stared at his hands, gathered in his lap. He blessed himself, the movements exaggeratedly grand. 'That is truly dreadful to hear. No one has the right to take another life. No matter how depraved that life might be.'

'That's not quite what you said last week, by all accounts,' Lucy commented. 'You defended the stoning of gay men.'

'Homosexual men,' Nixon said. 'I didn't defend their stoning, I said it was due penalty, the wages of their sin. There's a difference.'

'A subtle one.'

'Preaching is a subtle art.'

'Its effects aren't always subtle. You condone the stoning of gay people and seven days later someone stones a gay man to death.'

'A homosexual man,' Nixon repeated. 'Let's not sugar coat it. I have no control over my fellow man's actions. I preach the Word as I know it; how others act is a matter between them and their conscience.'

A young man sitting at the table, whom Lucy took to be Nixon's son, spoke now. 'Are you seriously accusing my father of being involved in someone's murder?'

'Of course not,' Fleming said. 'But . . . if we establish that the victim's sexuality was an issue in his death, I do think it would be prudent for the pastor to take account of the sensitivity of that in his next sermon.'

Nixon smiled. 'You want me to dilute the Lord's message. Because of sensitivities, Tom?'

'That's outrageous—' the young man started, though he was cut short by his father.

'Ian gets a little hot under the collar,' Nixon said, placing his arm around the younger man's shoulders, the size of Nixon's paw-like hand highlighting the narrowness of his son's shoulders, the fineness of his frame.

'We're asking you to tone down the inflammatory language in your service, Mr Nixon,' Lucy said.

'Pastor—' Ian began, but his father, tightening his grip on his shoulder, silenced him.

'Miss Black, the homosexual lobby has been furthering this agenda of theirs for years now. We see good people being taken to court because they won't compromise their morals by serving this agenda. Bakeries being vilified because they won't bake a "gay cake". Votes in Stormont on gay marriage, a referendum in the Irish Republic over the same thing. Ordinary decent people are sick and tired of being bullied and coerced into vindicating the lifestyle choices of sodomites. If my language is inflammatory, it is in the hope that it enkindles goodness and decency.'

'You think gay people shouldn't be served by shop owners who disagree with them?'

'I think each individual has to have the freedom to make that choice. If someone doesn't want to serve a homosexual, that's their moral decision.'

Lucy smiled. 'I heard a racist bigot use a similar argument to describe serving Roma immigrants,' she said. 'I'd caution you to be careful in what you say.'

'We're not curtailing your freedom to speak, Pastor,' Fleming began, but Nixon was focused on Lucy now, his hand raised imperiously to silence those around him.

'Every liberal on the planet was crying about the need for freedom of speech when that magazine was attacked in Paris. Everyone with their *Je Suis Charlie* badges and pictures. Then someone writes an article in the paper expressing her opinion that immigrants are cockroaches and the world vilifies her. The same liberals who defended freedom of speech three months earlier deplored it all of a sudden. That's the problem with the liberal agenda, Miss Black. You can't have your cake and eat it.'

'In Northern Ireland, you can't have your cake at all if you're gay, apparently,' Lucy retorted. 'To be clear, we're not asking you *not* to speak. But I've just left two parents mourning the death of their only son. I would have thought the Christian thing to do in that situation would be to not add to their pain any further with offensive comments. That's hardly unreasonable, Pastor Nixon.'

Nixon smiled coldly, then clasped his hands in front of him. 'Not at all, DS Black. Good day, Tom,' he added, nodding to Fleming, then he turned his back on them both and addressed those with whom he had been sitting.

'Shall we say grace after our meal?' he asked, though not all of those with him had even finished eating.

Chapter Twelve

FLEMING HAD SPOKEN little since he and Lucy had left their meeting with Nixon. Lucy couldn't tell whether his annoyance was with her for the manner in which she had spoken to Nixon or with Nixon for the manner in which he had been so dismissive of Fleming throughout the meeting. Either way, even when they had picked up a takeaway for their dinner, he had barely spoken beyond offering Lucy a share of his Lemon Chicken.

'I'm sorry I got a little heavy handed there,' Lucy said finally, as they pulled into the Strand Road station ahead of the 8 p.m. briefing.

Fleming acknowledged the comment with a nod. 'He has no intention of toning it down,' he said. 'Not now.'

'Maybe he'll have a chance to reflect on things before tomorrow evening,' Lucy suggested. 'Think about the impact on the Givens family.'

'Maybe,' Fleming said, though with little conviction.

THE BRIEFING STARTED at 8 p.m. sharp. The room was almost full, the air heavy with the smell of curry and sweat, the small windows at the back opened wide in a vain attempt to freshen the place a little.

Burns stood at the top of the room. He looked tired, his suit jacket crumpled, his tie loosened, the knot shifted across too far to the left so that the collar of his shirt sat up a little over it.

'Right, people,' he began. 'Quick update. We have the name of the victim now – Martin Givens. His family have been informed and, this evening, he was positively identified by his parents. Our thoughts are with them, obviously. It's imperative that we give them some answers as to why their eighteen-year-old son died last night. We know that Martin was at Paradise night club with a friend, Gareth McGonigle. We have CCTV footage of them leaving and going down the Strand Road, before we lose them on Princes Street. Clearly, at some stage, Martin ended up at Bay Road Park, at the end of the Strand Road, approximately two miles from where we last have images of him. McGonigle hasn't been seen since Martin's body was found.'

On the screen behind him, a blurred image appeared of Martin Givens and Gareth McGonigle walking down the Strand. In the image Martin's face was turned towards Gareth, his mouth open in laughter. Gareth had both hands jammed in his pockets, a small leather satchel hanging to his left-hand side.

'Were McGonigle and Givens partners? Sexually?' one of the DCs asked.

Burns raised a hand over his eyes to shield himself from the glare of the projector. In doing so, Lucy could see the ring of sweat-darkened material under the arm of his light blue shirt. 'We don't know. But in his continuing absence, it's hard not to think McGonigle's connected in some way to what happened to

Martin Givens. Finding him is our top priority. We also need to find this car.'

Another slide: a blue Peugeot, taken from an elevated angle.

'We picked this up on CCTV from the bottom of the Strand Road. We believe this car is the one in which Martin Givens died. You can see that the front passenger window is missing and we have what looks like a dent here.'

He pointed to the roof of the car above the passenger window.

'This was taken by the ANPR cameras at the fuel depot on the Strand Road. We've run the plates. The car belonged to an Eleanor Rea, in Dungiven. She sold it through a used car website a month ago. Whoever has been driving it has been doing so untaxed and hasn't re-registered the car in their own name.'

'Did Mrs Rea not get the name of the buyer?' Fleming asked.

Burns shook his head. 'It was her daughter's car. The girl has emigrated and asked her to sell it on for her. She got eight hundred pounds for it, in cash. All she could tell us was that the youth who bought it was local, looked to be in his twenties and had tattoos.'

'That narrows it down,' Lucy said.

'As for this evening,' Burns said, 'we know that the local kids congregate under the bridge for a drinking session on summer evenings. There's a possibility that some of them there last night heard or saw something. I know the shift ends at ten. The ACC has agreed overtime for those of us going to canvass the kids in Bay Road Park,' Burns continued. 'DS Gallagher and Sinclair will lead, with support from our colleagues in the PPU who've agreed to assist in the questioning of minors. I've asked for a team of uniformed officers to go with them to take statements and offer support, just in case, but ask that you hold back unless needed.

We don't want to spook the kids. I've assigned a second team to Paradise night club. I want you to do a canvass of those coming and going, with a picture of Martin. See if anyone remembers seeing him with anyone last night. And in particular, keep an eye out for Gareth McGonigle. Finding him is as important as finding this bloody car.'

Chapter Thirteen

ALL FOUR OF them travelled together in a marked car, Mickey driving and Tara in the passenger seat next to him, with Lucy and Fleming in the back.

'Did you enjoy your pizza?' Mickey asked, glancing up at Lucy in the rear-view mirror.

'It was grand,' she said. 'How was the stag?'

'Mental,' Mickey managed. 'It was tea time before I felt like I could keep anything down, you know.'

Lucy smiled mildly. 'When's your friend getting married?'

'Next weekend,' Mickey said. 'They're off to Majorca to get it done there.'

'That's the best way,' Tara opined.

'No sign of you getting yourself a man?' Mickey asked, nudging her.

'We should split up,' Fleming said. 'There are paths down to underneath the bridge on both sides of the carriageway.'

'What if they make a run for it? If there's drink or drugs and they're underage, they'll not want to be caught.'

Fleming shook his head. 'At the base of the bridge is a set of concrete steps. The kids tend to sit on those. If we come down the two paths, they'll be stuck in the middle, on the steps. We just need to make it very clear to them that we're not out for them. It'll be fairly unlikely any of them will have heard or seen anything of any use anyway; Givens' body was found a fair distance from where they sit.'

Mickey pulled into the lay-by on the side of the bridge serving the city-bound traffic. 'We'll head across and go down the far side,' he said. 'Save you having to cross the road, sir,' he added.

Fleming offered no argument. 'I'll ask uniforms to stay on the carriageway itself in case any of them try cutting up over the railings and up onto the bridge.'

Once the four uniformed officers had taken up position, Fleming and Lucy headed down the walkway that curved around the base and then met the pathway from the opposite side at the bottom of the steps which led up to the point where the bridge and ground met.

The bridge itself was a cantilever construction, its central arch spanning a quarter of a kilometre over the river and standing almost forty metres above it. A series of concrete pillars supported it across the river, the nearest of which sat just below where they now walked, at the edge of the river shoreline.

Even though they were some distance from the base of the bridge, they could already hear the noise of the youths assembled beneath the bridge's shelter. The bass notes of a song being played through someone's phone echoed against the underside of the concrete arch above them. The air filled with laughter and screaming and the odd obscenity being shouted in a verbal volley of insults between a youth sitting at the top of the steps and one further down.

As they reached the curve in the path they could see that a few of the youths had come down off the steps altogether and were standing in the tarmacked area below it, playing what Lucy first assumed to be a game of catch with a small ball. However, when one of them dropped the object and it exploded against the ground in a spray of froth, she realised they had been tossing a beer can to one another. The one who had dropped the can turned to pick it up and drink it, clearly the forfeit for having failed to keep the game going. In doing so, he was the first to see Lucy and Fleming approaching.

'Five-0!' he shouted, stepping back from the still discharging can.

The call was taken up by others in the group, rippling back up the steps under the bridge. Some of them scrambled to their feet, clearly gathering up their carry-outs. By this stage, though, Tara and Mickey had appeared along the opposite path and the gathered crowd seemed to realise that they were trapped between them. Despite this, a few scrambled round the concrete base of the bridge, trying to pick their way up the narrow grass incline and onto the upper carriageway.

'Shit!' one of them shouted, and Lucy guessed he had met the uniforms standing watch up there.

Lucy raised her hands and called to the youths standing watching her. 'Please, no one is in trouble. We need your help! We're not looking to catch you doing anything, so please calm down.'

The group, numbering forty perhaps, quietened a little, but most did not sit, waiting, their blue carry-out bags abandoned at their feet.

Fleming spoke now. 'There was an incident in the park last night,' he shouted. 'A young man died. We don't suspect anyone here, but we would like your help. If you were here last night, can you speak to one of the officers and tell us if you saw or heard anything unusual? You will not get into trouble, I promise you.'

This guarantee offered, some of the fellas among the group seemed to find their bravado again.

'Piss off,' one shouted, ducking his head behind the others around him so as to hide himself, somewhat ineffectually. Lucy scanned the group, shining the torch up towards the base of the bridge so as to illuminate the group but not blind any of them with the glare. The area at the top of the steps, in effect one of the support struts for the bridge, rising some twelve feet above the uppermost step, had been painted with graffiti. A large cartoon face winked down at her alongside several words in bubble letters, which she could not read.

She scanned the group now. A few of the kids looked wasted already, holding onto those around them for support. The steps on which they stood, which numbered over sixty, were much steeper than Lucy had realised. Some of the youths near the top were having some trouble keeping their balance, with several gripping onto the metal railing that bisected the stairway.

'A young man was murdered here last night,' Lucy shouted. 'A boy of your age. He died at the far end of the park. Did any of you see anything unusual here last night?'

'That was Marty,' a girl up to Lucy's right offered. 'Gareth knows him.' Lucy shone the torch towards her, careful not to direct it in the girl's face. The one who had spoken was small, with dyed blond hair, bright lipstick. Lucy guessed she might be fourteen. 'Gareth knows him,' she repeated and twisted her head, looking up to the top of the steps. Lucy directed the torch towards where the girl had indicated and there, for a moment, in the torchlight, she saw Gareth McGonigle.

Instantly, McGonigle shoved forward, causing the youths in front of him to lose their balance on the shallow steps and fall. Those around him scattered, taking the distraction as an opportunity to make a run for it, while below him, the falling youths created a domino effect of more and more falling. A girl screamed as the heavy-bodied youth on the step above her fell onto her, causing her to fall and strike her head on the steps.

Lucy and Fleming moved forward instantly, trying to get to McGonigle at the top of the steps, but the youths were chaotic now, screaming, stumbling down the steps. In the light of the wildly swinging torch she carried, Lucy saw a girl standing staring in shock at the blood badging her hands, which she had just wiped from her face.

'We have a suspect on the top of the steps,' Fleming shouted into the radio he carried. 'Pick him up on the carriageway. Bright blond hair. You can't miss him. Suspect is Gareth McGonigle. M-C-G-O-N-I-G-L-E.'

Mickey was attempting to scale the steps after McGonigle but those falling from higher up blocked his passage. Meanwhile, as the four PSNI officers moved into the morass of bodies tumbling down the steps, those at the bottom took it as a chance to escape, making a run for it down into the darkness of the park itself, away from the bridge and the uniforms who waited above them.

'Stop!' Fleming shouted. 'Everyone, stop!'

The youths remaining on the steps struggled to get to their feet, a number of them sporting cuts and grazes from the fall. 'Where's Gareth McGonigle?'

Lucy straightened, helping the boy next to her to his feet. She shone her torch along the bank of faces in front of her, but could not see McGonigle.

'He's not here,' she said.

'He didn't come down this way,' Tara said. 'I've been keeping an eye on who made it down to the bottom.'

'He must be on the carriageway,' Mickey shouted. 'He must have made it up and over the railings.'

Fleming clicked on his radio again. 'Any sign of the suspect?'

'Nothing,' the voice came back. 'We have a dozen up here, none matching the suspect's description.'

'Keep watch,' Fleming said. 'He must be here somewhere.'

Lucy felt her mobile vibrate and groaned when she recognised her mother's number. She'd have to be the one to tell her that they'd had McGonigle and lost him.

'Lucy,' her mother said without preamble when she answered. 'Did you and Tom go to see that pastor earlier? Nixon?'

Lucy looked across to where Fleming stood, scanning the park area below them, clearly looking for McGonigle. 'Yes. We warned him to tone things down.'

She felt her phone vibrate against her ear, even as her mother said, 'I've just sent you something. This appeared online earlier. The calls have already started coming in connecting it to Martin Givens.'

Lucy looked down at the screen, clicking through to Messages. The new message from her mother was a video clip.

The footage was a little grainy, taken as it had been on a mobile phone from someone sitting among the congregation. But it was clear enough for Lucy to see Pastor Nixon standing on a raised stage.

'Only last week, I read of an African nation, a heathen nation, a Godless nation, who arrested two men for homosexual acts,' he said on the video footage. 'One of these men was sixteen. Sixteen! And do you know what they did to the pair of them? They stoned them. They took them out of the town and they threw rocks at them until the pair of them were dead. And do you know what I thought? Shall I tell you?' He paused for a moment as someone called something incomprehensible from among the congregation.

'Stoning was too good for those men. Every rock that struck them was a just reward for their sinfulness, their immorality, their ungodly behaviour. Every drop of their blood that stained the ground was a reminder that they deserved to die. It was the wages of their sin!'

Chapter Fourteen

THE TEAM RECONVENED in the Strand Road station just after midnight. The soporific effect of the heat of the station, particularly after the chill of standing down along the river for so long, meant Lucy struggled to stop yawning throughout the briefing. Lucy's mother sat at the front, while Burns stood, debriefing the team.

'So McGonigle just vanished?' Burns said. He looked exhausted too, his eyes red and rheumy, his cheeks shadowed with a reddish stubble that seemed incongruous in contrast with the sandiness of his hair.

'He was definitely there,' Fleming said. 'Then he was gone. He caused a domino effect of kids falling down the steps, then must have run as we dealt with the injured.'

'Could he be in the water?' Burns asked cautiously.

'I suppose theoretically, he could be,' Fleming said. 'But no one up on the bridge saw him going in. None of us heard anything. You'd imagine at that height off the water someone would scream on the way down.'

'Or at least make a splash,' Mickey agreed. 'There was nothing.'

'Then where the hell did he go?' Burns asked. 'He can't just disappear.'

Lucy nodded. 'At least we had visual, sir. So we know he is still alive after last night.'

'And the fact he ran suggests he may well have been involved in Givens' death. Why run unless you're guilty?' Mickey offered.

'He's certainly guilty of something,' Lucy said. 'Maybe just not his friend's death.'

Burns raised his chin interrogatively, encouraging her to continue.

'We know McGonigle's old enough to go clubbing, which begs the question: what's he doing hanging around under the bridge with a group of teenagers?'

'Selling drugs?' Burns said. 'Or drink?'

Lucy shrugged. 'Or picking up underage girls.'

'Or maybe all of the above,' Tara added.

'Any one of those would be enough to leave him wary of speaking to us,' Lucy said.

'I'll keep the uniform watch on Rockmills, in case he goes home again,' Burns said. 'Though, if he knows we're looking for him, he might want to keep off the radar. What about Paradise? Any luck?'

The DS at the front of the room shook his head. 'A lot of people saw Marty Givens last night, but no one noticed who he was with or where he went afterwards. The doorman claimed he stopped him on the way in and Marty had ID. It was an over-twenty-one night, which means whatever he had was fake.'

'And is still missing,' Burns said.

'So, whoever attacked him must have emptied his pockets. Maybe it was an opportunistic mugging gone wrong. The whole gay thing might be a dead end,' the DS said.

'Whether it is or not,' Wilson said, 'we have a problem. Pastor Nixon's sermon from last week has been posted online. It's going . . . what's the word?'

'Viral, ma'am?' Mickey offered.

'Viral,' Wilson repeated. 'Apparently.'

'The PPU team was to speak with him?' Burns said.

'We did. We impressed on him how sensitive an issue it was and how a Christian response might be to try not to exacerbate the pain of Martin's parents,' Lucy said.

'DS Black warned him to tone it down or else,' Fleming explained to a ripple of laughter.

'And was he receptive to such a warning?'

'We hoped so,' Fleming said. 'This might change things, though. If the message is already out there, he may not see any point in mincing his words.'

'Maybe impress the message again even more firmly,' Burns said. 'Have we any idea who put it online?'

'We don't know,' Fleming said. 'But it shouldn't be too hard to find out.'

'Members of the local gay community are already making a connection between Nixon and how Givens died; we've had several calls reporting Nixon for hate crimes. Which makes it all the more important for us to establish the actual motive here quickly. Especially if it *is* a mugging gone wrong.'

If the comment was meant to pep the team up, it failed. Lucy glanced across to where Tara sat with her eyes closed.

'It's been a very long day, folks,' Burns said. 'I appreciate your staying on this evening. Go home and get a night's sleep. We'll reconvene at eight a.m.'

As they filed down the stairs, Fleming offered to get a taxi home rather than have Lucy go out of her way to drive him, but she refused. Consequently, he was sitting in the car with her when the call came through to her mobile.

'DS Black? This is Adrian Lupei. You were at our house last night?'

Lucy glanced at Fleming who was already frowning. *The son*, she mouthed to him before responding to the boy. 'I remember, Adrian. Is something wrong?'

'It's my dad,' the boy said. 'He's been beaten up. They've left him in hospital.'

Sunday

Chapter Fifteen

ANDRE LUPEI WAS unrecognisable. The left-hand side of his face was swollen, his eye ballooned shut, the skin livid red. His right cheek carried bruising and a gash, the edges of which had been sealed together by a series of paper stitches. The eye above the cut was already purpling. A small oxygen pipe sat on his upper lip, the two outlets embedded in crusted blood from his nostrils.

'His shift finished at ten thirty. He always walks home,' Constanta, his wife, explained. She sat next to the bed, one hand resting on the bedclothes, gripping her husband's hand. Occasionally, she would lean across and fix the oxygen pipe at his nose if it slipped with the movement of his head in his sleep.

There was little use in pointing out how foolhardy a practice this had been considering the threats that he had endured and the attack on the house, Lucy thought. Fleming had clearly reached a similar conclusion, for he nodded his head to show he understood, but said nothing.

'He normally comes in about eleven,' Constanta continued, 'but when he wasn't home by eleven forty-five I called Cezar.'

She nodded towards the door, against which Cezar Lupei stood, behind Lucy and Fleming. He raised his chin a little in acknowledgement of his name, but did not speak. His right foot tapped out an impatient tattoo against the wall behind him, his arms folded across his chest, his fist gathered in front of his mouth. His gaze shifted from Lucy to Fleming and then back to Constanta and the figure of his brother lying on the bed.

'Where did you find him?' Fleming asked.

'In the grass area in Greenway. Near the children's toys.'

'The play area?' Lucy said. 'The swings and slides and that?'

Cezar nodded. His foot slid from the wall onto the floor as he shifted onto his right foot, his left foot picking up the rhythmic tapping against the wall now.

'That's opposite the taxi stand,' Fleming said.

Another nod. Cezar straightened now. 'Yes. The taxis.'

Lucy turned to Constanta. 'Was that his usual route home? Across the playground?' she asked. The play area was at the centre of Greenway, while the Lupeis' house was to the periphery, on the side closest to the hospital. It made no sense that Andre would have walked as far as the playground if he were headed home.

'No. He doesn't have to go into the estate,' she said.

'Might he have taken a taxi home? Or a lift perhaps?' Lucy suggested.

Constanta shook her head. 'We don't know anyone in the estate,' she said. 'Andre keeps to himself. "Don't draw attention to yourself," he tells Adrian. He was annoyed that Adrian phoned you yesterday about the paint.' The boy, sitting next to his mother, lowered his head.

'You were right to call us,' Fleming said.

'It doesn't look that way,' Cezar snapped from behind them. 'Considering how it's ended up.'

'We are investigating,' Fleming said, 'both the leaflet and the attacks. We'll try to make sure that someone will pay for it.'

'How?' Cezar said. He moved into the room now, his limp pronounced. 'How will they pay? Will they pay Andre for the damage to his house? For the work hours he's lost because of this? What's the price for that?'

'If we find who did this, they will have their day in court. All that you've described will be taken into account—'

'How will that help *us*?'

'I understand your anger, Mr Lupei,' Fleming said.

Lupei grunted derisively. 'Adrian, come and we'll get some coke from the machine.'

Adrian stood, looking to his mother who nodded.

'Do you want anything?' he asked.

She shook her head, speaking in Romanian in response.

When they had left the room, Fleming sat on the opposite side of the bed from Constanta Lupei.

'Cezar?' he began. 'What happened to his leg?' Fleming asked.

'A motorcycle accident,' Constanta said.

Fleming nodded, then brooked the actual subject he wanted to address concerning Cezar. 'He'll want to get revenge for what's happened to Andre?'

Constanta nodded.

'Do you think he'll do something . . . violent?'

The woman considered the question, looking to her sleeping husband as if expecting a response from him.

'Men talk,' she said. 'Andre wouldn't want anyone getting into trouble for him. Cezar knows his brother: he knows that.'

'We need to look at getting you moved out of Greenway,' Lucy said. 'I know you don't want to move but . . . well, tonight could have been much worse. Andre will get better *this* time.'

Constanta nodded. 'We have no money,' she said. 'We bought that house; everything is tied up in it.'

Fleming nodded. 'We'll see what can be done,' he said. 'We can't promise anything, but there is a scheme, SPED, that allows the Housing Executive to buy your house from you if your life is under threat.'

Constanta's face brightened a little. 'That would be perfect,' she said. 'We could buy somewhere else.'

Fleming held up a cautioning hand. 'There are no guarantees,' he said. 'We would need a very senior officer to sign it off. An Assistant Chief Constable or higher.'

'Would he do it for us?'

'*She,*' Fleming said. 'She might. But we need to prove that a terror group is threatening your life.'

'What more proof do you need?' Constanta said suddenly, pointing to her husband, more animated now at the prospect of a possible escape from Greenway.

'I agree,' Fleming said. 'But we need to get our superior to sign it off, nevertheless. We can try but we're not promising anything.'

'But you'll do your best?' Constanta said. 'To convince her?'

Fleming glanced at Lucy who smiled and nodded. 'Yes, Mrs Lupei. I'll do my very best to convince her.'

Chapter Sixteen

LUCY WAS JUST drifting off to sleep when she heard Grace coming in downstairs and closing the front door. She heard her rattling around in the kitchen, making herself toast for her supper, heard the creak and pad of her footfalls on the stairs as she made her way up to bed.

'Night,' Lucy called sleepily.

Light spilled around the edges of the open door as Grace peered in.

'Hey. I thought you'd be asleep,' she whispered.

'How was work?'

'Fine. Some of *your* crew were there asking about last night.'

Lucy nodded, murmuring a little.

'What?'

'They were looking for info about the Givens kid,' she mumbled.

'What happened to him?' Grace asked, moving into the room now, one hand holding the door.

'Someone beat his head in with a rock.'

'Because he was gay?'

Lucy raised her head and turned the pillow over, pressing her cheek back against the cold linen. 'Maybe,' she said. 'We don't know yet. How was work?'

Grace moved across and lay down on top of the bed next to Lucy, her face turned towards the ceiling. Lucy could smell beer from her clothes and the tang of her deodorant beneath it.

'Porter went mental tonight. He said some cops were in earlier and found legal highs in the place.'

Lucy smiled sleepily. 'That was me.'

Grace nudged her. 'Thanks a bunch. We were checking the toilets all night for dealing. He was on the warpath.'

'Did anyone find anything?'

Grace shook her head. 'Nothing. Nothing at all.'

She turned her face towards Lucy, only to find that she was already asleep.

LUCY WOKE WITH Grace shaking her. The younger woman still lay on top of the blankets, but she held Lucy's mobile in her hand.

'Tom Fleming has been calling you,' she said.

Lucy sat up suddenly, glancing across to the alarm clock. It was just past 4.30 a.m. She took the phone from Grace, noted the disarray of her hair, the imprint of the seam of her duvet on the girl's right cheek.

'I fell asleep.' Grace shrugged. 'I'm going into my own bed.'

She got up and moved out of the room. Lucy sat up, fixing her T-shirt on her shoulder before calling Fleming.

'Lucy,' he said on answering. 'I thought you'd want to know. It looks like Charles Dougan's taxi company has been torched.'

She pulled back the duvet, sat up properly as she shifted the phone to her other ear. 'Do you need me to collect you?'

'I'm already here,' Fleming said.

'I'm on my way,' Lucy said.

SHE WAS BARELY halfway through the Greenway Estate when she saw the plume of smoke illuminated by the intermittent flashing of the fire-engine lights.

Most houses were still in darkness, though at a few, people had come out to see what was happening. Several late-night revellers staggered along the pavement on their way home. One man, in his twenties, Lucy guessed, stepped out onto the road in front of her, forcing her to brake, and crossed without even checking for traffic. Nor did he register that she was shouting at him from the open window of her car as he threaded his way down an alleyway between two rows of houses and, stopping, undid his trousers and urinated against a lamp-post. He swayed from side to side, drawing a line across the pavement in front of him. On the wall, next to where he stood, a large hand had been painted in red, white and blue. Lucy recognised it as the image that had been on the anti-immigrant leaflet the Lupeis had shown her.

As she rounded the corner towards the eponymous green area at the centre of the estate, Lucy saw the burning building properly for the first time. There were three fire tenders parked on the roadway, which was further blocked by two PSNI cars. The building continued to burn, the thick billows blooming upwards a result of steam as much as smoke as the fire hoses disgorged water into the taxi office. As she got out of the car at the cordon, she heard a number of quick pops.

'Some of the cars behind the offices were torched, too,' the uniform managing the cordon explained as she approached. 'DS Black?'

Lucy nodded.

'DI Fleming is waiting for you up at the site.'

Fleming was in conversation with one of the fire officers when he saw Lucy coming down towards him. He excused himself and came up the roadway to meet her.

'What happened?'

Fleming shrugged. 'No one's talking. The dispatcher is claiming he heard nothing.'

'What about Dougan?'

Fleming stepped back a little and indicated to where Dougan stood, at the far side of the road, deep in conversation with another man who was sitting on the kerb, a foil blanket around his shoulders. Lucy recognised the man but could not, for a moment, place where last she had seen him.

'He's having a quiet word with his worker,' Fleming said.

'Hard to feel sympathy for him,' Lucy said. 'Dougan, I mean.'

Fleming shrugged. 'I'd put an alert on his name in the station, so they called me when the owner of the business was identified.'

Dougan had finished his conversation and moved across to Fleming and Lucy.

'How is he?' Fleming asked.

Dougan nodded grimly. 'Fine. I think he was in shock. He seems to have come around now.'

'Was he able to provide any further information about what happened?'

Dougan pantomimed a grimace, inhaling sharply through his bottom teeth as he did so. 'He was smoking in the office and mustn't have stubbed out the cigarette properly. He must've been afraid he'd have been blamed for it.'

Fleming stared at Dougan. 'Really?'

Dougan shrugged. 'I'm telling you what he told me.'

'You know the fire investigators will be able to tell very easily if this was started deliberately.'

Dougan smiled. 'Now why would you say that?'

'You can smell petrol in the air, for goodness' sake.'

Dougan raised his head a little as if to inhale. He nodded. 'Must be some of the cars burning out the back. And we keep cans of petrol out there in case any of the drivers run out and need an emergency fill. Could be those went up in the fire.'

'You don't honestly expect us to believe any of this, Mr Dougan?' Fleming asked.

'Fuck I care?' Dougan laughed. 'Bobby dropped a fag butt.'

The mention of the name helped her place him. 'Bobby. Doesn't he work in McEwan's Printers?'

Dougan appraised her coldly a second then nodded. 'He does a few evenings here for me,' he said.

'Not any more, presumably,' Fleming said.

Dougan shrugged. 'It was a mistake. Insurance should cover it anyway.'

'That's very understanding of you,' Lucy said.

'I'm an understanding type of man.'

'A member of the Roma family you were campaigning against ended up in hospital this evening after being assaulted,' Lucy added.

'I wasn't campaigning about anything,' Dougan said.

'You were during a neo-Nazi rally in 2011? *There's no black in the Union Jack!*'

Dougan smiled briefly, though without humour. 'I'm proud of my country. That don't mean I had anything to do with an assault.'

'Where were you this evening?' Lucy asked.

'At home. With my family. You can ask them yourself.' He turned and strode back across to Bobby, the dispatcher.

'The Roma man is going to be okay,' Lucy called. 'In case you were wondering.'

Dougan turned to look at here. 'Like I said, fuck I care.'

Chapter Seventeen

THEY HEADED BACK out to the PPU. Burns had requested everyone be at the Strand Road for an 8 a.m. briefing and there seemed little point in going home for an hour. On the way to their own unit, they spotted a Cuisine de France lorry unloading at the twenty-four-hour garage on Dungiven Road and stopped to buy fresh croissants.

Once in the station, Lucy lay and dozed on the sofa in the interview room usually reserved for speaking to children in the unit while Fleming made them breakfast in the small kitchenette attached to it.

They ate breakfast in the interview room. The unit was deserted, though in the distance they could hear those coming in for the day shift shouting greetings to one another across the car park. Morning light was bleeding through the small windows of the room. They were narrow slits really, set high enough in the wall that those inside would not be seen by outside observers, and small enough that any external blast would shower only limited amounts of glass into the room.

'So, what're your thoughts on the fire?' Lucy asked, pulling apart her croissant and smearing butter across it with the back of a teaspoon, the unit's only knife having gone missing some weeks earlier.

Fleming shrugged. 'Could be an insurance scam,' he said. 'Dougan didn't seem annoyed. Or it might have been an accident. Maybe he *is* the forgiving type.'

Lucy had to look at him to be sure he was joking. 'You don't think it could be connected to what happened to Andre Lupei?'

'We'll not know until we get talking to Bobby, the dispatcher, without Dougan present,' Fleming said. 'I want to wait until the Fire Service is finished there and we get word back on how it started. They'll be able to tell pretty quickly if accelerant was used.'

'And if it was?'

'We look more closely at the Lupei family. Especially the brother, Cezar—'

Fleming's phone began to ring and he checked the screen, frowning as he did so. 'Norman Friel. Something must be happening with Nixon,' he said to Lucy, answering the call. 'Norman! Good to hear from you. How are things?'

Lucy peeled apart the final piece of croissant and chewed on it, listening to the tinny sound of the voice audible from the receiver, picturing the insipid man she'd met at the Gospel Hall on the other end.

'We'll be right up,' Fleming said, ending the call. 'We've got a problem,' he told Lucy.

As they approached the Gospel Hall, fifteen minutes later, they could already see the source of Friel's concern. A group of about a dozen protestors had gathered outside the gates. Among them,

Lucy recognised Shauna Kelly, the woman from the stall in Bedlam Market who had been a friend of Martin Givens. She held a hand-painted placard carrying the slogan, *Hate Is a Crime: Love Is Fine*. Several others standing with her bore similar sentiments on the cards and placards they held. Posters bearing the word *Pride* in rainbow colours had been tied to the fence in front of which they stood.

The group parted to allow Lucy to drive in through the gates and down into the car park. A half-hearted jeer rose as she and Fleming got out of the car and headed across to the doors of the hall where Norman Friel stood inside waiting for their arrival.

He unlocked the door and pulled it open. 'You need to do something about those people, Tom,' he said without greeting. 'Get them moved on.'

'Have they come onto the property?' Lucy asked. 'Or damaged anything?'

Friel shook his head. 'Not yet. But they're blocking the entrance way. We have the sermon tonight; they're going to drive people away.'

'Is the pastor here?' Fleming asked.

'He's praying at the moment,' Friel said. 'He can't be disturbed.'

'We can wait,' Fleming said. 'And Norman, would you be able to pull up any security camera footage you have from inside the hall during last week's sermon?'

Friel glanced at Lucy, then back to Fleming. 'Why?'

'Someone leaked footage of the sermon onto the internet last night, which is why you have the demonstration outside this morning. I'd like to see if we can find out who was filming the pastor last week.'

Friel nodded. 'I suppose that's okay,' he said. 'I'll get it for you.'

'We'll have a word with the people outside while you do,' Fleming said. 'Tell the pastor we'd like to speak with him when he's finished his prayers.'

SHAUNA KELLY VISIBLY steeled herself when she saw Lucy and Fleming approach, while the others around her, a mixture of men and women, though almost all under thirty, seemed to coalesce behind her.

'Miss Kelly,' Lucy began, 'can we have a word?'

Shauna stood her ground. 'Yeah. What?'

Lucy nodded, glancing at the others behind Shauna, glaring at her, as if challenging her to take a side.

'You probably shouldn't be here,' Lucy said.

'We have a right to peaceful protest,' Shauna said. 'It's completely legal.'

Fleming shook his head. 'There is no such thing as a right to peaceful protest,' he said, 'regardless of how many times people invoke it. You have a right to peaceful assembly.'

'Then we're assembling,' Shauna said. 'In protest at what he's done.'

'I understand you're angry at what he said—' Lucy began.

'This is about Martin,' one of the women behind Shauna snapped. 'He was killed for being gay. That man in there told people it was okay.'

Lucy nodded. 'He didn't say Martin's death was—'

'He said gays should be stoned,' Shauna interrupted. 'Which is how Martin died. That man in there is as guilty as whoever picked up the rock that killed Marty.'

'Standing out here protesting isn't going to change his mind,' Lucy said. 'Nor those of the people who attend his sermons. You do realise that?'

'We're not trying to change their minds,' Shauna said. 'But we won't be silenced or shamed either. It's people like him should be ashamed.'

'You need to stay off church property,' Fleming said. 'No matter how provoked you might feel, you need to keep things peaceful. And legal.'

Shauna nodded. 'You'd be better warning him in there about what he does and says. Thinks because he's got "Pastor" in front of his name he's got the right to say whatever he wants.'

'We'll speak to Pastor Nixon,' Lucy said. 'Just mind yourselves out here.'

She turned and followed Fleming into the grounds of the hall again. 'I didn't know you were such an expert of the European Convention on Human Rights,' she said.

'Full of surprises, me,' Fleming laughed. 'I just get fed up with people spouting off about rights they have that don't actually exist. All these people claiming their rights and do you know what? They don't seem any happier. The whole world just seems to be getting angry about everything.'

'It's just as well you stay clear of social media, then,' Lucy said.

They pushed back in through the double doors. Norman Friel was standing with Pastor Nixon, wringing his hands.

'Are they going to leave?' he asked.

Fleming shook his head. 'They invoked their right to free assembly. We've warned them to stay outside the grounds.'

Nixon laughed. 'Homosexuals and their rights,' he said. 'Missing the irony of their protesting my right to freedom of speech.'

'Have you considered toning things down, sir?' Lucy asked. 'In deference to the grieving parents of Martin Givens.'

Nixon shook his head. 'I'll pray for them and for their son this evening,' he said. 'But I won't curtail my own beliefs for anyone. Their pain is a result of their son's sinfulness. He is wholly responsible for what they are going through. Besides, now that my words from last week are all over the World Wide Web, there seems little point. Everyone knows my views. Those who come to hear them are coming because they agree with me. I'd be failing my own congregation and myself otherwise.'

'And we wouldn't want that, would we, sir?' Lucy said. 'We will be present tonight, Pastor Nixon, to ensure that at no point does your right to freedom of speech overreach into the realms of incitement to hatred. Just so you know.'

'I look forward to seeing you, DS Black.' He nodded, as if dismissing them.

'Did you get that for me, Norman?' Fleming asked Friel.

Friel nodded and moved across to the desk opposite on which sat a brown envelope. He picked it up and handed it to Fleming.

'What's this?' Nixon asked, smiling.

'Footage from last week,' Fleming said. 'I wanted to see if I could find out who had been filming you on their phone. We might be able to get to the source of who leaked the footage last night.'

'Very good,' Nixon muttered, but his expression darkened. He glanced askance at Friel, then excused himself and pushed his way through the doors into the prayer room again.

Chapter Eighteen

THEY DROVE UP through Greenway in order to get back to the PPU block at Maydown. As they passed through the centre of the estate, Lucy glanced across at the smouldering remains of Greenway Taxis. Dougan and his dispatcher Bobby had gone now. Only a single fire tender remained and Lucy could see the men, still in high-vis jackets, picking their way through the debris of the building.

'Give me a second,' Fleming said, as Lucy drew up alongside the cordon. Undoing his seat belt, he slid out of his seat and ducked under the cordon tape. Lucy parked up and followed him across to the still smoking shell.

The air was damp, the breeze that blew across the green so rich with the scent of burnt wood it made Lucy's eyes water. Unbidden, the smell brought to mind an image of Mary Quigg, so clear and sharp, Lucy felt her breath catch.

Mary Quigg was a child Lucy had met during her first case with the PPU. She had been looking after her younger brother and herself, her mother being an alcoholic who had fallen in with a low-level recidivist named Alan Cunningham. Cunningham had stolen from the house and set it alight one evening with the rest of the family still inside. Mary and her mother had died. Lucy had sat outside her smouldering house, in tears, retching against the acridity of the smell.

The younger brother Joe had survived and was adopted by a couple living on the Culmore Road. Lucy occasionally drove by the house to get a glimpse of the boy, to ensure he was okay. She had once considered calling with the child, but had decided against it. How would it have profited him to know, at such a young age, the horrors that had been inflicted on those who loved him most?

Cunningham, however, had been in the wind since the killing. Lucy had managed to convince a local hoodlum with links to Limerick, where Cunningham was hiding out, to withdraw their support for him, but since then, he seemed to have disappeared. Lucy knew that he would eventually answer for what he had done to Mary Quigg and that Lucy herself would be there when it happened. Until then, Mary's picture remained pinned to Lucy's office wall as a reminder of that. The difficulty was, as time went on, and Cunningham remained free, that Lucy was finding it harder and harder to look at the girl's image each time she went into the room, as if bowed by the shame in having failed her.

She took a breath, held it, then allowed herself to move forward towards where, ahead of her, Fleming was talking to one of the firemen at the scene. The man had pulled down the breathing apparatus from his face in order to speak more clearly, the mask leaving an outline of grime haloing his features.

'Morning, Sergeant,' he said at Lucy's approach. 'Long night.' A statement, not a question.

Lucy nodded. 'For us all.'

'Kevin here was just saying that the fire was started deliberately,' Fleming offered.

'Not from a dropped cigarette, you mean?'

Kevin shook his head, the breathing mask bouncing lightly against his chest as he did. 'Not unless two cigarettes were dropped at two different parts of the office into petrol.'

He turned, leading them towards the building. 'Two points of origin,' he said. 'We followed the burn patterns in from the front and from the back. Had there been a single source, the two patterns would have converged. They didn't.'

'Was an accelerant used?' Fleming asked.

Kevin shrugged. 'We'll not know until we take residue samples from the points of origin. Even so, the owner claimed there were canisters of petrol in the office which could have gone up accidentally.'

'But definitely not a cigarette butt being dropped accidentally?'

'I'm pretty certain that's not what happened,' Kevin agreed.

Fleming thanked him and turned to Lucy. 'Why don't we call with Bobby ourselves and find out what really happened?'

'Where is he?'

Fleming feigned surprise. 'Getting his compo claim ready, of course, in A&E.'

THE EMERGENCY WARD was buzzing despite the early hour. Some of those seated looked to have just arrived, perhaps hoping that early on a Sunday, the waiting times wouldn't be too bad. Others appeared to have been there most of the night, including one woman who was stretched across four plastic chairs, fast asleep, one leg hanging off the edge of the seat, twitching involuntarily every few seconds.

'We're looking for a man who was brought in this morning from a fire in Greenway,' Fleming said to the receptionist.

'Which one?'

'Which fire?' Fleming asked incredulously.

'No, which patient? We have five in from the Greenway fire.'

'There was only one person there when it happened,' Fleming said.

'Apparently not. Four of them are waiting to be seen in triage. The fifth's already in with the nurses.'

'Bobby someone, we're looking for,' Fleming said.

'McLean. He's already being seen,' she said. 'Head on through.'

BOBBY MCLEAN WAS sitting up in bed when Lucy and Fleming pulled back the curtain of the partitioned area in which he had been left. He held an oxygen mask in one hand, the top of the index finger of his other hand enclasped in a small white clothes-peg-like monitor.

'Mr McLean?'

Bobby nodded, took another hit off the oxygen.

'You were in the fire at Greenway Taxis last night?' Fleming asked.

The youth nodded. Lucy studied him more carefully now. He was in his early twenties at most. His hair was slick with gel, combed over to one side, hanging limply in a fringe over his fore-head. His eyes darted from Fleming to the waiting room beyond, restlessly. He sniffed nervously, and as he did Lucy noticed a scar transverse the bridge of his nose. A few smudges of soot dirtied his cheek on one side, accentuating the acne pockmarks his skin carried. He wore a white tracksuit jersey over a football top. A thin gold chain hung round his neck and it was with this that he fidgeted as he spoke to them.

'You work in McEwan's Printers, too, isn't that right?' Fleming said.

'That's right.'

'We're just following up on what happened in the taxi office this morning. Can you describe in your own words what you saw?'

Bobby stared at him blankly, then looked to Lucy, as if hoping she might help him out.

'Just in your own words, Bobby,' she echoed.

'Charlie's already told you,' he said. 'I dropped my fag.'

'I know. But maybe in your own words. What happened after you dropped it?'

Bobby shrugged. 'I don't know. The place went up in flames. I panicked. I think I must have breathed in smoke or something. Smoke immolation.'

'Inhalation,' Fleming said.

'What?'

'Smoke inhalation. Immolation suggests you set *yourself* on fire rather than just the taxi office.'

'Inhalation,' Bobby repeated drily. 'Big difference!'

'We know that the fire was started deliberately, Bobby,' Lucy said. 'The fire service have identified two separate points of origin, which means your cigarette story doesn't add up. Either you torched the place deliberately, in which case you'll be done for arson, or else you're lying to cover up what really happened. In which case we'll do you for obstruction. Which would you prefer?'

Bobby stared at them across the top of the mask he held, still clamped over his mouth and nose.

'I think you could probably breathe on your own for a few minutes, Bobby,' Fleming said. 'What happened last night?'

'Do I need a lawyer?' Bobby asked, lowering the breathing equipment slowly.

'Only if you're planning on lying to us,' Lucy said.

'I only work in the place,' Bobby said. 'It's nothing to do with me.'

'The fire or the business?'

'Both.'

'You didn't start the fire. We know that.'

Bobby nodded.

'So, who did?'

He took a deep breath through the mask then lowered it again, coughing a little, raising his hand to wipe the spittle from his mouth, then finding the cord on the heart monitor was too short and prohibited him from so doing. He used the back of the hand holding the mask, then shook his head. 'I don't know. They didn't say.'

Lucy, realising that he would talk in his own time now, said nothing and waited for Bobby to continue.

'It was just after four they came in. Most of the drivers had finished up for the night and a few of them had left their cars round the back like they normally do. I was sitting watching the TV when two guys came in with two petrol canisters. I thought maybe their car had broken down and they wanted a taxi to the nearest garage, but when I stood up to talk to them through the grille, between the office and the waiting room, they told me to get out. One of them started pouring petrol around the waiting room and the other waited for me to come out of the office and went in and did the same in there once I'd opened the door. He went out back and I heard him smashing the windows of the cars out there and he must have doused them too. I could hear the whoosh of the flames catching in the cars. He came back in and threw a match into the office and then one more into the waiting room. That was it.'

He stared at the two of them, waiting.

'And they said nothing more?' Fleming asked.

'They told me not to call 999 for ten minutes. They said they'd be watching.'

'Where did they go then?'

'They cut over the green, up through the playground into the estate.'

'Did you notice anything unusual about them? Their clothes, the way they spoke, anything like that?'

He let the question hang while Bobby considered the question. 'I couldn't be sure.'

'You couldn't tell by their accents?' Lucy asked.

Bobby shook his head, took another breath through the mask before removing it. 'I was in shock. I can't remember much, what with the smoke and that.'

'You were outside the building before it was set alight,' Fleming said. 'The only smoke inhalation you would have suffered would have been from your cigarette.'

'Did they say why they were burning the taxi office?' Lucy asked.

Another headshake. 'No. They just told me to get out and then they left.'

'And what about the other four?' Fleming asked.

'What other four?' Bobby said quickly. 'There were only two of them.'

'The other four in the taxi office at the time? The ones in here claiming to have smoke inhalation too?'

Bobby raised his chin lightly, then lifted the mask and clamped it over his mouth, indicating that for now, he was done talking.

'WE'LL RUN BACKGROUND on Bobby,' Fleming said as they walked out to the car. 'It seems a little coincidental that he works in the printers which Dougan used to print the anti-immigrant leaflets and he's also involved in the fire at Dougan's taxi rank.'

'It doesn't bring us any closer to finding out who set the place alight, though. Could it be something to do with the Lupeis? Cezar, the brother, maybe?'

Fleming nodded. 'Maybe,' he said. 'We'll run his details, too. I want to head back to Greenway: Bobby says the attackers headed across the green. We can ask around about the fire, see if we can't find some witnesses. Maybe slip in the odd question about the attack on Andre Lupei while we're at it. If he was beaten and dumped in the green, someone living there must have seen or heard something.'

Chapter Nineteen

THEY RECEIVED NO response at the first house, though a car was parked in the driveway and music played through the open windows.

The woman who answered at the second house expressed shock at what had happened but could offer no assistance. She'd been working nights over the weekend and hadn't been home.

The owner of the third house, an older man, a cup of tea in his hand when he answered the door, stood for some time with them, but did not invite them inside. He listened to their questions, then set off at a tangent, complaining about the lack of facilities in the estate, seemingly believing they were there to canvass his views on Greenway as opposed to looking for witness statements relating to either the fire or the Lupei attack. Despite Lucy bringing him back to the topic twice, he still managed to include complaints about street lighting (too little), bin collections (too infrequent) and police patrols (too many). He continued calling his complaints after them even as they walked down his pathway to move on to the next house.

It appeared to be the same story in the next house, with the occupant, a woman this time, starting on a rant about antisocial behaviour in the area. This time, however, she did at least invite them into the house. She introduced herself, finally, as Stella, as Lucy and Tom Fleming sat together on the sofa that dominated her living room. She stood at the window, leaning against the sill, a cigarette in one hand, her wrist arched so that the ash curved precipitously, ready to fall onto the linoleum floor. Eventually, unable to stand it, Lucy lifted the ashtray sitting on the table next to her and handed it to Stella, who took it without thanks and flicked the column of ash into it.

'People here are angry,' she said. 'Fed up with it all.'

'I don't doubt it,' Fleming said grimly, casting a surreptitious glance around the room, but Stella had already moved on.

'This used to be a nice place to live; people got on with things. It felt safe, among your own. Then they start letting outsiders in, it's not the same any more.'

Lucy nodded, attempting to appear understanding.

'They brought in the drugs, you know?' Stella added conspiratorially. 'Those ones.'

'Which ones?'

'The gypsies.'

'The Roma?'

Stella nodded. 'That's why I'm voting out.'

Fleming frowned as he attempted to work out what she meant.

'The Brexit!' she explained. 'We're sending £350 million a week to Europe. We're going to have it to spend on our hospitals when we leave.'

'I've seen the posters,' Fleming said. 'You were saying that the Roma family in Greenway were involved with drugs?'

Stella nodded. 'I heard they were bringing in drugs. Last year. They tried bringing them into the estate, but some of the fellas soon stopped it.'

'The family who are being attacked didn't live here last year, Miss . . .' Fleming said.

Stella waved away his protest, wafting a trail of smoke from her cigarette and snowing ash from the newly formed tip onto the floor. 'I'm telling you what I heard. They were selling it in the schools. My Ronnie came home one day and I found it in his pocket.'

'Found what?'

'Drugs!' she snapped. 'What do you think I'm talking about?'

'What kind of drugs?' Fleming asked.

'Those highs. Ronnie said they were all right, but I didn't believe him.'

'Was this legal highs?' Lucy asked. 'You found a legal high in your son's pocket?'

'Aye. His blazer was dirty and I stuck it in the wash.'

'What did the drugs look like?'

'Like herbs,' Stella said. 'It was in a packet, like a rubber johnny packet. I thought that's what it was to start with, until I opened it.'

'Did it have a name?'

Stella closed her eyes as if trying to picture it again. She shook her head. 'Not that I can remember. It had a picture on it. A yellow whatsmecallit. A dinosaur.'

'A dragon?' Lucy asked.

Stella opened her eyes again and clicked her fingers. 'That's it,' she said, taking a drag on her cigarette, then screwing it out on the ashtray. 'A dragon.'

Fleming leaned forward. 'When did this happen?'

'Last Hallowe'en,' Stella said. 'He was off for the holidays. That's why I was washing the bloody blazer,' she added, as if this should have been self-evident.

'Did you tell anyone?'

'The school! They said they'd deal with it. That's the last I knew.'

Lucy wasn't hugely surprised. If Ronnie had bought a legal high, there wasn't a massive amount that could have been done about it last year: the legislation outlawing them had only been passed the previous month. Besides, if the school had been con-tacted, they'd probably have wanted to keep it quiet, which would explain why she'd not read about legal highs being in a local school in the papers. 'Which school was this?'

'The High.'

'Did you ever find any more of them?' Fleming asked.

Stella shook her head. 'I went to see Jackie in the end. That was the last of it.'

Fleming glanced at Lucy. 'Jackie Moss?'

'Sure what other Jackie is there?' Stella snorted. 'Jackie takes care of the people.'

'You don't know anything about the attack that happened out-side your house last night. A man ended up in hospit—'

'I bet it was the gypsies that done it,' Stella said.

She pulled another cigarette from the box on the windowsill and lit it, staring at them both, as if challenging them to disagree.

Chapter Twenty

THE BLUEBELL CAFÉ was not quite as busy as it had been the previous morning. Moss was standing behind the counter this time with the same two women who had been there during their last visit. After they'd finished canvassing the houses, Moss himself was the obvious final port of call. When he saw them enter, he feigned surprise.

'Twice in as many days! What can we get you, Inspector?'

'I'll take a tea,' Fleming said, 'and a pastry or something.'

'What about you, love?' said the woman, whom Lucy thought she remembered Moss calling Annie.

'The same,' Lucy said, 'please.'

'I'll bring it down, if you want to grab a wee seat,' Annie said, turning and lifting a large silver teapot.

Fleming led them to a table near the window, the same one in which Moss had sat the previous day.

A moment later Annie appeared with a tray bearing mugs, spoons, tea and milk and a plate with three large Danish pastries on it.

'There's youse are,' she said unnecessarily. 'On the house.'

'That's not—' Fleming began, but Moss, who had been coming down behind the woman interrupted him.

'I insist. It's the least I can do for the local constabulary.'

He carried a mug of tea in one hand while he leaned heavily on a crutch with the other as he walked. Lucy didn't remember seeing it the day before.

'My hip,' he explained. 'It plays up. I'm waiting eighteen months to have it fixed. Annie says I should go private and get it done but what's the point?'

'You'd not be hopping along like a bloody pirate is the point,' Annie retorted before heading back to the counter.

Moss rolled his eyes in mock exasperation. 'What can I do today?'

'There was a fire in Greenway last night,' Fleming began.

'I heard about that. Bad business. A dropped fag or something, was it?' Moss sipped at his tea, watching Fleming from over the rim as he did so.

'Apparently not. Two men went in and set the place alight.'

Moss put down his tea and shook his head. 'That's dreadful business altogether. No one was hurt, though?'

'There's five in the hospital as we speak getting checked over,' Lucy said.

'Five?' Moss laughed. 'I'd say someone's taking the piss there,' he added, lifting one of the Danish and unfurling the swirl of pastry, then tearing off the end and shoving it in his mouth. He wiped the loose flakes from his fingers onto the plate in front of him.

'You haven't heard anything about it, then?' Fleming asked.

Moss shook his head. 'I heard it had happened. I was told it was an accident.'

'Seems not. You've no idea who'd want to hit Dougan's place? Locals? Foreign nationals? Maybe a bit of a turf war?'

Moss shook his head. 'I've had some people complain to me in here about antisocial behaviour in the area. Those leaflets you were asking about and the like. It's created some bad blood.'

'And was burning Dougan's business an example *of* antisocial behaviour or a punishment *for* it?'

Moss shrugged. 'I'm just trying to keep peace. A bit of graffiti, paint on walls, you have to accept, you know. I'm not saying it's right, but it's understandable, maybe.'

'Not to the Lupei family. The father was beaten up the other night and left in hospital. Andre Lupei,' Lucy said. 'The family are living in terror.'

'Have they thought about moving? There are plenty of young couples trying to get a start on the housing ladder that can't get a place. People from the estate. I'm sure they'd jump at the chance to get a wee house like that. That family could get their money back and find somewhere else.'

'It's the Lupeis' home,' Lucy said.

'No it's not, actually,' Moss said, his voice soft and reasoning. 'Their home is Romania. I'm not saying they *should* move, but you pick your battles. One family can't change the nature of a place like Greenway.'

'You said you'd help.'

Moss's expression darkened. 'And I have helped. The man's in the hospital, not the morgue. I'm trying to keep a lid on things in Greenway. Since they arrived, things have started to boil over a bit. It seems to me that the easiest thing for everyone involved is if they get rehoused and the louts here trying to stir up trouble lose a key element in their recruitment drive.'

'That's not very hospitable.'

'That's reality,' Jackie said. 'We work with what we have.' He hobbled to his feet, gripping his crutch with his right hand.

'We spoke with a resident whose son brought home legal highs from the local school last Hallowe'en. She says she came to see you about it.'

'Did she now? I wouldn't remember.'

'She claimed the Roma were involved in selling drugs.'

Moss shrugged. 'That wouldn't surprise me.'

'It would have been quite a feat, seeing as how they weren't living here last year.'

'As I say, I don't remember that,' Moss said. 'Enjoy your breakfast.' He turned and hobbled back towards the counter.

Lucy left her pastry untouched, the tea suddenly dark and bitter in her mouth.

'Will we go?' she asked.

Fleming nodded. 'Dougan must have borrowed Jackie's colours,' he said. 'I think Jackie's taking them back.'

Lucy looked across to where the big man had reached the counter, puffing his cheeks with the exertion.

'Jesus, someone watch the toaster,' he shouted. 'The last thing we need's this place going up in flames,' he added, as he looked down to where Lucy and Fleming now stood.

Lucy pulled a five-pound note from her pocket and tossed it onto the table next to her plate, then left.

Chapter Twenty-One

THEY ARRIVED IN the PPU just after lunchtime. The Maydown complex was fairly quiet, it being a Sunday afternoon, and many of the trainees who would normally be milling around the compound during the week were away for the weekend.

Lucy ate the last of the morning's croissants in the kitchenette, having been unable to touch anything Moss had offered her in the café. Fleming had gone into his own office to take a look at the CCTV footage from Pastor Nixon's service. She, meanwhile, wanted to process the SPED form for the Lupeis and run checks on Cezar Lupei and Bobby McLean.

She completed the SPED application first. It was a scheme that had been devised to allow the Housing Executive to quickly purchase property from people whose lives were under threat. A number of officers had been able to avail of it when warned of threats to their safety and it precluded having to wait for an estate agent to find a buyer for the house in question. Lucy hoped that by completing the form herself, it might expedite things when it reached her mother who would have to sign off on it as the ACC.

That done, she began running the checks on Lupei and McLean. There was nothing on Lupei in the system, though that wasn't totally surprising: he'd lived in the North for so short a time. She put in a request to the National Central Bureau to run a check for international warrants on Lupei through Interpol's ASF, though she knew that to do so, she might be waiting some time to get the information. The recently established National Crime Agency, long delayed in the North due to political reluctance to have a police force here that could not be held to account by the area's Policing Board, wouldn't be interested in such a low-level crime, unless Lupei had been involved in a major criminal organisation. The possible burning of a taxi stand hardly seemed to fit that criterion.

Having logged her request, she searched HOLMES for information on Bobby McLean. He had been at McEwan's Printers the day they had gone there and now appeared to be trying an insurance scam in the Dougan fire, she reasoned, so he was, at the moment, the only overlap between the incidents in Greenway.

McLean's name appeared several times. He had been cautioned for drunk and disorderly when he was seventeen after PSNI Community officers found him and his friends trying to set alight the swings in the playground at the centre of Greenway at 3 a.m. one morning. He'd also been arrested on suspicion of affray in May 2014. He and two others had been involved in an incident in which a fight broke out outside a pub on the edge of Greenway between two gangs and someone had thrown a breezeblock into the midst of the squabble. Ultimately, the charges had been dropped. In both instances, the responding officer was named as Constable Jason Lloyd.

Lucy called through to the Strand Road to be told that Lloyd was a member of one of the community policing teams and was actually based in Lisnagelvin, in the Waterside. He was due to start his shift at six that evening. She had just hung up after leaving a request for Lloyd to call her when he arrived for his shift when Fleming called and asked her to come down to his office.

As she passed the noticeboard that dominated the wall opposite her own desk, she raised her left hand and lightly touched Mary Quigg's photograph, as if to reassure the child that she was not forgotten.

When she went into Fleming's office, he was sitting at his computer. 'Can you bring up that footage of the Nixon sermon that went online?' he asked.

Lucy took out her phone and, opening her mother's message, clicked on the video link. She moved around to where Fleming sat and turned on the video.

'Can you pause it?'

She nodded and did so. The image froze on Nixon standing, his hands raised, his eyes half closed as if caught mid blink.

'Look at this,' Fleming said, pointing to the row of heads between the pastor and the person recording the footage. 'The filming was being done in the third row; there are two people in a direct line in front of the camera. The person at the front had grey hair and . . .'

He leaned forward, squinting at the screen. Lucy angled the picture. 'A red top of some sort,' she said.

'Now, look at the CCTV footage taken in the hall.'

He directed her to the computer screen where there were four small squares of images, all taken inside the hall, but from different angles. 'We need the one facing the front rows,' he said, clicking on the appropriate box which then expanded to fill the screen.

'There's the grey-haired woman,' Lucy said, pointing to a lady seated at the front wearing a red cardigan.

Fleming nodded. 'So, if we go back two seats we have—'

He stopped, peering closer at the screen. There would be no doubt about the identification of the man holding his own phone slightly aloft, clearly filming his father's sermon.

'Ian Nixon leaked the footage of his own father?' Lucy asked.

Chapter Twenty-Two

'MAYBE HE WANTED to embarrass his father,' Lucy suggested. 'Maybe he doesn't agree with what the old man's preaching.' Even as she made the suggestion, she wasn't convinced. The impression Ian Nixon had given was that he was just as hardline as his father, more so perhaps.

Fleming shook his head. 'I know Nixon and the boy both. The apple didn't fall far from the tree, trust me. He's drumming up support for his father. Spreading the word among his followers.'

'Nixon's target audience are hardly the most computer literate when it comes to social media, I'd imagine.'

'Haven't you heard of the Silver Surfers?' Fleming joked. The name had been appended to a group of older officers who had received special training in ICT after the force decided that a certain generation of officers was technophobic. Fleming had been a proud founding member, though he'd dropped out soon after.

'No; I mean the most likely people to see that footage on social media would be younger users. Users who are more likely to disagree with the message being delivered, I'd have thought. Disagree enough to arrange a demonstration outside the hall where Nixon is speaking, maybe?'

'A demonstration that will attract a lot of attention,' Fleming agreed. 'And will bring out the waverers who might have given it a miss otherwise.'

Lucy nodded. 'Ian Nixon is doing his father's PR work. And Shauna Kelly and her friends are doing exactly what he wants.'

Fleming nodded.

'We should get them warned off before this evening's sermon,' Lucy said.

'Do you really think they'd listen? They're as evangelical in their own way as Nixon.'

Before Lucy could respond, her phone rang. She recognised the number as Adrian Lupei's, but when she answered, it was actually Constanta who spoke.

'Andre is awake,' she said. 'I thought someone should know.'

ANDRE LUPEI STILL lay in the bed, a second pillow placed behind his head, raising it slightly so that he could see Lucy and Fleming where they stood next to him. The injuries to the left-hand side of his face were as pronounced as they had been earlier, though the eye had opened slightly, the swelling darkening. The gash on his right cheek had leaked a globule of blood around the paper stitches. He fixed the oxygen supply attached to his upper lip with a thickly bandaged right hand. Constanta stood at the opposite side of the bed, hovering nervously, ready to provide him with whatever he needed.

'How are you feeling, Mr Lupei?' Lucy asked unnecessarily, moving across to take one of the seats next to where he lay.

'Tired,' he muttered. Lucy realised he was reluctant to be too animated in his speech lest it put increased tension on his facial wounds.

'We'll not take too much of your time,' Fleming said. 'Can you remember anything about the attack last night? Anything at all?'

He managed a single, light nod, his head barely shifting on the pillow.

'You left the hospital at ten thirty to walk home, is that right?' Another nod.

'Did you make it to Greenway?'

Another movement, neither a nod nor a shake of the head. 'Too lip.'

'Tulip? Tulip Drive.'

A nod. 'There.'

Lucy knew the place. Tulip Drive was the first street on the way into the estate. When it had first been built, as if to deflect from the grimness of the boxed housing and paucity of greenery in an area ironically called Greenway, the designers had named each of the streets after flowers: Daisy Way, Tulip Drive, Primrose Crescent.

'They were waiting,' he said. He smacked his lips a little and Constanta, who had been standing silently, lifted the small polystyrene cup of water next to him and angled the straw into his mouth. He took a short suck on the straw, then angled his head to indicate he was finished.

'They?'

'Four men. They pushed me into a car and drove to—' He winced as he attempted to straighten himself, the water he had taken catching in his throat when he had swallowed.

'The toys,' he managed when he had got his breath.

'The playground?' Lucy asked. 'The swings and that?'

A nod. 'The grass there.' He glanced now at his wife, his one good eye swivelling towards her, as if aware that what he said next would upset her. 'Then they hit me,' he said in the end.

'Did they use anything? Sticks, bottles?'

A brief shake. 'Their hands and feet.'

Lucy nodded. 'Did you know any of them?'

'No.'

'Did you see their faces?'

'They wore hats pulled down. With the eyes cut.'

'Balaclavas?' Fleming asked.

Andre shrugged lightly, then looked to his wife. The word played on her lips as she tried it out in the hope it might trigger some recognition. Finally she shook her head. 'Sorry,' she said.

'Don't worry. Were they young? Old?'

'Young, maybe. I didn't see faces.'

'Fat, thin, tall, short? Did any of them stand out?'

Andre nodded. 'One of them looked to be in charge. He told the others when to stop.'

'What was he like?'

'Thin. Muscles on his arms. He had a tight shirt with short arms.' He indicated the upper muscle of his own arm. 'A T-shirt.'

'Colour?'

'White, I think.'

'Did it have anything on it? A symbol? A picture?' Lucy asked.

'No,' Andre said. 'But his arm had a . . . a . . .'

Both Fleming and Lucy instinctively leaned forward, as if encouraging him to speak.

'A tattoo?'

A curt shake of the head. 'A scar. A red scar on his arm.'

'A scar or a cut?'

'A scar. Like a burn.'

For a moment, Lucy wondered whether this might be connected in some way to the taxi office, but the fire there had happened hours *after* Andre Lupei had been beaten.

'You're sure?' Fleming asked.

'He came over when they stopped. He said, "Next time, you'll get a bullet in your head." That's all I remember.'

He raised his hand towards the gash on his right cheek. 'A bullet,' he repeated, as his wife finally let go the tears she'd been holding on to since his story began.

'Mrs Lupei,' Lucy asked gently, 'I know you're upset. But we need to ask *you* a few questions, is that okay?'

The woman nodded, rubbing away the tears as best she could.

'What time did you get home last night? From here?'

She shook her head. 'Nearly seven, I think.'

'Did Cezar and Adrian stay here with you all evening or did they leave and come back?'

She glanced at her husband who frowned at the tenor of the question.

'They stayed with me. Cezar brought us home. He stayed until morning to be sure we were safe.'

'So he was here until almost seven this morning, with you?'

Constanta nodded. 'Yes.'

'Would the staff here have seen him too?'

Constanta nodded, then seemed to realise the significance of the question. 'Why? What happened?'

'There was another incident in Greenway last night,' Lucy said. 'We just wanted to be able to eliminate Mr Lupei from our inquiries.'

'What happened?' she repeated.

'IT'S JUST GOING to get worse,' Lucy said, as they made their way up the corridor.

Constanta Lupei had remained in the room with her husband. She sat on the bed next to him, gesturing wildly as she spoke, the tears running freely now. Andre held one of her hands in his, trying to comfort her.

'It's escalating, certainly,' Fleming said. 'The Lupeis are at stage five or six now.'

Lucy remembered the training day they'd had to attend with divisions from all around the North about hate crime. It had been as a result of a series of attacks in Belfast two summers previous. The speaker had outlined the seven stages of hate crime attacks. Stage 1 was when the haters gathered together, forming groups, in either the real or the digital world. Stage 2 involved them defining themselves with symbols or motifs, sharing racial jokes or material on social media. They moved onto disparaging their target next to the wider public, which, in this case, probably meant the leaflet drop that had been done in Greenway. The graffiti and paint attack on the house would be classed as stage 4: attacks just short of physical contact.

'The only thing left for them now is to follow through on their threat,' Lucy said.

Fleming nodded grimly. 'We need to get that family moved as soon as we can. Before someone is killed,' he said.

Chapter Twenty-Three

AS THEY DROVE out of the hospital grounds, Lucy looked at the bulking Lisnagelvin PSNI station across the dual carriageway. She glanced at the clock and saw that it was approaching six. Jason Lloyd would be on site now to start his shift, she reasoned, though he had yet to phone her as she had requested.

'I want to take a quick check with someone,' she explained to Fleming, cutting across the carriageway and swinging in towards the station.

She had just parked in the station grounds when she recognised two uniformed officers exiting the main block and heading across to a marked vehicle, each wearing the light flak jackets that were standard issue for going out on patrol. Constable Lloyd, she now realised, had been the officer who'd spent an inordinate amount of time recording the 'Romans Out' graffiti on the Lupeis' wall, while Constable Huey, his partner, had been sitting inside with the family when Lucy had first arrived.

Lucy got out of her car and jogged across towards them. 'Constable Lloyd,' she called.

Lloyd turned to see who was calling him, then he and Huey stopped to allow her to catch up.

'DS Black,' Lucy explained. 'I left a message for you to call me.'

'I got the note,' he said. 'I was late in and needed to get out on patrol. There's a crowd of gay protestors gathered outside the Gospel Hall in Greenway.'

'I've heard,' Lucy said. 'This won't take a moment.'

'Do you want to go and get the car?' he said to Huey who nodded at Lucy and, taking the keys from Lloyd, cut on across the yard towards where the marked cars were parked. 'You're the Roman woman, Sergeant. I know you now.'

Lucy nodded. 'I'm looking into a guy called Bobby McLean,' she said.

'I know Bobby,' Lloyd said. 'What's he done this time?'

Lucy hesitated a moment. 'He claimed to have accidentally started a fire in the taxi rank where he works in Greenway last night. Then he changed his story and said the fire was started deliberately by two masked individuals.'

Lloyd shook his head. 'That sounds to be Bobby; by this evening he'll have another version of events for you. He's not the brightest bulb in the pack.'

'He was charged with affray previously, is that right?'

Lloyd thought for a moment. 'The pub fight,' he said, snapping his fingers in acknowledgement of the memory. 'He lobbed a brick into the middle of it.'

'But the charges were dropped?'

Lloyd nodded. 'The people in Greenway are tight. They have a don't-rat-on-our-own mentality. No one would positively identify anyone else as having been involved in the row. Even the CCTV footage from the pub went missing before we had a chance to look at it. There was no point pursuing it.'

'And he was drunk in a playground before that? Setting the swings on fire?'

Lloyd nodded. 'A lot of the local kids – the teenagers, like – tend to congregate there on a weekend evening. We usually have to move them along. He was trying his best with a BIC lighter, but he wasn't getting anywhere with it.'

'You know Greenway well,' Lucy said admiringly.

'It's our beat,' Lloyd said. 'We spend a lot of time there.'

'Then you know the house we met at the other evening?'

Lloyd grinned. 'Romans Out. I only got it afterwards.'

'The husband of the family was beaten last night in Greenway, near that kids' playground. You didn't hear anything about that, did you?'

Lloyd frowned. 'No. We were off last night. Is he okay?'

'He's still in hospital. He was threatened, though, that he'd be shot if he didn't leave the estate.'

Lloyd shook his head. 'The poor family,' he said. 'But, you know what? He might be best to get out while the going's good. Before things get worse.'

'We're working on that,' Lucy said. 'He said the man who threatened him had a burn scar on his arm. That doesn't ring any bells, does it?'

Lloyd stood for a moment, considering the question. 'Nothing. Was Bobby involved in that, too?'

'We don't know,' Lucy said. 'Why do you ask?'

'You'd mentioned him first,' Lloyd said, 'that's all.'

'What about Charlie Dougan?' Lucy asked.

'The taxi rank owner?'

Lucy nodded.

'I'd heard rumours he was squeezing in on Jackie Moss's turf, but nothing concrete. He has money all right, but nothing behind him. Not like Jackie. I wouldn't be surprised if it was Jackie who hit the taxi rank last night. Putting Charlie Dougan back in his box.'

'Jackie Moss did it?' Lucy said.

Lloyd shrugged. 'I've no idea. But don't let the limp fool you; Jackie rules Greenway with an iron fist. Maybe he wanted to bring Dougan down a peg or two.'

An unmarked car pulled up alongside them now and Huey leaned across and opened the door.

'We have to go,' she called. 'The crowd's getting bigger, apparently, and the congregation is beginning to arrive.'

'I need to go.' Lloyd smiled. 'I'll be in touch if I can think of anything else,' he added.

'I'll be right behind you,' Lucy said. 'We're heading the same way.'

Chapter Twenty-Four

BY THE TIME they reached the hall, the crowd of protestors had swollen considerably and there were now at least thirty gathered on the pavement outside.

Shauna Kelly was standing to the front. Behind her, several people held aloft a rainbow atop bamboo canes, the banner extending almost the width of the crowd. Others had lit candles of various colours, which they held in cupped hands. As Lucy parked up the car and got out, she noticed a few of the arriving congregation stepping out onto the road to pass the gathered group, their heads bowed, eyes averted.

Lloyd and Huey were ahead of them, though, and approached Shauna Kelly. Lucy could tell that Lloyd was telling them to move across the street to the facing pavement so as not to obstruct people trying to enter the hall. So far, Shauna seemed to be refusing.

'Why are you taking *their* side?' she snapped. 'We're doing nothing wrong.'

Lucy jogged across to assist. 'Ms Kelly,' she said, 'maybe I could have a word?'

Shauna glared at Lloyd and Huey, as if afraid that if she moved out to speak to Lucy, they would somehow manage to convince the others to cross to the other pavement. Finally she stepped down off the kerb, handing her placard to someone standing next to her as she did.

'What?'

'I think you should move.'

'There's a surprise. We have a right to peaceful *assembly*, you know.'

'You do,' Lucy agreed. 'And the people attending Nixon's sermon, regardless of how repugnant you might find his content, have a similar right to free assembly and worship.'

'You call *that* worship?'

Lucy raised a hand in placation. 'I didn't say I agreed with anything that man says. But you are blocking access to the hall. Many in the congregation are elderly. You're going to force them to step out onto the road, into traffic, in order to attend their place of worship.'

'Imagine! Such an inconvenience.'

'You're looking to convince these people that Nixon is wrong. Does antagonising them seem like a good plan? Do you think standing in their path, with slogans shoved in their faces, is going to *change* their opinions? Or *entrench* them?'

Shauna smiled. 'Do you think anything could change their opinions? Maybe seeing that the people he wants to see stoned are brothers and sisters and sons and daughters of their neighbours, their friends might make them see past the label and recognise the person.'

The comment sounded like something she had learned by rote.

'That's fine,' Lucy said. 'But there's something else you should know. The footage of Nixon's sermon? It was leaked by a member of his own entourage.'

Shauna stared at Lucy, as if unsure whether she could believe her. 'Why would they do that?'

'To create some PR, presumably. The footage leaked, you arrived to protest this evening's event, giving it all the free publicity Nixon could want.'

'You're wrong.'

'I saw other footage from last week's sermon; the hall was fairly packed. Let's see how many more attend tonight's.'

Shauna glanced back now to the rest of the protestors, her certainty wavering.

'Don't play into Nixon's hands. He wants people to see homosexuality as a threat to them, to their way of life. Don't become his best recruiting agent.'

Shauna nodded once, then moved back to the rest of the group. Lucy heard her uttering something and, one by one, the protestors began to peel away and move across to the opposite side of the road.

'We're not moving another inch!' Shauna called back to Lucy.

'That's fine,' Lucy said, allowing her the impression of some small victory.

'Good work,' Fleming said, sidling up to her, having evidently thought it best to let Lucy speak with Shauna alone. 'I'll tell Crockett and Tubbs over there to stay in the grounds of the hall, make sure no one tries to get in who shouldn't. We can keep an eye on the protestors out here.'

As the starting time of the sermon neared, it became clear that Shauna Kelly would keep her word. The protestors did not speak to those attending the sermon, nor did they block their entrance to the hall. Despite this, in the absence of a visible uniformed presence outside the hall, some members of the congregation were not so respectful. While most glanced at the protestors as they entered, some lowering their heads, some straightening as if in pride or defiance, some shaking their heads and tutting, a few were more vocal. Several women in a group together stopped and stared pointedly across at them.

'Shame on you all,' one of them called, wagging her finger at them angrily. 'You should be ashamed of yourselves.'

'Vile,' one of her friends said, joining in. 'Vile animals.'

Lucy moved towards the group in the expectation of something starting, but the women moved on into the hall and the protestors stood their ground.

'We're not going to hit old women,' Shauna said. 'Some of us have parents that age.'

'And that nasty,' one of the men added.

'Faggots!'

Lucy turned as a car drove past and into the grounds of the hall, the rear window being wound up quickly as it passed. The face inside was young, male, but she could tell little else. She called over to Lloyd to stop the vehicle but by the time she'd got his attention, the car had passed him and was rounding the corner towards the rear of the hall.

'What's wrong?'

'The car—' she began.

Her comment, though, was drowned out by the sound of jeering. Looking around she realised that a black car had drawn up alongside her and was indicating to turn in to the grounds of the hall. Pastor James Nixon sat on the back seat, behind the driver, looking out at the protestors. When they saw him they began to boo and jeer more loudly, actions that Nixon met with an ever-widening smile.

He wound down the window and addressed Lucy and Fleming. 'Tom. Lucy. Glad you could make it. Are we ready to begin?'

Chapter Twenty-Five

FLEMING ASKED LLOYD and Huey to stand at the gate, explaining that he and Lucy needed to go in to keep an eye on what Nixon was saying, as requested by ACC Wilson.

Despite having watched the congregation entering the hall, the piecemeal fashion of their arrival meant even Lucy was surprised by the sheer size of the crowd inside. In addition to the spare seats that had been placed to the rear, the back and side walls were lined with people standing. The room seemed to heave with expectation, heightened perhaps by the presence of the protestors just outside the hall. Lucy and Fleming stood inside the door and waited for Nixon to appear.

The pastor did not keep his flock waiting. At 7 p.m. on the dot he strode onto the stage, one hand raised in acknowledgement of the applause that greeted his appearance.

He started by bowing his head, as if in silent prayer, an action which encouraged the murmurs and whispering of the congregation to quieten and cease. Then he raised his head and began.

'I see some familiar faces here this evening, folks,' he said, smiling and receiving, in response, reciprocal grins of recognition.

'I thank you for your support and for your warm, warm welcome. And I hope you won't mind that much of what I have to say, you heard last week, too. But I need to say it again tonight, not just because we have among us friends who didn't hear my words last week but because, as we saw when we came in here tonight, we have disturbed a bed of sin and those sinners are at our very door, desperate that you do not hear my words. They tell us they have a right to be the way they are, as if it's something over which they have no choice. They say we have to respect that right, respect their choice. Well, that's a two-way street.'

'Yes it is,' someone called from the front with such enthusiasm it elicited a ripple of laughter from the rest of the congregation.

'Yes it is,' Nixon echoed, smiling at the speaker. 'They have to respect my right to speak my mind. We've seen just this past year or so, in the events in Paris, what people will do to silence speech.'

The reference to the Paris attack seemed to immediately charge the atmosphere in the hall again.

'And what happens when we have no respect for religious belief.'

He bowed his head a moment. Lucy wondered at the breathtaking moral gymnastics that had allowed him to appropriate seemingly opposing viewpoints in order to support his right to spew his own vitriol.

'So *they* have to respect my right to be who *I* am. And I am a man disgusted by depravity, a man weeping for the morality of our young people, a man determined not to let perversion parade as normal behaviour. And all good people say . . .?'

He raised his hands to usher the chorus of 'Amen' from those sitting in front of him.

Fleming leaned towards Lucy. 'He does this, getting people to say Amen,' he muttered. 'He's legitimising personal opinion using the language of prayer.'

'Now, let us all admit. We are all sinners. I am a sinner.' Nixon smiled bashfully and paused, as if waiting for some cries of disagreement. One of the women near the front, the one who had described the groups outside as 'vile animals', rose to the task with a cry of 'No' that was greeted with more light laughter, which spread down through the hall.

'I am,' Nixon continued. 'I am guilty of many things. And tonight, I want to confess to you my greatest guilt. Last week, I mentioned the killing of two homosexual men in Nairobi. I believe I said their deaths were the wages of their sin. They were stoned to death for their perversion. I was told a man died yesterday. A homosexual. I pray for that man tonight. Not for his sin, but for the sinner. I hope his family find comfort, I really do.'

Those in front of Nixon hung on his words, the faces of some drawn in bewilderment at so pastoral a tone.

'Two police officers came to me and one told me she thought it was my fault, that I was to blame for this homosexual's death.' A few of those standing near Lucy and Fleming stared round, some with open hostility. As Lucy returned their stares she noticed Jackie Moss, sitting across to her right, smiling over at her. He leaned on his crutch, his upper body heaving with each breath he took. Behind him sat four youths, one of whom was looking across at her too; she assumed he was one of Jackie's men.

Nixon continued. 'As a result, I intended to curb my words tonight, to swallow my principles and pour oil on troubled water.

I was tempted to turn from the truth and lie to you good people. *That* is my sin. So I confess it freely to you and I promise you: I will not be silenced; I will not deny my belief; I will not be afraid to speak the truth. Just as the people of Sodom burned for their sin, the sinners outside our door will burn for their licentiousness, will burn for their lustfulness, will burn for their depravity.'

Some of Nixon's followers moaned ecstatically at his words, the movement of those words mirrored in the listeners' rocking back and forth as he spoke to them.

'And I will not mourn the purging of their sins!' Nixon shouted, stepping around from the podium and raising his arms aloft.

At that moment, Lucy noticed the side door of the hall, through which Nixon had entered, suddenly fly open. Nixon turned towards the disturbance, just as Shauna Kelly ran into the room.

'Murderer!' she screamed, flinging an object she held in her hand. Lucy's view of Nixon was obscured by some of the others in the crowd standing up in shock. By the time she'd shoved through, Lucy realised that, though Nixon was still standing, blood was spreading across the white fabric of his shirt. Shauna threw a second object just as Fleming reached her, grappling her to the ground.

Nixon recoiled from what she had thrown, but without effect. It glanced off his shoulder and exploded, blood bursting from it onto his face and neck.

Lucy glanced to where Shauna lay now, Fleming kneeling on her back to restrain her, a pool of blood widening around them both on the floor.

'Witch!' someone screamed, and Lucy saw a few of the congregation motioning towards the girl. Fleming tried to stand, one hand on the girl's back, pushing her to the ground, the other held out in an attempt to ward off the congregation. Lucy moved towards her too, both to protect her from Nixon's followers and to help Fleming get her out of the building.

'Friends!' the pastor shouted, causing those around them to stop. 'It's okay. I am unharmed.'

Lucy looked up again to where Nixon stood, his arms outstretched, his clothes and face incarnadine, the whiteness of his smile bright against the crimson of his skin.

Chapter Twenty-Six

'IT'S ONLY PIG's blood,' Shauna told them a few moments later.

Fleming had bundled her through the side exit of the hall to protect her from blows from those present while Lucy checked that Nixon was not injured. Now, outside, Fleming hurried her across to Lloyd and Huey to have her brought to the station.

'Are you hurt?' Lucy asked, catching up with them.

'It was a water balloon,' Shauna said. 'I fell on it when *he* jumped on me,' she added, indicating Fleming.

Fleming shrugged and glanced down, realising that he'd managed to get blood on his own clothes. 'My Sunday best, too,' he managed.

'Sorry,' Shauna said.

'What the hell were you thinking, Shauna?' Lucy asked, leading her along the pathway towards the front of the hall.

'He's a murderer. He killed Marty Givens.'

'He didn't kill him.'

'He may as well have done,' she said.

'How did you even get in?' Fleming asked. Lloyd and Huey were meant to have been standing patrol outside.

'I slipped past the two cops out front. I knew if I came in the back I'd get stopped by some of the congregation. It was quicker to get in through the side door.'

'That's why you've been here all day? Doing a recce on the place?' Lucy asked.

But Shauna was no longer listening. Looking up the path, she suddenly straightened and, wriggling from Fleming's grasp, pulled at her T-shirt. They heard the cheering and realised that those outside had been waiting for her to appear. She pulled the T-shirt over her head and held it aloft, waving the bloodstained cloth like a flag of victory. Fleming pulled off his own jacket and placed it around her shoulders to cover her while Lloyd and Huey, seeing their approach, ran down to meet them.

The gathered crowd cheered again as Shauna was helped into the squad car. She beamed at Lucy. 'Now Nixon literally has blood on his hands. Let's see how he likes it.'

IN FACT, NIXON seemed to revel in it. Lucy had expected that the man would have cut his sermon short in light of the attack, but she was wrong. He stood, his jacket off, his white shirt stained with blood, at the front of the stage, away from the lectern, his voice rising as if re-energised. Lucy looked around at those listening to him, their faces flushed as they leaned towards him, their attention focused solely on him.

'They ask for respect!' he shouted. 'Respect! Was this respect?' He gestured to the bloody shirt, now a prop in his performance.

'No!' the crowd intoned.

'Is it respectful to lay down with another man, to defile the temple of your body for lust? Is that respect?'

Another catcall of disapproval.

'I will not be silenced, good people. Blood will not silence me, for I am cleansed in blood. I am reinvigorated in my mission. I will not be silenced, by threat or law of man. In blood I am renewed!'

The front row of the crowd, peopled partly by members of Nixon's entourage, rose to their feet at this, leading the rest of the room in a standing ovation. For his part, Nixon stood on the stage, basking in the adulation, his hand raised in blessing.

'YOU'LL BE CHARGING her,' Ian Nixon said.

They sat in the anteroom after the sermon, the crowd now dispersed. The protestors had left before the sermon even ended, Shauna Kelly having achieved what they had planned, though perhaps not with the desired effect on Nixon.

'If your father wants to press charges,' Lucy said.

'Why wouldn't I?' Nixon asked.

'That's your prerogative, sir,' Fleming said. 'Your sermon last week heightened some people's emotions in light of Martin Givens' death. The girl who attacked you was a friend of the victim.'

'You sound like you're excusing what just happened,' Ian said.

'Not at all. Though it is interesting that no one would have known about your sermon from last week had it not been for the leaking of footage onto social media.'

'I suppose that was my fault too?' Nixon snapped.

'Not yours, sir,' Lucy said. 'Your son's.'

Ian Nixon swallowed back his words, clearly caught off guard by the accusation. By the time the denial came, it was too late and even his father realised it.

'You leaked that film?' he said, leaning over the boy.

Ian moved back a little, though still in his father's shadow. 'You saw the crowd out there. I knew it would drum up support. Especially among younger people.'

Nixon considered the comment, then nodded. 'There were more young men out there this evening than usual.'

'That might have been in response to the protest beyond,' Lucy said. 'People hoping for some fireworks.'

'Well, they got them.' The pastor shrugged. 'It's all grist to the mill.'

'Members of the LGBT community might feel that some of the comments made on the stage out there are tantamount to incitement to hatred and incitement to violence, Pastor,' Fleming said. 'Spreading the word is one thing. Spreading hate is something else entirely. Ask Martin Givens' parents.'

'I'm surprised at you, Tom,' Nixon said. 'I deny, unequivocally, any responsibility for what happened to this homosexual man,' he added, unbuttoning his shirt to change. 'And as a Christian, I feel it incumbent on me to speak as I believe. Without compromise. I thought you'd understand that.'

'To be honest, Pastor, I'm surprised at how little Christianity has featured in your sermons. I've heard a lot of your opining on the lives of other people. Christ hasn't been mentioned so much,' Fleming said, his tone even, his voice soft.

'God is judgement, Tom. God is retribution.'

'Not the one I believe in,' Lucy said.

'In your profession, Sergeant, you must get sick and tired of those who are persistently unrepentant for their crimes?'

'The benefit of my job is that I don't have to claim insight into the private thoughts and prayers of others. I don't judge,' Lucy said.

Nixon held her stare. 'I think we can all see that's patently untrue,' he said, turning his back on her to peel off the bloody shirt.

Chapter Twenty-Seven

'WELL, THAT WENT well,' Fleming muttered as they headed back to their car. The grounds of the hall were deserted save for the cars in which Nixon and his entourage had arrived.

'We should probably speak with Shauna Kelly. Let her know that Nixon wants to press charges,' Lucy said.

'He might not.'

Lucy stared at Fleming sceptically. 'Really?'

Fleming nodded. 'He's got what he wanted out of it. Shauna proved his point as far as the congregation is concerned. And no doubt we'll see some of the pictures of the event leaked. He'll come across as forgiving and merciful; the LGBT protest will be seen as aggressive and disrespectful of his right to practise his faith. He stands to benefit more by not pressing charges than he does from pushing for it.'

'I'd not thought about it that way,' Lucy admitted.

'His son's a different matter, though,' Fleming added, getting into the car.

As Lucy opened her own door, she could hear the building crescendo of a siren, the tone sharpening as it got nearer. Soon after, a second joined the first, different in tone and speed, a note lower and a beat slower, so that they seemed to compete with one another a moment before merging discordantly and parting again.

Lucy stood, waiting, already able to see the thin branches of the trees on the roadway beyond sporadically illuminated blue as the vehicle approached. An ambulance wailed past, followed closely by a PSNI vehicle. Somewhere, deeper into the Waterside, Lucy could hear a third siren join their chorus.

'Something's happened,' Lucy said, getting in.

Fleming leaned over and flicked on the police radio in the car. '... fired. 147 Greenway. One injured. Paramedics on rou—'

Fleming turned down the volume. 'Let's get moving.'

'What is it?'

'147? That's Jackie Moss's address.'

THE AMBULANCE CREW was working on Moss when Lucy and Fleming pulled up at the cordon already established outside his house. Several squad cars were parked there. Lucy could see Moss lying on the driveway. His car was parked in the drive, the passenger door lying open, the chatter of the PSNI officers' radios and the clicking of the blue flashing light on the ambulance, the siren now silenced, mixing with the incessant pinging of the alert from the vehicle whose door remained ajar.

Fleming was out of the car and at the cordon before Lucy had cut the engine. She followed him across, ducking under the tape being strung across the roadway by a uniform, and moved over to where Moss lay. He was on his back, his shirt pulled open by the ambulance crew. One was applying pressure to a wound on his chest, pressing down on the seal around the bandage he'd applied just to the right of Moss's sternum. Another worked at his shoulder, where she was applying a dressing to a second injury there.

'You'll be okay, Mr Moss,' she was saying. 'We're just stemming the bleeding, then we're going to have to lift you. Okay?'

While Lucy could not hear Moss reply, it was clear that he had, for the paramedic smiled. 'We'll see how we manage,' she said.

The medic working at his chest raised his head. 'Eh?'

'He says we'll need more than just the two of us to lift him,' the woman said, smiling.

'You don't know Janine here, Mr Moss,' the man joked. 'She could bench press all of us.'

'What happened?' Fleming asked the uniform standing next to them who was watching the proceedings open-mouthed.

'He was shot,' the man managed.

'I'd guessed that much. Where's his missus?'

'Inside,' the man said, nodding in the direction of the house but never taking his eyes off the work of the paramedics.

'Come on,' Fleming said to Lucy, and the two of them stepped past the uniforms and, crossing the front lawn, went into the house.

Lucy recognised the woman sitting on the sofa as Annie, who had served them in the Bluebell Café both times they had gone to see Moss. She sat now, diminished by the events occurring on her own doorstep, a cup in her hand from which she barely drank. One of the uniforms had placed a coat around her shoulders, while a female uniform sat with her arm around her. Her blouse and skirt were stained with blood, though the absence of medics working with her suggested the blood was not her own. Lucy thought instinctively of Nixon's appearance moments earlier. The blood there had been part of the theatre: the blood here reflected harsh reality.

'They'll do their best, love,' the uniform was saying. 'It's a good sign that he's able to talk.'

Annie nodded, then looked up to see Fleming and Lucy.

'Tom,' she said, smiling in gratitude at a familiar face.

'Annie.' Fleming moved across the room and took her proffered hand in his. 'Are you okay?'

'We only saw you ten minutes ago,' she said. 'At the pastor's talk.' She offered this as if amazed at the speed with which things had changed for her.

'That's right,' Fleming agreed. 'I saw you there. What happened?'

Annie stared at him blankly. 'We just came home. I was driving. I pulled up and went round to get the door for him. This bike pulled up at the end of the drive. One of them pulled out a gun. Jackie pushed me to the ground. I heard the bang, the sound of . . . of it . . . I just knew they'd shot . . .' Her mouth continued to move for a few seconds, though she made no sound, as though her thoughts had raced past her speech.

'He's a tough old bird,' Fleming said, still holding her hand. 'I heard him joking with the ambulance crew out there. They'll take good care of him.'

Annie smiled, though without humour. 'He pushed me to the ground.'

'He saved your life, love,' the uniform next to her said, squeezing her a little closer.

'He's a hero,' Annie said, nodding. She looked to Lucy who had not spoken. 'He's a hero.'

Lucy tried to nod and smile but the idea of calling anyone a hero who, thirty years previous, had murdered four teenagers because of their religion did not sit easily with her.

'How many were on the bike?' Fleming asked, squatting in front of Annie.

'Two,' the uniform replied, earning a scowl from Fleming. He needed Annie to remember for herself, to be as clear as possible in her recollection of the events. Lucy knew that, in her present state of shock, she would be suggestible, easy to influence.

'Two,' Annie agreed.

'Male, female?'

'Both men, I think,' she said.

'I know this is tough to recall, but did they both shoot at you and Jackie, or just one of them?'

Annie considered the question. 'Just the one at the back. He pulled it out of his jacket.'

'Was it a pistol? Bigger?'

'A pistol,' Annie said. 'He fired a few times, then they drove off.'

'That's good, Annie,' Fleming said. 'Thank you. One more thing. Can you remember, did they say anything?'

She shook her head. 'Nothing.'

Fleming nodded and stood. Lucy moved next to him.

'Has anyone threatened Jackie? Any rows with anyone?'

Annie shook her head again. 'Nothing. No one has been near him about anything in months. He just gets on with things. I couldn't tell you the last time any of you lot came to see him about anything. Until you two did this week.'

Shouting from outside ended the conversation. Fleming and Lucy went out to see that the paramedics were ready to left Moss onto the stretcher and, as he had foretold, needed a few extra hands to help. Fleming moved forward and did so, while Lucy stood with Annie, who gripped her arm.

'I'll need to go up with him,' she said. 'I need to get him some things.'

She turned and went back into the house. Lucy crossed to the paramedics. 'His wife wants to come with him,' she said.

The female paramedic nodded. 'If she's quick.'

Lucy looked up to see two unmarked cars pull up at the cordon. She recognised a DCI get out of one and, a moment later, saw her mother climb out of the other car. The investigating team had arrived.

Chapter Twenty-Eight

'HIS WIFE SAYS you've been to see Jackie twice in the past few days,' the SIO, Sean Mulholland, said. He was leaning against his desk in Lisnagelvin PSNI station. The small windows high up on the wall showed only blackness. The room itself was organised, neat, the files piled on the in-tray seemingly stacked according to some colour coding that Mulholland himself must have understood. Two pictures in frames sat on the desk, facing Lucy and Fleming where they sat. One was of Mulholland and presumably his wife, young, blond and pretty, though hard featured, while the other showed two children playing in the garden, wearing shorts and T-shirts. A boy and a girl, the former red-headed, the latter brunette. A gentleman's family. That the pictures were turned to face the two seats sitting in front of the desk suggested that Mulholland wanted everyone to know it, too. Lucy wondered why he felt the need to do so.

'That's right,' Fleming said. 'We were looking for his assistance on something.'

'Anything that might have resulted in him being shot?'

Fleming shook his head. 'I'd not have thought so. There have been several attacks on a Roma family in Greenway. We traced a batch of racist leaflets back to a guy called Charlie Dougan. He owns a taxi—'

'I know Dougan,' Mulholland said. 'What's Moss's involvement?'

'We don't know that there is one,' Fleming said. 'I knew Annie back in the day. And Jackie too, of course. By reputation. Dougan's name came up in connection with the leaflets and, as I'd not heard of him before, I went to ask Jackie about him.'

'What did he say?'

'Not much,' Fleming said.

'Not much is something. Did he make any comment about Dougan?'

'Why is this important?' Fleming asked, shifting in his seat a little; he'd clearly decided he'd given Mulholland enough to get started.

Mulholland looked across to ACC Wilson who had pulled out the office chair from behind the desk and had positioned it at the corner instead, allowing herself a clear view of the other three in the room.

'You know Jackie was the Commander of the local district,' Wilson said. 'Has been for years.'

Despite the ceasefire and Good Friday Agreement, it was an accepted fact that most areas, particularly working-class areas of cities, were still under the control of the paramilitaries who had run them during the Troubles. Even with the seeming end of hostilities, they had retained their titles, their influence and their feudal taxation systems, which meant that companies paid their tithes to the local commanders in order to stay open for business. For many, it had been a form of pension, to sustain them in the retirement years. Lucy had noticed that the Bluebell Café was a cash-only business, presumably a way for Moss to launder such payments.

Fleming nodded.

'Charlie Dougan had worked his way up to be his deputy.'

'He must have worked quickly then,' Fleming said. 'I'd never heard of him before this.'

Mulholland nodded. 'Very quickly. Jackie decided a year back that he was losing control of some of the younger fellas around the estate. I investigated them then over drugs in the area when I was working with the Drugs Squad. They were doing their own thing, not paying their dues to him. And they weren't afraid of him either. A lot of his hatchet men had passed on or passed away. Moss himself is in no state to be dealing out six packs.'

'Moss's favoured form of punishment,' Fleming explained to Lucy. 'A bullet in each elbow, kneecap and ankle.'

'Those days are past for him, now,' Mulholland said. 'Dougan, on the other hand, seemed to have some influence with the younger crews running round the estate; he was that bit younger himself and wasn't seen to be resting on the stripes he earned in the eighties the way Jackie has been.'

'So Jackie promoted him?'

'Better inside the tent pissing out, so to speak,' Mulholland said. 'It looked to have worked, too.'

'Until now,' Lucy said.

Mulholland nodded.

'So is Dougan a suspect or a potential next target?' Lucy asked.

Mulholland shrugged. 'His taxi firm was torched last night.'

'We know,' Lucy said.

'Any ideas on who hit it?'

'The father of the Roma family we were dealing with was attacked last night. We wondered whether his brother might have had something to do with it,' Lucy said. 'Though he has an alibi.'

'Jackie himself was suggested as a possible suspect, too. We told him about Dougan's involvement in the anti-Roma campaign. Maybe Jackie thought he was getting a bit too big for his boots and brought him down to size,' Fleming added.

'That's what we've heard on the estate,' Mulholland said. 'The feeling was it was a local attack. The question is whether it's a power play from Dougan or a new group looking to take control.'

'Which new group?'

'We've noticed graffiti appearing on some of the walls around Greenway lately; a red, white and blue hand of Ulster?'

'I've seen it,' Lucy said. 'The same thing was on the leaflets we saw.'

'Ulster First, they're calling themselves,' Mulholland said.

'We think Dougan is involved in some way with them, then,' Lucy said. 'Certainly we know he collected the anti-Roma leaflets from the printers where one of his men works.'

Mulholland straightened. 'Which printers?'

'McEwan's,' Lucy said.

Mulholland nodded grimly. 'You heard about Mr McEwan? He broke his leg falling down the stairs at home yesterday.'

Lucy raised a sceptical eyebrow. 'That's a pity.'

'He lives in a bungalow,' Mulholland said.

'Ulster First?' Fleming suggested. 'McEwan gave us Dougan's name. He was being watched by his own son and Dougan's guy, Bobby McLean.'

Mulholland nodded.

'We spoke to Jackie about the targeting of the Roma. He said he'd look into it. Dougan, who we've connected to the leaflets from Ulster First, gets hit twenty hours later. Twenty hours after that, Jackie gets shot,' Lucy said. 'That's a lot of bad blood. Maybe Ulster First decided to let it.'

'Unlikely,' Wilson interrupted. 'Jackie Moss has been unassailable for years. I don't see some group of kids trying their luck on him. Even if they did kill him, some of his people are still there. They're not going to start supporting Dougan or a group of young fellas just because they had the balls to take out Jackie.'

'Maybe they don't need to,' Fleming said. 'You said yourself, Jackie's been unassailable. Five years ago would someone have taken a pot shot at him?'

Lucy shook her head. 'The attack is enough to show he's gotten sloppy, careless.'

'Jackie's swanning around the Bluebell on crutches talking about his hip problems, for dear Lord's sake,' Fleming continued. 'He's been relying on a forty-year-old reputation to keep him alive.'

'A regime change?' Wilson said.

'Dougan uses Ulster First or whatever they're called to make it look like there's a feud between them and Jackie,' Lucy said. 'Then he can negotiate the peace on Jackie's behalf, with himself. Bring Ulster First in under the wider umbrella and give himself a better seat at Moss's table.'

'But you knew this already,' Fleming said.

'We didn't know about Ulster First's activities with the Romas,' Mulholland said, 'but we did suspect Dougan. We lifted him half an hour ago. Ostensibly for his own protection.'

'What did he say?'

'Not much so far,' Mulholland said. 'He's waiting for his solicitor.'

'How's the Lupei man now?' Wilson asked.

Lucy, caught off guard by the question, had to angle herself a little to better see her mother where she sat.

'He's recovering. I submitted a SPED form this morning; we need to move them.'

Wilson nodded. 'Leave it with me.'

'Can I tell them a timeline for when it might be done, ma'am?' Lucy asked.

Wilson shook her head. 'It's a delicate one, DS Black.'

'They've been threatened,' Lucy said.

'I know. By a group that has only just come into existence. And may be at the centre of a loyalist feud. Naming them on a SPED form gives them a lot of legitimacy all of a sudden.'

'I don't think the Lupeis will mind, ma'am,' Lucy said.

'Let's wait and see what happens. If Dougan plays this the way we think he will, Ulster First will vanish very quickly once he takes control. The Lupeis are just a prop he's using to bolster his position.'

'And what if we're wrong?' Lucy asked, twisting now to see her mother properly. 'What if this isn't Dougan's doing at all?'

'Then we're going to have bigger problems than a Roma family,' Wilson said. 'Regime change at the top is one thing. An all-out war in a housing estate is a very different matter.' 'Signing a SPED form won't cause a war—' Lucy began, but her mother raised a hand to stop her.

'Do you think if a local hack hears that an ACC has named a new paramilitary grouping on an official SPED request, that won't be headline news tomorrow? At the minute this crowd are spreading the word on leaflets and graffiti. They're small, limited within Greenway. The last thing I want to do is to give them any extra oxygen, bring them to a wider audience.'

'If they kill one of the Lupei family, they'll get all the oxygen they want,' Lucy said.

'The ACC is right, Lucy,' Fleming said quietly.

'Thank you, Tom,' Wilson said. 'Sean's team will be handling the Moss shooting. Mark Burns' team is continuing with the inquiry into Martin Givens' death. I'll ask that you continue to liaise with both teams and support where necessary.'

'What about the attack on Andre Lupei?'

'Continue to investigate it, by all means. But be aware of where your inquiry crosses Sean's.'

Fleming nodded. 'Yes, ma'am,' he said, standing.

LUCY CAUGHT UP with him at the top of the stairs down to the car park.

'Have we just been straitjacketed?' she asked.

Fleming stopped, took a breath. 'That's one way of putting it.'

'We can't just leave the Lupeis unsupported.'

Fleming considered the statement for a moment, then nodded once. 'We need to tackle things from the bottom up. Tomorrow morning, we go back to McEwan's Printers and start putting some pressure on Bobby McLean.'

Chapter Twenty-Nine

LUCY DROPPED FLEMING home, then drove down the Crescent Link, with the intention of cutting up the Limavady Road and heading home. At the roundabout, though, she turned right instead and a few moments later, pulled into the parking bay at the secure unit in Gransha Hospital, where her father had been a patient for several years. He'd been committed following an incident in the woods near his home that had resulted in the death of a serving PSNI officer named Travers. Over the course of her father's incarceration, the Alzheimer's which afflicted him had developed to the point that he frequently did not recognise her. Despite this, she still called on him every few days, though the duration of her visits had shortened. Usually, he was asleep when she came in. But not this evening.

'Hello, love,' he said, smiling mildly at her. He sat upright, in the easy chair next to his bed. His pyjamas were buttoned up the front, though incorrectly, so that the left-hand collar sat higher than the right, grazing the bottom of his ear. He swatted at it as he spoke, as if it were irritating him.

'Hi, Dad,' Lucy said. 'You look well.' She leaned in and hugged him lightly. She could feel the change in his mass, found herself momentarily shocked at the thinness of his frame, the sharp edges of his shoulder blades. His cheek bore sparse stubble, which scraped her skin as they separated from their embrace. His breath was warm and milky. 'How are you this evening?'

He nodded, then swatted at his collar again. 'I had fish for dinner. I told them I wanted it without bones but there was a bone in it anyway.'

Lucy nodded. 'These things happen, Dad.'

'They do it on purpose, Jane. They're trying to kill me. I could have choked.'

'I'm sure they didn't mean it.' She ignored his calling her Jane, her mother's name.

'They did!' he snapped. 'I told them I didn't want—' He swatted at his ear again. 'This bloody fly.'

'Let me get it,' Lucy said. She leaned across and unbuttoned his pyjama top, then buttoned it up correctly, smoothing down the collars. As she did so, she noticed that two of the buttons had come off, which was presumably why it had been buttoned the way it had. 'Have you no better pyjamas?'

'They're all being washed,' he said. 'These are my best.'

'I'll bring you some down tomorrow,' Lucy said. 'You can't be wearing ripped nightclothes.'

'Did you ask him yet?' her father said.

'What's that?' Lucy had grown more accustomed to the non-sequiturs her father made. 'Ask who what?'

He nodded. 'About the promotion?'

Lucy sat back, smiling uncertainly. 'What promotion?'

'The inspector's posting.'

'I'm not going for inspector,' Lucy said.

'He told you you were a cert for it, Jane.'

'Who did?'

'Grant,' her father said. 'He promised us.'

'I don't know anyone called Grant, Dad.'

'I don't think your father is too happy.'

Lucy stopped herself responding. She guessed he wasn't just mistaking her name for her mother.

'He doesn't like me.'

'I'm not Jane, Dad,' she said. 'I'm Lucy.'

'I'd know you anywhere, love,' he said, reaching out and taking her hand in his. 'I know you.'

Lucy nodded. 'I'd best be getting on,' she managed. 'I didn't want to pass without calling in and seeing how you are.'

'Okay, love,' he said. 'Will you have a word with him?'

'Who? Grant?'

'Your dad,' her father said, rolling his eyes at her foolishness. 'Tell him what I'm like. Tell him that I won't let you down. I'll stand by you. He doesn't like me; I can tell. Will you say to him?'

Lucy nodded, her eyes filling. 'I'll tell him.'

'I'm on a good wage. And we'll move. We'll get away from here, once we have kids. Somewhere nice. Someone with a big garden.'

'I'll see you later, Dad, eh?'

'Tell him, Jane. Tell him how happy we'll be. You and me. Against the world.'

LUCY SAT IN her car outside the unit and wiped her eyes, checking herself in the mirror to see how red they looked. In all the time she had thought about her parents' divorce, about its impact on her and her relationship with her mother, she had never really considered the impact it had had on them. How full of hope her father had been just now, how ambitious for a future which had already happened and which had turned to ashes in his mouth; their marriage failed, their relationship destroyed, her own child-hood spent living with the barely suppressed anger of his house. There was no big garden, no move beyond that required when their family was threatened and which was the beginning of the dissolution of their world. All of it had resulted from her father's infidelity with a teenage girl who had herself been tarred and feathered for consorting with RUC officers, publicly shamed and abandoned by her own parents for her sin. In a way, Lucy could understand why her father had, at least mentally, returned to that point in time before anything went wrong, when the world was still rich with possibilities and his only concern was whether or not his future father-in-law liked him.

Lucy started when her phone rang. She glanced at the caller ID before answering. It was DS Tara Gallagher.

'Hey you,' Tara said.

'Hi, Tara.'

'You okay?'

Lucy nodded, then realised the futility of the gesture. 'Fine. Just visiting my dad.'

'Burns was wondering where you were this evening, for the briefing. He was raging about the blood attack on Nixon.'

The event seemed some time ago now. 'We got caught up in something else,' Lucy said. 'There was a shooting—'

'Jackie Moss? You were involved in that?'

'Not quite. We'd had dealings with Jackie over the past few days.'

'Was it bad?'

'He'll live,' Lucy said. 'Did we miss anything at the briefing?'

'Just Burns in a mood,' Tara said. 'He gave Mickey a bollock-ing over the blue car. Mickey found it online – an '05-reg blue Peugeot 306. Whoever bought it had done it up and posted it on *Gumtree* to sell it on again. The posting is still on but the number's a dead end.'

'What about Givens' friend McGonigle? Any luck finding him?'

'Nothing. I think Burns fancied getting the Moss shooting, but the lack of progress on the Givens killing hammered him. He's looking for someone to blame.'

'And Mickey got the brunt of it.'

'In your absence!' Tara joked. 'Listen, the reason I'm phoning: a few of us are going out on Friday night, to Limavady. Do you fancy coming along?'

Lucy leaned across in her seat to get a better view of the Foyle Bridge, which arched above the river just beyond the hospital grounds, lit up against the night sky. She could see, suspended from the bottom of the bridge, a large mechanical cradle in which workmen could stand as they carried out repairs on the underside of the structure. The cradle sat near the Waterside end of the bridge, swaying gently in the breeze running up the Foyle valley. Lucy wondered at the head for heights required to work in such a contraption, hanging in mid-air forty metres above the river.

'Sure,' she managed, straightening up again. 'Who's going?'

'A few of the girls,' Tara said. 'We're going for dinner about eight. There's a nice place that opened a while back: Granny Annie's.'

'Sounds good,' Lucy said.

'It's a date.' Tara's voice sounded suddenly brighter. 'I'll see you then.'

'I'll see you in the morning,' Lucy said. 'For the briefing.'

Tara laughed. 'Yeah, of course; see you then.'

Lucy hung up and glanced back up to the unit in which her father was kept, but the light no longer showed at his window.

Monday

Chapter Thirty

LUCY WOKE LATER than she had intended, the time already gone 7.15 a.m. She grabbed a quick shower, ate a bowl of muesli standing in the kitchen, then headed out. The sky was grey, the air fresh and pregnant with rain. Indeed, as she pulled out of the driveway, the first droplets splattered on the windscreen. She glanced up at the curtained window of the front room. Grace must have been working late, for Lucy hadn't heard her coming in. They'd been passing one another in the doorway, though Lucy had Wednesday off and hoped the two of them might manage to catch a movie.

Having Grace in the house had changed things for her. She felt now as if the property were hers rather than her father's. The redecorating was almost completed. She'd toyed with the idea of inviting some of the team from work for a housewarming party, but wasn't really sure how many might reasonably turn up. It wasn't that she feared there would be too many; quite the reverse. Tom Fleming might, but he didn't drink. Tara would, and some of the other female officers. Mickey would turn up to nosy at the living arrangements. She'd decided against in the end; she hadn't wanted them to know about Grace. Taking her in had felt like a personal act of kindness, and one that would be somehow diluted if she shared it with others. Now that she'd been with her a while, Grace'd become almost like the younger sister Lucy had never had. She knew that not everyone would understand that.

THE BRIEFING HAD already started by the time she made it up to the incident room in the Strand Road. Tara sat on a worktop at the back of the room and moved over to make space for Lucy when she arrived at the door. A still warm mug of coffee sat waiting for her. Burns stood with his back to them, pointing out spots on a map he'd projected up onto the wall.

'Thanks,' Lucy whispered. 'Have I missed much?'

Tara raised her eyebrows but said nothing.

'Good of you to join us, DS Black,' Burns said, having noticed her arrival now that he had turned back to address the room. 'The briefing started at eight.'

'Sorry, sir,' Lucy said.

'We were just discussing the fiasco last night.'

'Which one?' Lucy asked innocently, hearing Tara suppress a nervous snigger to her left.

Burns held Lucy's stare a second, before continuing. 'The attack on Pastor Nixon. The papers have picked up on it and, more importantly, the reason behind the attack. The radio this morning was running a headline story about Nixon's possible complicity in murder. We wanted to keep the situation contained.'

'In fairness, we had a very narrow window for that,' Tom Fleming commented. Lucy had spotted him, sitting in the corner. He looked tired, as if the events of the weekend had caught up with him. 'Had we made more progress on the Givens murder, sir, we might have been able to disprove any accusations of a connection between it and Nixon. Unfortunately, we're not in a position to do that.'

'If we could find this bloody car, we'd take a big leap forward,' Burns snapped, turning his attention now to Mickey. He moved across to his laptop and jabbed a finger at the keyboard. The map on the wall dissolved to an image of a Facebook posting advertising a blue Peugeot for sale.

'I've tracked it to four other sites, sir,' Mickey said, a note of desperation in his voice. 'But we can't get a reply to the phone number on the ads; whoever owns it could have dumped the phone, for all we know. The last time it was used was three days ago, in the city centre. I'm trying to trace who posted the adverts; the one on Facebook is from a fake account. It's not that unusual; people afraid that the tax man is watching them, making up false accounts to do business online.'

'That's of no use to me,' Burns snapped. 'Get some of the IT people down in Maydown on it.'

Lucy inclined her head a little to the side as she studied the picture on the wall. The car was parked on tarmac, sitting at an angle to best show off the alloy wheels. Behind it were grey buildings, though too out of focus to be recognisable. Just to the left of the car's roof was an image of something sitting in what appeared to be a bucket of some sort.

'Finding this car is our priority. Or finding Gareth McGonigle. I assume PPU have had no joy in locating him?'

'We've been a little busy, sir,' Fleming said. 'He's not returned to Rockmills?'

'Not yet,' Burns admitted. 'With the shooting of Jackie Moss taking all our manpower, we're all going to have to work extra hard today; we have little uniformed support unless we have a compelling reason to request it. So work smart, people. I want updates throughout the day.'

Lucy drained her mug of coffee. 'Thanks, Tara,' she said. 'Do you want me to wash your cup?'

Tara shook her head. 'Leave yours and I'll do them later. If the Chief Super sees any of us washing dishes instead of working smart, we'll be for it.'

'Smart's an adjective in this instance,' Tom Fleming said, joining them. 'He was looking for an adverb. Smartly? More intelligently, perhaps? Though even that wouldn't be great.'

Lucy raised her eyebrows at Tara who smiled in return.

'So, we're off to see Bobby McLean,' Fleming said. 'Shall we go?'

Lucy nodded. 'We can find out what McEwan's son thinks about his father being left with a broken leg, too.'

Fleming nodded. 'That's assuming it wasn't the son himself who broke it, of course.'

Chapter Thirty-One

As it transpired, only the son was in McEwan's when Lucy and Tom Fleming arrived. One of the machines was running, while he stood next to it, stacking piles of the leaflets it disgorged into boxes.

'Frankie, isn't it?' Lucy said, stepping into the unit.

'Frank,' he said, straightening. 'Only my da calls me Frankie.'

'How is he?' Lucy asked. 'We heard he'd had an accident. A broken leg?'

Frank snuffed into the back of his hand, his gaze flicking from Lucy to the steadily building pile of leaflets between them.

'He fell,' Frank managed. ''S all right.'

'That's a pity. He was saying business was tight. I hope he's okay.'

'You fall yourself?' Fleming said.

Lucy realised that, from where Fleming stood, he had a better view of the left-hand side of Frank's face, which, she saw now, was bruised above the cheekbone.

Frank nodded his head, angling his cheek a little in acknowledgement of the comment.

'That looks nasty.'

'What do you want?' he asked, lifting the pile of leaflets and placing them into another free box.

'Is Bobby McLean here?' Lucy asked.

Frank looked around him. 'Do you see him?'

Fleming moved forward and lifted one of the pages from the box that Frank had just filled.

'You can't touch that,' Frank said, but too late, for Fleming had already lifted a second and passed it across to Lucy.

PUBLIC MEETING: GREENWAY ESTATE: MONDAY 5 P.M., the heading ran. Lucy scanned through it: it listed a number of recent events in the Greenway estate – the burning of Greenway Taxis, the shooting of Jackie Moss, the events in the Gospel Hall – and called on the people of Greenway to unite against the attacks on their community and culture. The bottom of the leaflet carried the red, white and blue hand, with 'Ulster First' printed beneath it. It was the first time Lucy had seen the name appear alongside the logo. The group was growing in confidence, their logo now recognisable enough in the estate for them to begin appending their name, building their brand.

'Who ordered this?'

Frank shook his head. 'I don't know.'

'Have you the order sheet?'

'Dad handled it,' he said. 'He must have lost it, what with the fall and that.'

'Who's collecting it?'

Frank shrugged.

'Where's Bobby?'

Another shrug.

'And you know nothing about this?' Lucy asked, holding up one of the flyers.

'Just what's on it,' Frank said.

'See here's the thing, Frank. This refers to the shooting of Jackie Moss and the attack on Pastor Nixon. Those happened last night.'

Frank nodded. 'And?'

'Well, I can't see how your father could have taken the order for a leaflet that could only have been written in the past twelve hours or so, when he's housebound with a broken leg.'

'I can't help you,' Frank said, breaking her stare and shifting one of the boxes near him unnecessarily.

'Your dad was punished for giving us Charlie Dougan's name, wasn't he?'

'I *can't* help you,' Frank repeated.

'You let someone break your own father's leg? You're a piece of work.'

'Fuck you!' Frank snapped. 'You know nothing about it.'

'That's right,' Fleming said. 'So tell us. What happened? Was it Dougan?'

Frank moved another box. 'I have to work.'

'Bobby?'

A snort of derision.

'You? Did they make you do it? Maybe you'd be more careful than—'

With a sudden movement, Frank was at Fleming, his hands grappling at Fleming's shirt front, his face pulled in a snarl. Just as quickly, before Lucy could reach him, Fleming had grabbed Frank's arm and twisting it, had managed to free himself from the youth's grip and force Frankie to bend slightly to prevent his own shoulder becoming dislocated.

'That's assaulting an officer,' Fleming said. 'You'll do time for that, Frankie. And your dad's business will be finished. Can't see Bobby McLean running things too well in your absence, eh?'

'I'm sorry, I'm sorry—' Frank jabbered, suddenly cowed.

'Then tell us the truth. Who ordered these leaflets?'

'Bobby set them up this morning,' Frank said. 'He'll kill me if I say anything.'

'Who broke your father's leg?'

'I don't know, I swear,' Frank protested.

'You have the right to remain—' Fleming began.

'I swear,' Frank said, his register a little higher. 'Bobby must have told Dougan about you being here.'

'Where's Bobby now?'

'I don't know. He's coming back for these. They need to distribute them before this evening, to get people to the rally.'

'Is Bobby part of Ulster First?'

Frank nodded. 'It's not really like that. We were all mates. A few took it a bit further, that's all.'

'The attack on the Roma – was that Ulster First?'

Frank winced again. 'I—'

'You okay, Frankie?'

They all looked to where Bobby McLean stood in the doorway now. Neither Lucy nor Fleming had heard his vehicle approaching over the noise of the machinery running.

'What's going on?' Bobby asked. He held in his hand two white paper bags, both stained with grease, having clearly been on a bun run for their break. He must have been peckish, for his mouth was bulging, his words a little indistinct.

'Frank here assaulted an officer,' Fleming said, though he did loosen his grip on Frank's arm enough for him to straighten up again.

'You're a fucking madman, Fran,' Bobby laughed.

'These are yours, I believe,' Lucy said, holding up the flyer. 'Ulster First.'

Bobby shrugged. 'That's not mine. Someone called in the order this morning. A quick job. Who said it was me?' He glowered at Frank now, who rubbed at his shoulder sullenly.

'There was an attack on a Roma man on Saturday night.'

'I know.'

'You'd nothing to do with that?'

'I was working. You know that.'

'And you didn't see anything? You didn't see someone being dumped out of a car on the green across the street from your office?'

Bobby shook his head. 'Sorry. I don't recall.'

'Must have been the fumes playing with your memory. All that smoke immolation.'

'Must be,' Bobby agreed drily.

'What about last night? Where were you last night?'

'Why?'

'Someone shot Jackie Moss.'

Bobby laughed, spluttering bits of the bun onto the floor. 'You think I'm mad enough to be involved in anything with Moss!'

'So where were you?'

'In the pub,' Bobby said. 'Plenty of people there saw me, too. Frank was there. Weren't you, Frank?'

'That's right,' Frank said, straightening himself. 'I was there too. The Greenway Arms. All evening.'

'We'll hold onto this,' Fleming said, indicating the flyer in his hand.

'Take a handful,' Bobby said. 'Pass them round the station. Some of your mates might want to come along and support it.'

LUCY AND FLEMING moved out to the car parking area. Bobby McLean had parked a silver BMW diagonally across three of the spaces outside, including a disabled parking spot.

'You try to see the best in people,' Fleming said, 'but with that young fella, you'd need a microscope.'

Lucy wasn't listening, however. As she'd moved round to get into her car, she'd glanced across at the other industrial units, all closed now. Some carried no signage above them or signage in such a state of disrepair that it was unreadable. But the one at the very end caught her eye. The unit had previously been a Pet Grooming Salon. Above the door, stretching the width of the unit, remained a black sign for the business, outlined in pink. To one side of the name was an image of a cat wearing curlers. The other side was bookended by a cartoon of a dog sitting in a wooden bath.

'That's the picture,' Lucy said. 'The blue car. That's the unit visible behind it.'

Fleming stood and looked at it. 'Are you sure?' He reached into the car to his folder, rifled through the loose pages and pulled out a printout of the car, taken from the advertisement. He held it up in front of him, in line with the actual unit opposite, and squinted a little. 'You know, I think you're right.'

Lucy was already on her way back into the printers. Frank and Bobby were deep in discussion when she came back in, though the conversation seemed to be a one-way affair with Frank doing all the listening.

'Did someone take pictures of a blue Peugeot 306 outside here over the past week or so?'

'What?' Bobby turned.

'A blue Peugeot 306? It was photographed outside here for a For Sale advert.'

Bobby shrugged. 'I know nothing about that. You, Frankie?'

Frank shook his head, but he watched her intently.

'You sure about that?' Lucy pressed.

'Certain,' Bobby said. 'Why?'

'The car was involved in a killing a few nights back. A youth was killed in Bay Road.'

'The gay boy?' Frankie said.

'Sergeant, let's go!'

Fleming stood behind her, frowning at her for having already said too much. But when she turned again to Bobby and Frank, she could see that the latter stood taller now, his expression clouded.

Chapter Thirty-Two

'YOU SHOULDN'T HAVE said that,' Fleming cautioned her, a little unnecessarily, as they got back into her car.

Lucy nodded. She'd known as she'd spoken it that she was going too far. But she'd also grown frustrated at Bobby McLean's seeming indifference to their investigation. And, if she was completely honest, the intolerance that she had witnessed with regards the Lupeis had annoyed her, too. Her comments had been a twist of the knife; she had no doubt that at least one of them knew something about the car. Turning their intolerance against themselves might shake something loose.

Fleming phoned through to Burns to pass on details of the unit where they believed the car had been photographed, while Lucy cut down through Greenway. As they passed the green, they could see a small scaffold was already being erected.

'There's a surprise,' Lucy said, nodding to where now stood Pastor Nixon and his son along with another man Lucy didn't recognise, watching the workmen putting the scaffolding in place.

'Let's say hello, shall we?' Fleming said, unbuckling his belt again and getting out of the car as soon as Lucy pulled to a halt.

Nixon smiled broadly. 'Tom, Lucy, our paths just seem to keep crossing.'

'Indeed, Pastor,' Fleming said. 'You recovered from last night.'

Nixon laughed lightly. 'That was nothing. All part of the theatre of preaching.'

'A lot of the local media are very interested in the events,' Ian said. 'The pastor has already done two radio interviews this morning.'

'I hope you've exercised caution in your remarks,' Lucy said.

'I need no advice on caution from you,' Nixon said. 'Some caution last evening could have avoided all sorts of unpleasantness.'

'But look at the attention it's drawn,' Lucy said. 'You couldn't buy that kind of publicity.'

'The Lord works in mysterious ways,' Ian Nixon said, earning glances from all three of them. Only the stranger, with whom they had been standing, had remained aloof from the conversation.

'Are you speaking this evening?' Fleming asked. 'At this rally?'

Nixon nodded. 'Stephen here has been kind enough to invite me along.'

Fleming turned to the man now for the first time. 'I'm sorry, I don't think we've met.'

'That's right,' he said, smiling, his eyes creased at the corners as he did so. Lucy guessed he was in his late twenties, early thirties at most, around the same as herself. He wore jeans and a light V-neck sweater over a white T-shirt. The sleeves of his jumper were pulled down and gathered in balls in his fists. He waited a beat, then extended his hand. 'Stephen Welland. We own the local, the Greenway Arms.'

'DI Fleming. This is DS Black.'

'I've heard,' Welland said. 'Some of the neighbours were commenting on your being around yesterday.'

'We were investigating the attack on a Roma man here on Saturday night. We still are.'

Welland's smile did not falter. 'Not the attack on the taxi rank. Or on Pastor Nixon. Or Jackie Moss. You're here about a Roma man getting roughed up?'

'Do you not think we should?'

Welland nodded. 'By all means. I'm just a little bemused by the way you've prioritised your investigations.'

'There are other teams working those other cases,' Lucy explained. 'What's your role here?'

'I'm one of the organisers of tonight's rally,' Welland said.

'I thought Ulster First was arranging it.'

'I'm part of Ulster First,' Welland said.

'You're also the first person to openly admit to it,' Fleming said. 'Anyone else we've spoken to denies knowing anything about it.'

'I wouldn't know about that,' Welland said. 'I can only speak for myself.'

'I suppose tonight is a sort of coming-out party, then,' Lucy said, earning a glance of disapprobation from Pastor Nixon. 'Up until now, everything's been in the shadows: leaflets threatening immigrants, graffiti on walls, that sort of thing.'

Welland laughed, looking to Nixon to see how he was reacting to this. For Nixon's part, he remained impassive. 'You've the wrong end of the stick, Sergeant,' Welland said. 'Ulster First is an umbrella term to cover a number of concerned groups and individuals in the Greenway community. It was something dreamed up in our pub; a way for people to vent their frustrations at the erosion of the old Greenway way of life. A release valve, if you like.'

'And when talking in the pub isn't enough, what then?'

Welland shrugged. 'Bringing people onto the streets. Having a referendum. We'll see what happens on Thursday with this Brexit thing; I suspect people are angrier than the politicians think, fed up with their taxes being wasted on migrants. Certainly, the overwhelming sense I've been getting from the people of Greenway is that they've had enough. You can only push a community too far before something snaps.'

'And then people end up in hospital,' Lucy commented.

'I can't comment on the attack on Saturday night,' Welland said. 'Though, if you ask me, if I moved to an area where I wasn't wanted, I wouldn't stay too long. Common sense would tell you that.'

'Common decency would make you want to welcome strangers rather than chase them,' Fleming responded.

'I think we're going round in circles,' Nixon said, clasping a thick hand on Welland's shoulder. 'What I hear, as an outsider, is a community crying out to be heard, not one crying out to be told what to do. Good people will always bend to accommodate things, but you can force them a step too far. Homosexuals among us we can stomach; having their agenda shoved down our throats, having to accept their shams as a real marriage? That's a step too far. So, too, is allowing drug dealers and criminals to move into our estates.'

'So far, the only crimes we've seen in Greenway have been committed by people who live here.'

'Then you're not looking too hard,' Welland said. 'Come along tonight and you'll get a sense of how people here really feel.'

Chapter Thirty-Three

LUCY DROVE THEM both back to the PPU in Maydown. As she reached the roundabout, she realised that she'd forgotten to leave in the new pyjamas she'd brought for her father.

'Do you mind if I call in with dad?' she asked Fleming. 'I've clean nightclothes for him.'

Fleming nodded. 'No problem. Have you been to see him recently?'

Lucy nodded. 'Last night.'

'How's he doing?'

Lucy raised her shoulder in a half shrug. 'The same. A little worse. He thought I was my mum.'

Fleming laughed lightly, causing Lucy to glance. 'Sorry, I'm not . . . it's just not that surprising. You're very like her, your mum, when she was your age.'

'Really?'

Lucy realised that in her memories of her mother from her childhood, she looked as she did now, not as she had then. In fact, Lucy wasn't sure she could quite picture her as she had been.

'She had her hair cut short, too,' Fleming said. 'You're very similar.'

'In looks, maybe,' Lucy accepted.

'Not just in looks,' Fleming said. 'Was your dad lucid, apart from thinking you were your mum?'

Lucy was reluctant to let the previous comment go, but knew it was pointless to pursue. Fleming was entitled to his opinion; trying to convince him he was mistaken would do little to disprove what he had said.

'He wanted me – Mum – to convince *my* father that he was a good prospect. He talked about how happy they'd be together. It was sad, knowing how things turned out, realising that he'd imagined things would be so different.'

'It's almost better that he doesn't remember how things turned out.'

Lucy nodded. 'For him, maybe.'

IN FACT, HER father was asleep when she went in, still wearing the same nightclothes as before, the jacket lying open now. Lucy left the new pyjamas with the orderly at the main desk and headed back out to the car. The sky had cleared and Fleming was standing outside, leaning against the bonnet.

'It's brightening,' he said unnecessarily. 'Sadly. If it had been bucketing down, that rally this evening might have struggled to make it past a handful of hardliners.'

'You think it'll be busy?'

'Knowing Greenway? I'd say it'll attract a right crowd.'

Lucy got back into the car and started the ignition. As she did so, she glanced out towards the bridge, as she had done the previous night. The yellow works cradle still hung under the bridge but, as she looked, Lucy realised that it had moved to the centre of the bridge now.

'Do you see that?' she asked, pointing out through the windscreen.

'What am I looking at?'

'The cradle under the bridge. It's moved from when I was here last night.'

'There must be workmen in it, then,' Fleming said.

Lucy squinted to see if she could better discern whether there were any figures standing in it.

'How do they get into it?' she asked. 'There's no access from the ground, is there?'

'They must go through the—' Fleming began. 'God! They go *through* the bridge. McGonigle!'

'McGonigle!' Lucy echoed.

THEY DROVE ACROSS to the city end of the bridge, turning in at the lay-by and driving along the footpath that led down to where the teenagers had congregated on Saturday night. As they rounded the bend in the path to reach the bottom of the set of concrete steps, Lucy could see clearly now that there was indeed someone working in the cradle.

The place looked very different in daylight. The steps, which ran from the path up to the base of the bridge, were steep and narrow, their edges sharp. Here and there the concrete was stained with blood, presumably from the injuries caused during the incident on Saturday night. A beer can, lying on an upper step, was shifted by the wind enough that it clattered down a few steps towards them. At the top of the steps was a wall stretching up about ten feet to the underside of the bridge itself. This wall, as Lucy had seen on Saturday, was covered in graffiti.

She was beginning the ascent up the steps when she heard the siren begin blaring below her, causing her almost to stumble.

'Can we speak to you?' Fleming shouted, his hands cupped around his mouth, the siren having got the attention of the man in the cradle suspended forty metres over the water. Whether or not he had heard Fleming's shout, he clearly had heard the siren for, a moment later, they saw him climb onto the rail of the cradle and disappear up into the underside of the bridge.

Lucy continued up the steps, towards the back wall, where she had seen McGonigle standing on Saturday. Only as she neared the top did she realise that the back wall was not quite what she had expected. Due to the darkness during her previous visit, she had not seen that, in fact, a second outer wall sat out about a foot from the main wall and stood about four feet tall, acting almost as a stepping ledge up to the main wall. The step was just a little too high for her to climb unaided. As she stood, she heard a grating sound and, a second later, a door opened above her head. A workman stood, in high-vis vest and hard hat, five feet above her. The door had been impossible to distinguish from the rest of the wall, due to both the lack of handle on the outside and the graffiti, which had helped camouflage it. The shelf, created by the second wall, was actually the threshold step of this entrance.

'What's wrong?' the man asked.

Lucy stared up at him, unsure where to start. 'We were going to ask how you got into the cradle there, but now we know,' she managed.

'Seriously? You brought me back in for that?' he scowled. 'Quiet morning on duty, was it?'

Lucy looked down to where Fleming was beginning his ascent, stopping after five steps and resting one hand on the silver hand-rail running up the centre of the steps.

'Not much of a head for heights,' he called up in explanation, setting off again.

'I'm DS Lucy Black.'

The man nodded. 'David Harkin,' he said. 'Is he all right?' he asked, glancing down towards Fleming.

'He'll be fine,' Lucy said, without confidence. 'Look, we're sorry for bringing you in from your work. A youth vanished here on Saturday night.'

Harkin grimaced. 'Into the water?'

'Not quite. He literally vanished. He was standing at the top of these steps and he just vanished. He caused a distraction and made off. The problem is, he didn't go up onto the roadway above and he didn't come down the steps. We couldn't work out where else he could have gone.'

'Until now,' Fleming wheezed, having finally joined them. 'It's higher up here than you'd think,' he said. 'You'd wonder how the kids manage it when they've had a few cans.'

'You want to try hanging out there,' Harkin said, nodding towards the cradle. 'The wind up the valley would cut you.'

'I don't doubt it,' Fleming said. 'Is this door always locked?'

Harkin nodded. 'You have to sign out the key from Road Service, and sign it back in again.'

'What's in there?' Lucy asked.

'Come up and I'll show you,' Harkin said. He disappeared inside the doorway and returned with a small ladder, which he lowered down to her. She climbed up onto the ledge and stepped in. Fleming followed after her, muttering a quiet prayer as he did so.

Chapter Thirty-Four

THEY WERE STANDING in a small antechamber which, when they moved across to the left, opened out into the interior of the bridge. The structure was hollow in the middle, a space about eight feet square. A metal walkway ran up the centre of the hollow, with criss-crosses of pipes and support struts on either side of it. The floor just under the struts was covered in thin metal sheeting, though Lucy could see that in several places the sheeting was hinged and could be opened back, giving access to the outside. A series of lights were spaced a few feet apart along the length of the right-hand side of the interior.

'Is it like this the whole way across?' Lucy asked.

'It narrows as you get to the centre of each section,' Harkin explained, 'where the bridge arches, then it widens out again towards the other end.'

'But you can walk the entire length of the bridge?'

'Walk and crawl, if you really wanted to,' Harkin said.

'You didn't notice anything unusual today when you arrived, did you?' Lucy asked.

Harkin shook his head. 'Mind you, I've not gone the whole way through yet.'

'You came in this end, though?' Fleming asked.

A nod.

'Was it locked when you arrived?'

Harkin nodded again, though this time he glanced to the floor as he did so.

'Are you sure?'

'Pretty much,' Harkin said.

'Was it or not?'

Harkin quickly glanced to his left, then stared at Lucy. 'Look, someone could get fired. If the wrong person got inside here and planted something, well, you know yourself, like.'

'What happened?'

'One of the lads lost the key to the door I let you in through a while back. It was meant to be replaced but they never did. He told them it fell out of his pocket while he was working in the cradle and went in the water.'

'Did it?'

Harkin shrugged. 'So he said.'

'You don't believe him?'

'The key falling in the river is bad luck but at least the key's gone for good; dropping it in a place where someone else could find it is the type of thing you could lose your job over. Which story would you tell if you were the one who'd lost it?'

Fleming nodded. 'So, theoretically someone could have found the key and could be using it for access.'

'In theory. We've been checking it for devices every so often, just in case, but there's been nothing unusual.'

'What about today?'

'I've not checked, to be honest,' he admitted.

'Can we?'

Harkin nodded. 'I suppose so. Mind your head as you move in towards the centre; it gets tight.'

'If someone came in through this end, could they get out the other side?'

'Not unless they had a key for that door, too. It's a deadbolt, so it can't be opened from inside.'

Lucy glanced at Fleming to see if he was coming with her, then set off. Once she was inside the body of the bridge, she felt suddenly vulnerable, aware that only a few centimetres of metal separated her from a 120-foot drop to the ground below. The grille beneath her feet vibrated with the rumbling of traffic above her head. As she moved further in, she realised that the bridge was shifting suddenly to the right. She gripped the handrail running the length of the walkway and turned to Harkin, who was following behind Fleming.

'We're moving!' she called.

'It's the wind,' Harkin said. 'It feels worse in here.'

Lucy held steady, gripping the handrail white-knuckled as she waited for the swaying to stop. Instead, the walkway seemed to tilt even further.

'We're moving to the right,' she said, turning now and moving back towards the entrance.

Harkin laughed. 'The bridge is split along its length into two halves,' he said. 'Left and right. There's a gap between the two sections. Look.'

He pointed just to their left and Lucy saw a gap, no thicker than a pencil, which showed straight through to the river below. She realised that as they'd stood under the bridge, looking up, she'd seen a crack of light running up the centre along the entire length of the structure.

'Because of the height,' Harkin explained. 'High winds hit us side-on. If the bridge were solid, it would take too much pressure and crack. The gap lets the two halves shift and reduces the pressure overall. It's safer. But it does mean it can move in one direction on one side and not the other. It's safe, trust me.'

Lucy paused a moment, then steeling herself, turned back. As she did so, the bridge swayed once more, buffeted from outside. This time, Lucy swallowed slowly and stepped forward.

They moved in such a procession for three or four minutes before Lucy became aware that the walkway was actually on a slight gradient upwards and she found she had to crouch a little as she walked.

'We're getting near the middle,' she said.

By the time they had reached the apex of the arch in this section, Lucy had to crawl to get through the space. She realised, as she inched her way through the space, that with Fleming and Harkin behind her, she was pretty much trapped. She could feel the shuddering of the HGVs above her, vibrating through her hands pressed against the walkway. The movement of the bridge had become increasingly exaggerated as they moved out fully over the water. Suddenly, they seemed to lurch sharply to the right again and Lucy felt certain she was going to be sick.

'You okay?' Harkin called.

'I can't . . .' she said.

She felt a hand on her calf as she crawled and let loose a brief, involuntary scream.

'It's me,' Fleming said. 'You're okay. You're doing okay.'

'I was,' Lucy muttered, aware that his gripping her leg had been well intentioned whatever the outcome.

'Are we nearly there?' Fleming asked.

'It should be widening out again,' Harkin said.

Even as he said it, Lucy realised that the ceiling above her had raised a little and she could straighten herself up slightly, which, in turn, allowed her to breathe more freely.

It was here, finally, that Lucy saw something.

Gareth McGonigle was leaning against the central pillar, his back to Lucy, his head laid on the metal grille of the floor.

'It's him,' Lucy shouted.

As she reached him, she saw for the first time a scattering of empty packets of Magic Dragon on the floor around him, a pool of vomit haloing his head. He was pale, his head clammy, his skin sticky with sweat.

'I think he's overdosed,' Lucy said, pulling out her phone to call for an ambulance.

Chapter Thirty-Five

'THANKS TO THE efforts of our colleagues in the PPU, we have what seems to be definitive proof as to why Gareth McGonigle was in Bay Road Park on Friday night and, possibly, why he was in Paradise night club.' Burns was standing at the head of the incident room, his carriage more erect than it had been previously. 'Unfortunately, Mr McGonigle took some of his own produce while hiding out inside the Foyle Bridge and is currently in Altnagelvin. We're waiting for word about if or when he'll be fit to be interviewed.'

'Was Givens selling too?' Mickey asked.

'We got the impression from anyone we've spoken with that Givens was a good kid,' Lucy said.

'I spoke with his parents this morning. We're waiting for toxicology results on the remains, but that will take a few weeks. The parents, however, also claim that he was not a drugs user, nor had they ever a reason to suspect that he might be.'

'Said every parent ever,' Mickey muttered, though without his usual brio.

'Quite,' Burns said tersely. 'We'll know better when tox comes back. Again, thanks to DS Black, we suspect we know where the car Givens was in was photographed prior to being put on sale, which may lead us to the owner. Mickey, can you update us on that?'

'We called at the printing works, sir,' Mickey said. 'The owner is off work with an injury. We spoke with his son and another worker, Robert McLean, following on from DI Fleming's call. Neither of them knew anything about the car, had never seen it being photographed, could tell us nothing about it.'

'Is that it?'

'We did take away some photographic equipment from the unit, sir. I have it down with technical to see if maybe it was used to take the pictures. They're working on it as we speak.'

'Update me as soon as you hear anything. Do we have anything on either of these men?'

'A few drunk and disorderlies on McLean,' Tara said. 'McEwan is clean, pretty much; just a caution for careless driving.'

'Keep digging on him. Tara, I want you to get back to Paradise and find out a bit more about the drugs scene there and how McGonigle fitted into it. Whatever the manager might say, there's bound to be one. And Mickey, you need to get me something quickly on that bloody car. It can't just have vanished.'

MICKEY PASSED LUCY in the doorway but could not look at her. He stormed across the open-plan office and out to the stairs beyond, slamming the door behind him.

'Someone's missing his Scooby snack,' Tara said, coming up alongside Lucy.

'So I see.'

'Well done on getting McGonigle,' she added. 'You're on a roll. I hope you didn't mind my mentioning the legal high we found . . . you found, in Paradise.'

Lucy dismissed the comment. 'Not at all. We were there together. It's all teamwork.'

'I'm heading back up again; you fancy coming along for the ride? See if you can find anything else?'

'I'm afraid I need DS Black to taxi me about,' Fleming said, joining them. 'Are you ready?'

'Where are we going?'

'Burns talking about the drugs scene reminded me: Stella, our concerned Greenway citizen, mentioned Magic Dragon being sold to her son by the Romas. We were to call at the High and find out if that's actually what happened.'

Tara sniggered. 'The *High*? That's a bit unfortunate. In the circumstances,' she said.

Chapter Thirty-Six

THE HIGH WAS situated at the heart of the Waterside. It was one of a number of newer schools which were actually amalgamations of existing colleges. Northern Ireland had retained a two-tier secondary system with children sitting an examination at eleven to determine whether they attended a grammar or secondary school from eleven to eighteen. When devolution saw Sinn Fein taking responsibility for the education portfolio, the party had scrapped the eleven-plus exam, as it had been called. Many of the grammar schools had protested and, rather than accepting pupils of all abilities, had instigated their own entrance examinations. In effect, Catholic grammars now used one test for admission while Protestant grammars used a different one. As a result, the scrapping of the eleven-plus, intended to do away with division and segregation, had ironically strengthened both. As a way of counteracting that, a policy was introduced of amalgamating local schools, grammar and secondary, into one building so that, in essence, the tests might eventually become pointless. The High was an example of one such amalgamation.

The alliance of the two schools had not been without problems; rural and urban children both brought different sets of experiences and expectations, as did the staff from the two separate schools. Managing all of this transition was the headmistress, Sheila Gormley.

She was a small woman, barely passing five foot in height, with cropped blond hair, styled into a ragged quiff. As she spoke, the collections of bangles on her right arm rattled against her office desk. Occasionally, as if only aware of them for the first time, she would raise her arm and, with a shake, slide them back towards her elbow but, with her next movement, they would slither back and rattle against the desk once more.

'I'm the wrong person to ask, really,' she said, when Fleming told her the reason for their visit.

They waited for her to explain why, but no explanation was forthcoming. 'You *are* the one in the charge, though?' Fleming asked.

Gormley laughed lightly, flicking her head a little, like one accustomed to having longer hair. Lucy suspected her cropped cut was a recent change and, presumably, a significant one. Something must have prompted her to do it.

'Of course,' Gormley replied. 'What I mean is that we passed on all the relevant information.'

'Did you get to the bottom of who was selling drugs in the school?'

Gormley glanced to the window. 'We're not even sure drugs were being sold *in* the school.'

'To school children, then,' Fleming said, his patience going.

'I can't really recall if . . .' Gormley began, though the sentence petered out. Despite this, she sat, her hands folded together on the desk in front of her, looking at the two of them as if she had answered them and was waiting for their next question.

'It must be difficult managing the amalgamation,' Lucy said.

Gormley flashed a brief smile, nodding as she did so. 'A lot is riding on the school being a success. A lot of funding has gone into it. It's not in anyone's interests to see it fail.'

'And a story about drugs being sold in the school would be very damaging,' Lucy agreed. 'I can see that.'

Gormley's smile grew more brittle. 'Yes.'

'So you can rest assured that we won't be making any of this public,' Lucy said. 'A parent claimed that her son was sold drugs in school. She implied that members of the Roma community were responsible for this. We're simply looking to see if there's any truth in that claim.'

Gormley swallowed, then reset her smile. 'None,' she said. 'There was an issue with substances being sold – *outside* the school grounds, I should add. The person responsible for selling them was not a member of the school community.'

'Do you know who he or she was?'

'I, ah, I don't recall,' Gormley said.

'It wouldn't have been Gareth McGonigle?' Lucy asked, taking a punt.

But Gormley shook her head. 'No. It was Mc something. McClean. McLean.'

'Bobby McLean?'

Gormley smiled. 'That's it. Robert McLean. He was a pupil of the old secondary so, you see, it really has nothing to do with me. He'd left long before I took over.'

'You said you passed on this information to the authorities,' Fleming said, sitting up a little straighter in his seat.

'That's right. The Community Policing Team were involved.'

'Can you remember which officers?'

Gormley smiled again. 'Of course. Officer Huey. She comes in every term and talk to the kids about antisocial behaviour and drugs and that.'

FLEMING WAITED UNTIL Gormley had left them, having retrieved their visitor badges to be returned to Reception.

'We need to have another word with Huey,' Fleming said.

'About McLean?'

Fleming nodded. 'And about why there was no record of his selling drugs to school kids in the files on him.'

'The SIO handling the Jackie Moss shooting mentioned that he'd been involved in investigating the young fellas in Greenway over drugs. Maybe he came across McLean?'

'Let's go ask him,' Fleming said.

Chapter Thirty-Seven

MULHOLLAND AGREED TO give them five minutes. Despite being in the middle of the shooting investigation, Lucy noticed that he appeared calm, his clothes fresh, his manner businesslike but relaxed in comparison with Burns who seemed to be unravelling over the Martin Givens investigation. Lucy wondered why her mother had assigned the case to Mulholland. Perhaps she was preparing him for bigger things.

'You've heard Jackie Moss is on the mend,' he said, having invited them to sit. He leaned back in his seat, ran his hand through the loose straggles of hair that hung over his forehead.

'That's good to hear,' Fleming said. 'Any luck with Charlie Dougan?'

'None,' Mulholland said. 'He reckoned he had no reason to take out Jackie. They were friends, he says.'

'Until Jackie hit his taxi rank.'

Mulholland shrugged. 'We'll get him on something else at some stage. That's the way these guys work. He'll walk this afternoon, though. You mentioned you had a few questions on the phone?'

He was keen to get them moving.

'We spoke to a school principal who claimed that Bobby McLean had been selling legal highs in the High last year,' Lucy explained. 'I remembered you mentioning having worked the Drugs Squad.'

Mulholland nodded. 'The name sounds kind of familiar. I'll need to go back through my notes for you. There was a whole bunch of them. A fella called Welland was the ringleader.'

'Stephen Welland?'

A shrug. 'I think so, yeah. They were local muscle. We thought there was an Eastern European gang trying to move into the North. They were bringing in shipments but needed someone to sell into the local communities. Some of those young lads got involved in it. It was short-lived, to be honest. The Provos didn't take kindly to Roma trying to sell in Derry. They were supplying a head shop in town. One of the Republican splinter groups shot dead the owner. Then a few of the Roma shipments got hit and they pulled back. I'd heard they were still selling in Dungannon. Jackie Moss got involved at that stage and ordered Dougan to bring the young fellas in under his wing.'

'That might explain the reaction to the Roma family living in Greenway,' Fleming said. 'One of the locals claimed they were selling drugs in the area, but the family only moved there a few weeks back.'

Something in what Mulholland had said registered with Lucy. She remembered the shooting of the head shop owner the previous year. 'Head shops?' she asked. 'For legal highs?'

'Among other things,' Mulholland said.

'Is that what this gang were selling?'

'Again, among other things. But yes, primarily legal highs. They were bringing them in from China.'

'Legal highs have come up a few times in the past few days. Stuff called Magic Dragon.'

Mulholland grunted. 'That's a common one.'

'If they were legal back then, why were criminal gangs getting involved in them?'

Mulholland shrugged. 'Until the Act a few weeks back, it was all a grey area. The Roma gangs figured they'd found a gap in the market; some of the paramilitaries were handling the heavier drugs. Now, it's different. The highs are illegal, but there are still plenty of them in circulation that need to be sold and can be shifted pretty cheaply. How does that connect with your Greenway case?'

'It doesn't,' Lucy said. 'At least not yet. The suspect in the Martin Givens killing was selling MD.'

'I see,' Mulholland said. 'Speaking of which, I heard in the canteen there that they've found that car they'd been looking for out at an abandoned quarry just past Gobnascale.'

Chapter Thirty-Eight

THE QUARRY ACTUALLY lay closer to Newbuildings than Gobnas-cale, on the Old Strabane Road which ran along the rear of Prehen Park, a few miles out of town. It had once been used as a dump of some sort, judging by the remains of a weighbridge at the entrance and the sealed-up hut which still carried the rusted metal signage of a now long-closed waste disposal company.

Mickey and Tara were standing talking to Burns when Lucy and Fleming arrived. They led them all up, past the entrance hut and round a bending path into an open part of the quarry. The ground was thick with vegetation, which extended even up the sides of the spoil heaps sitting to the right of the open area. It was in the shadow of these that the blue car now sat, while several forensic technicians examined it.

Even at a cursory viewing it was clearly the same car, though the number plates had been removed before it had been aban-doned. The passenger-side window was missing, the paintwork around the frame dinged and dented. Lower on the door were two more dents, close together, which looked like someone had struck the door. The relative position of the damage suggested some-one kicking the car had caused the dents. Burns broke off from the rest of them and moved across to speak to one of the SOCOs examining the bodywork.

'You found it? Well done,' Lucy said to Mickey, earning only a scowl in return.

'Police 44 found it,' Tara explained. 44 was one of the PSNI's helicopters which was being used increasingly to cover areas of the city where dissidents were thought to be operating. Lucy guessed they'd been over Gobnascale for some reason and had caught sight of the vehicle. That it had taken until now to find it suggested that it had only recently been dumped here.

'That was lucky.'

Tara nodded.

'Excuse me,' Mickey said. 'See you later. Sir.' He nodded at Fleming then went across to Burns and the forensic technicians.

'What's eating him?' Lucy asked.

'We only found the car because 44 picked it up and we only found out where the pictures of it had been taken because youse found that. Mickey was in charge of locating the car and everyone else did the work for him. Burns let him know that he was aware of that fact.'

'That can't have gone down well,' Lucy guessed.

'You saw for yourself—' She stopped short as Burns reappeared.

'We're interviewing Gareth McGonigle this afternoon,' he said. 'If we can find anything to connect him to this we'll have it all sewn up by tea time,' he added, nodding across towards the carcass of the car.

Mickey approached them again. 'They're finishing up here,' he said.

'What did they find?'

'Blood around the passenger side. Someone tried to clean it off with bleach, but there's some in the creases of the upholstery. They reckon someone smashed in the passenger window. There are several dents on the roof which suggest they attacked whoever was inside with a rock; bloody grip prints on the door suggest it was opened and the victim pulled out onto the ground. There is some evidence of damage to the other side and rear and a chip mark on the back windscreen. And there are traces of something on the passenger seat and footwell which forensics think is semen. It pretty much confirms what we'd suspected happened.'

'Still, expedite getting it tested for confirmation. I want to have as much concrete evidence as possible to take to McGonigle when I speak to him.'

'Yes, sir,' Mickey said.

'DS Black,' Burns said, 'the ACC and I would like you to sit in on the interview with McGonigle. Having been the one to find him, he might be more forthcoming with you there.'

'Yes, sir,' Lucy said, blushing. 'Of course.'

As she turned to follow him, she could not help but notice Mickey's expression.

Chapter Thirty-Nine

'I DIDN'T DO it,' McGonigle said, wincing as he swallowed a mouthful of water. He sat up in his hospital bed, pillows piled behind him to keep him upright. His colour had improved significantly. 'He was just lying there and . . . I turned and ran.'

He glanced at his lawyer, a slim, red-haired man, who sat next to the bed. He nodded his head encouragingly.

'So, who did?' Burns asked.

McGonigle shrugged. 'I don't . . . he was just there.'

'Maybe take us back to the start of the evening, Gareth,' Burns said. 'We'll get to what happened to Martin in a minute. Talk us through where you went on Saturday from the start.'

Lucy knew what he was doing. They'd managed to trace some of Martin's movements through CCTV footage. By getting McGonigle to retrace the events of the evening, they could assess how honest he was being with them. It would also give them a sense of where they could pin him if he started lying.

'I got my stuff and headed out early with Martin,' he said.

'Your stuff? What does that mean?'

McGonigle looked again at the solicitor.

'It's fine, Gareth,' the man said. They'd found McGonigle with a bag full of Magic Dragon; there was clearly little point in his not admitting to having it or trying to claim it was for personal use only.

McGonigle nodded. 'Stuff. The MD,' he said, looking to Burns again.

'Magic Dragon? You mean legal highs?'

McGonigle nodded. 'Yes.'

'So, where did you go first?'

'We stopped off under the bridge,' McGonigle said. 'The kids gather there on weekends. I made a few scores there. Then we headed on. There was a gay disco on in Paradise and Martin wanted to go. He thought he was gay.'

'*Thought* he was gay?'

'He was,' he said. 'He wanted to find out what the gay scene was like in Derry. He asked me if he could come with me. I think he thought it would be easier if he was there with a wingman.'

'So you went, too?' Burns paused and Lucy guessed he was wondering whether he could ask McGonigle if he too was gay. 'Just as a wingman? Or were you interested in finding out about the gay scene in the city, too?'

'I'm not queer.' McGonigle laughed.

'But you didn't mind going to a gay disco.'

McGonigle hesitated a moment. 'Naw. I was there to sell.'

'Magic Dragon?'

'Yeah.'

'How long did you stay there?'

'A few hours,' McGonigle said. 'It was mental busy; I sold out of stuff.'

'Then what?'

'We went back down to Bay Road Park.'

'Why?'

'To get the late crowd there.'

'But you'd sold out.'

McGonigle looked at him. 'What?'

'You said you sold out in Paradise. But you went back to the bridge. How did you stock up?'

'I called into my flat.'

Fleming shook his head. 'No. We've checked the CCTV there. You didn't go back to your flat.'

McGonigle straightened in the bed and glanced to his lawyer. 'I called someone to help me restock. He met us in Paradise after midnight.'

'Who?'

'A friend. I'm not ratting him out.'

Fleming didn't speak for a moment, allowing the silence to descend in the room. It made no difference, though, for McGonigle folded his arms, his jaw set.

'So, what then?'

'He drove us down to Bay Park and I went across to the kids there. I left Marty in the park. When I came back, he was just lying there, on the grass. I panicked and ran.'

'You didn't call for help?'

'I was scared,' McGonigle said, and looking at him, Lucy believed it. His eyes had filled and he looked down at his hands, folded now in his lap, as if ashamed to meet their gaze.

'Did Marty wait with anyone in the park?'

McGonigle shrugged.

'Was he with your friend?'

'I don't know,' he said, snuffling his nose against his hand.

'Is this your car?' Burns asked suddenly, presenting McGonigle with a picture of the blue car.

'I don't have a car.'

'Do you know who owns this car?'

McGonigle shook his head.

'We've recovered various fibres and samples from this vehicle, Gareth,' Burns said. 'We know it was the car in which Martin was killed. If we connect your DNA to the samples taken from this car, you know what that'll mean. Do you want to think again?'

McGonigle blanched, as if something had only struck him for the first time. 'Do you think I killed Marty?'

'You're the last person to be seen alive with him,' Burns said.

'He was my friend!' McGonigle said. 'I'd not hurt him.'

'You saw his injured body but didn't think to contact an ambulance? The police? Nobody?'

'I was . . .' McGonigle swallowed. 'I was scared in case I got into trouble. I couldn't . . .'

'Who owns the car, Gareth?'

McGonigle looked at his lawyer, but the man had nothing to offer him.

'My supplier. He gave us a lift down to the park. He came to Paradise to give me more stash and dropped us down there afterwards. I left him and Marty in the car. They'd messed around a few times before. Marty fancied him.'

'Who is your supplier?'

McGonigle swallowed hard again, looked to his hands, fidgeting with the edge of the blanket.

'He'll kill me if he knows I said.'

'You're going to be charged with murder if you don't,' Burns said. 'It's your choice.'

'Bobby,' McGonigle said at last. 'His name's Bobby McLean.'

Chapter Forty

'WE NEED TO find Bobby McLean as a matter of urgency,' Burns said as they strode down the hospital corridor. 'And we need to place him in Paradise night club to substantiate McGonigle's claims. You know what he looks like; help DS Gallagher to work through the footage from the club, see if you can spot him.'

'Yes, sir,' Lucy said. 'There's a rally in Greenway this evening. Pastor Nixon is speaking at it. It's been organised by Ulster First so McLean may put in an appearance there, unless he knows we're after him for Givens' killing.'

'We'll have a presence there anyway,' Burns said. 'I've asked Mickey to lead it; DI Mullholland wants us to keep an eye out for Dougan. It'll be interesting to see what happens when he gets home.'

'You mean, will he try to take control in Greenway?'

'I mean, will anyone take a pot shot at him in retaliation for Jackie Moss,' Burns replied.

THE INCIDENT ROOM was markedly busier through the afternoon. Burns had gathered the team together for the afternoon briefing and run through McGonigle's statement. It was clear that his direction now was focusing on proving McLean's complicity.

'Mickey, see if forensics can place both Givens and McLean in the car. Get DNA profiling done on the semen found at the scene. We can always run a comparative analysis against McLean whatever time we get him.'

Mickey nodded. 'Yes, boss.'

'Tara, DS Black will assist with the CCTV footage from Paradise. If we can place McLean there, it'll strengthen our hand, too.'

Tara nodded and smiled at Lucy.

'I want all eyes on the lookout for McLean,' Burns continued. 'We'll have a presence at Greenway tonight for this rally. DS Sinclair and DS Gallagher will lead our team there, but keep it low key. We don't want to spook him if he does show his face.'

'Nor do we want to start a riot with the residents,' Fleming muttered.

LUCY AND TARA sat at a desk at the far end of the room, the blinds pulled shut to help them see the hazy images on the screen in front of them as they worked through the CCTV footage provided by Paradise.

The images they were watching were taken by the CCTV camera over the club's front entrance. The main thoroughfare of Strand Road was visible to the far right of the screen, the headlights of each car taking the corner onto the Strand momentarily dazzling at the edge of the screen. Two doormen stood at the entrance, one with his back to the camera but still identifiable by the cable hanging from the earpiece he wore. Occasionally they stopped people going in, clearly asking for ID, though at no point did Lucy see them refuse entry to anyone.

'This'll take all afternoon,' Tara said, putting her feet up on the empty chair to her left. 'May as well get comfortable.'

'McGonigle said it was after midnight when McLean arrived,' Lucy said. 'We can probably skip ahead until then. Maybe half an hour before, just in case his timings were wrong.'

Tara leaned forward and pressed the twin arrow key. The people coming in and out of the bar moved now at triple time. Finally, she slowed it again as the time in the bottom left-hand corner hit 11.29 p.m.

Some of the patrons were leaving the bar now, their exit briefly halted by the doormen who made them transfer the contents of their glasses into plastic cups before they could go on their way. Occasionally, a member of staff came out to retrieve the tottering pile of empties and take them back inside.

It didn't take more than ten minutes of scrolling through the footage before they spotted Bobby McLean entering the bar at 12.20 a.m. Lucy recognised him almost immediately. Neither of the doormen stopped him, though as they watched they saw McLean swiftly shake hands with the security man with his back to the camera. The gesture was quick, almost unnoticeable, the man's hand barely raised past his hip.

'He slipped him something,' Tara said. 'A free sample?'

'Or a sweetener to turn a blind eye to what was being sold upstairs,' Lucy said.

They continued scrolling through the images, waiting to see McLean reappear. It was during this period that Lucy recognised someone else leaving the bar behind a group of revellers. While he initially looked to be part of the group, once they were outside, he peeled away from them and moved off across the Strand Road on his own. He wore skinny jeans and a white T-shirt, despite the cold of the evening. He paused at the kerb and called a taxi, giving Lucy a final clear look at his face.

'Pause it,' she said. 'I want to get DI Fleming.'

She returned with Tom a moment later. 'Who does that look like?' she asked.

Fleming studied the screen for a few seconds. 'Pastor Nixon's young lad, Ian,' he said at last. 'Where was this taken?'

'Outside Paradise night club,' Lucy said. 'He's leaving the gay disco.'

'On his own?'

Lucy nodded.

'Sussing out the enemy?' Fleming offered unconvincingly.

'I don't think so,' Tara said. 'I watched on a little.'

She hit the play button. A second figure appeared from the bar, another man, wearing a coat of his own and carrying another. He approached Nixon and put the coat around his shoulders. Nixon turned and smiled at him, one hand placed proprietarily on the other man's arm.

'Sleeping with the enemy more like,' Tara added.

'He looks happy,' Lucy said. 'It suits him better than the permanent scowl he wears with his father.'

'If he is gay, it must be a nightmare having to sit through his father's sermons,' Fleming said.

'Maybe his leaking the footage online in the wake of the Givens killing wasn't ever intended to bolster support for his father,' Lucy suggested. 'Maybe his intention all along had been to shine a light on the pastor's views.'

'It backfired,' Fleming said. 'Nixon's never been more popular.'

'Maybe not. It galvanised support on both sides,' Lucy said. 'It brought out the protestors, too. Maybe he wanted to bring things to a head.'

'Can we check for McLean going again?' Tara asked. 'CS Burns will be looking for something soon.'

Lucy nodded, retaking her seat and pulling across the extra one which Tara had been using to rest her feet for Fleming to sit.

It was a further minute or two before McLean left the club, turning down the Strand Road towards Princes Street. There was no handshake this time, just a barely perceptible nod exchanged between the doorman and Bobby.

About fifteen minutes later, Martin Givens and Gareth McGonigle spilled out of the club, Givens laughing silently at something McGonigle had said. Tara paused the video.

'That's us,' she said. 'McLean was definitely there. It bears out what McGonigle said. We'll be heading up to Greenway soon for this rally.'

Lucy nodded, studying the faces on the screen.

'What's up?' Tara asked.

'Martin Givens,' she said. 'He looked happy, too.'

Chapter Forty-One

A CROWD OF a few hundred residents had already gathered on the green by the time Lucy and Fleming made it to the centre of Greenway. A scattering carried placards which had clearly been mass produced, each bearing the logo of Ulster First. Most, though, stood around, phones in hands, passing the time until the speeches started. Younger kids were clumped near the front, as if in expectation of a rock band taking to the stage of the hastily erected scaffolding, the rear now covered in a blue tarpaulin against the rising wind that cut across the green. Other residents stood further back, some on the roadway or on the pavement opposite, standing outside the charred husk of Dougan's taxi office, separated from them with a few strands of tape wrapped around traffic cones.

Several of the major incident team were in attendance, most in plain clothes, in the hope of spotting Bobby McLean but without spooking the crowd by having a heavy police presence. There were, however, also a few uniformed teams on the periphery of the group and, Lucy noticed, some of the community officers, including Lloyd and Huey. It was this pair that she pointed out to Fleming.

'Officers,' Fleming said as they approached their two uniformed colleagues.

'Inspector,' Lloyd said. 'Sergeant. What's with all the plain clothes here?' He glanced around, clearly having recognised so many of the officers across from the Strand Road. 'Expecting trouble?'

'Expecting Bobby McLean, hopefully,' Fleming said. 'Have you seen him?'

Lloyd shook his head. 'Why?'

'You didn't mention that he was involved in selling drugs.'

'Bobby?' Lloyd said incredulously.

'Bobby,' Fleming repeated. 'We spoke with the head of the High. She said he'd been selling to students last year. She said it had been reported on to the community team.'

Huey nodded. 'That's my bad; *I* spoke to Bobby about that. Legal highs. It was a grey area.'

'Supply isn't that grey.'

'Tell that to the head shops that were selling this stuff openly last year.'

'We can't,' Lucy said. 'Most of the people who owned them have been shot.'

Huey smiled. 'Exactly. That's how I told Bobby he'd end up if he didn't catch a grip of himself. I'd not heard anything more about it.'

'Why, he hasn't started selling again, has he?' Lloyd asked.

Fleming nodded. 'Supplying and running sellers targeting school kids.'

Lloyd shook his head. 'The fucking muppet. Bit of overkill, mind you, all this to pick up someone for selling legal highs.'

'Oh, this is different,' Fleming said. 'Bobby's wanted for murder.'

'Murder?'

'Bobby was the driver of the car Martin Givens was in when he was beaten to death.'

'Givens?' Lloyd said. 'That the gay fella killed down Bay Road?'

'He's the teenager murdered in Bay Road Park,' Lucy said, 'when someone stove in his head with a rock. He'd been last seen in the car with McLean.'

'*With* McLean?' Huey asked.

'*With.*' Fleming nodded.

'I never took Bobby for gay,' Lloyd said. 'You?'

Huey shook her head. 'Nothing would surprise you about some of these youngsters.'

'That's not really the issue here,' Lucy said. 'His being implicated in a murder is.'

'No one's saying being gay is wrong,' Lloyd said. 'I'm just surprised is all.'

'Have you seen him?' Fleming asked.

Lloyd shook his head. 'He's normally with Welland and McEwan,' he said.

'Not Dougan?'

'Dougan's out on his own now,' Huey said. 'After the Moss shooting, he's short of friends. Bobby might be steering clear until he knows how the wind's blowing.'

'I think it's pretty clear how the wind is blowing,' Lloyd said, nodding past them.

They turned to where he had indicated, where Charles Dougan stood at the edge of the crowd. Despite the relative mildness of the weather, he wore an overcoat, which served to considerably bulk his size.

'He's wearing a bullet-proof vest under his coat,' Fleming muttered, clearly having noted his size at the same time.

Dougan stood alone, looking around him, as if trying to catch the eye of any of his fellow bystanders. Most, though, seemed determined to ignore him. One or two couldn't help themselves and nodded, or offered a quick word of greeting, but most had already decided that Dougan was guilty. If his plan had been to take control of Greenway after taking out Moss, it wasn't going to be quite so easy to gain the support of the locals. Finally, he stuffed his hands into his pockets and waited for the speeches to start.

'He has brass balls, I'll give him that,' Lloyd said. 'Coming out here. Does he not realise he's target number one after what he done to Jackie?'

'He knows just fine,' Huey said, before anyone else could speak. 'That's exactly why he's here. To show everyone he doesn't care. Besides, two days ago, he would have been the main attraction on the stage this evening.'

'Not any more,' Lucy said, turning as Stephen Welland took to the stage, tapping the microphone a few times both to check that it worked and to call those gathered in attendance to quieten down. Only when they had done so did he start to speak.

'Ladies and gentlemen,' he began. 'Friends. Thank you for joining us here this evening to express, peacefully, our disgust at the recent events that have blighted Greenway Estate. Local businesses burned, local businessmen attacked, religious freedoms stymied. These are dark days for Greenway.'

A grumble of agreement rose among the crowd.

'No mention of the attacks on the Lupeis,' Lucy muttered to Fleming, who nodded.

'But,' Welland continued, 'your presence here shows that we are not alone in fearing for the future of our community, fearing for our safety and security. When all else fails, when the police and those in authority fail us, we always have ourselves. We can rely on ourselves, to stand firm, to stand together, to stand in strength. And we can rely on the good Lord to protect us in our righteousness.'

He stumbled over the last sentence, as if the sentiment did not sit easily with him. He did not have the charm or polish of Nixon, his tone earnest, his mouth drawn tightly as he spoke.

'And to help us with that, can I welcome on your behalf, onto the stage, Pastor James Nixon.'

The mention of the pastor's name created more of a reaction. He strode towards the microphone, hand already raised in greeting to the crowd, as Welland melted back towards the rear of the stage and then moved down the steps to join the group standing there, among whom Lucy could see Nixon's family. There, at the centre of the group, following with his gaze his father's movement, for just a moment his bitterness barely concealed, stood Ian Nixon.

Chapter Forty-Two

NIXON'S SPEECH WASN'T markedly different in either tone or content to the ones Lucy had already heard. He started once more by calling those gathered in front of him 'All good people'. Several times, he appended his comments with a call for 'Amen', but the crowd in front of him was there for primarily political reasons, and their response was a little more tepid than perhaps he had expected. He must have realised he wasn't quite engaging his listeners, for after a few moments he changed tack and paused. He stared at those in front of him, his gaze slowing as he took in Lucy and Fleming. Then he unbuttoned his suit jacket and pulled the microphone free of the stand.

'Do you know what I see when I come to Greenway?' he said, then continued quickly before anyone had a chance to shout suggestions. 'I see the end of our culture.'

The reference to 'culture' reclaimed some of the crowd's attention. Those at the back, who had been engaging in their own conversations, stopped talking and glanced towards Nixon again.

'I see people who have been forced to give up *too* much. To make sacrifices *too* often. To compromise an inch *too* far.'

He clearly sensed that he had captured their attention again, for he began pacing on the stage, the microphone held close to his mouth, his breath fuzzing against it as if indicating the urgency of his message.

'That's what these people don't get,' he said, pointing beyond the square, into the distance, as if towards an unseen enemy that lay just beyond the borders of Greenway. 'They tell us we have a shared future. They tell us we have to accept change. They tell us we're being unreasonable in our demands. Well, I say, we need to see something back. This shared future promised jobs. Where are the jobs for Greenway? It promised investment. Where is the investment in Greenway? It promised new hope. Where is the hope for the young people of Greenway?'

A spattering of applause now and a few voices rose in support. The crowd began to shift, its ragged edges tightening as those on the periphery moved closer to the stage.

'We're not allowed to march where once we marched. We're not allowed to fly our flag where once it flew. We are discriminated against in our own police force where you get a job because of your religion, not because you're the best person for the job. Is this fair?'

A murmur of agreement rippled through the crowd, but Nixon was already being carried away on his own rhetoric.

'Where is this promised wealth? This peace dividend? They never told us it was for the middle classes only. They never said that the poor would stay poor. They never said that our kids would still leave school barely able to read or write. They never told us that there would be no jobs, no houses, no future for us.'

Lucy could see his speech was having the desired effect on the crowd, the faceless 'they' who had imposed these privations being set in contrast with the amorphous 'us' amongst whom Nixon clearly counted himself.

'Greenway is a special place. You know that, don't you? A final bastion of what it means to be *us*. But it is a forgotten place. They don't care about what happens here. Businesses attacked, shootings and violence, drugs in our schools. Local people who can't get housing, young couples unable to get their foot on the property ladder while homes are being offered to strangers, outsiders who aren't part of our culture, don't understand our history, don't appreciate what makes Greenway so truly special.'

The audience's response was warming now, those listening more intent in their attention, the crowd a collective held breath as if waiting for Nixon to make good on the promise of his reputation and say something inflammatory. Nixon himself must have sensed this for he paused, the microphone shaking slightly in his right hand, his left hand stroking his right cheek, his gaze locked in the middle distance in a fugue of contemplation.

'As I'm sure you know, the PSNI are keeping a careful eye on me. On all of us, in fact. I spoke out about aberrant behaviour in church and they challenged me on it. But I can't watch all that is happening around us, to us and to our communities, and not say, "Enough." We have compromised enough. We have surrendered enough. Ulster isn't allowed to say "No" any more, apparently, but it can surely say "No More!"'

A cheer rose now from the crowd. Lucy glanced across at Welland who had moved from the side of the stage to nearer the front, joining those who had themselves shifted a little closer to Nixon's platform.

'No more attacks on God's people. No more migrants tak-ing our homes. No more roads blocked to us. No more flags taken from their rightful spots. Enough. No more in Greenway. No more businesses burnt. No more infighting within our own community.'

This comment elicited a number in the crowd to turn to glance at Dougan where he stood, alone, at the rear. If he noticed their gaze, he didn't react, staring over their heads, as if transfixed by Nixon's words.

'We must turn our attention to those who would attack us, who would dilute our faith, our culture, our sense of ourselves. It is against these forces we must stand; against those who would trample our values, our beliefs, underfoot, who would force us to accept those into our neighbourhood who are not welcome, those who are not worthy of the name human: drug dealers, paedo-philes, gypsies, queers.'

'We need to stop him,' Lucy said. 'He's putting it up to us.'

'He's playing us,' Fleming said. 'Don't move. If we go near him, we're proving his point.'

Lucy scanned the crowd, looking for colleagues. 'Tara!' she said.

Across to the right, at the front of the stage, Lucy could see Tara making her way towards the steps, Mickey following desper-ately behind, though whether his haste was to stop her or assist her, Lucy couldn't tell.

'What are they—They're going to start a riot,' Fleming snapped. 'Stop them.'

They pushed their way up through the crowd. Tara was already on the steps and Nixon had spotted her. He dropped the micro-phone, the thud of it striking the floor of the stage reverberating in a screech of feedback through the speakers. Some in the crowd started booing while others began pushing forward themselves, presumably to protect Nixon.

Welland was taking the steps on the left-hand side of the stage two at a time, clearly hoping to beat Tara to Nixon. Ian Nixon followed, already shouting in protest.

'It's too late. Position yourself in front of the stage,' Fleming shouted. 'Grab whoever you can to help.'

Lucy nodded. Some of the others who had been in the crowd, including Lloyd and Huey and others in the Neighbourhood Policing Teams, were joining them now.

Lucy looked up to where Tara was with Nixon, already cuffing him, while Welland's protests could be heard through the microphone lying at his feet.

'You can't do this,' he shouted. 'The pastor has done nothing wrong.' Behind him, Ian Nixon and his mother joined in the chorus of disapproval. Nixon himself stood at the centre of the scene, smiling beatifically, while Tara and Mickey on one side and his disciples on the other debated his arrest. He caught Lucy's eye and, smiling broadly, winked once.

Lucy turned her back to him and stood, shoulder-to-shoulder, with Fleming, trying to stop the building crowd from pushing their way up onto the stage.

Chapter Forty-Three

THOUGH THE CROWD only numbered around one hundred, they still easily outnumbered and outweighed the PSNI officers who had managed to make it to the front. Lucy and Fleming locked arms, as did the officers on each side of them, and held the already straining line against the assembly.

A few of those in front of her shoved against them, their bodies packed so tightly together than she couldn't discern who owned the various limbs flailing and grabbing through the crowd. Likewise then, she could not tell whom it was who grabbed at her breast. The action caught her so off guard that, by the time she glanced down, she could see several arms reaching through, shoving and pushing. But there was no doubt that the gesture had not been accidental.

She loosened her arm lock with Fleming, found herself involuntarily stooping a little, curving her shoulders, bringing her arms across her chest. She could still feel the pressure the hand had exerted on her skin, the squeeze hard enough to hurt her. She scanned the faces in front of her, most pulled in leers and jeers, the odd one turned in anger.

'Are you okay?' Fleming asked.

'Give me a minute,' she said, grateful to escape the line and turn from the crowd. Surreptitiously, she rubbed her chest lightly, as if in doing so she could wipe away the touch of whoever had grabbed her. She looked up to the stage to see Nixon being led off by Tara and Mickey. The crowd were shifting now, over towards the left of the stage, as if to intercept them.

Lucy took the steps to the right, going up to where Welland and Nixon's family stood. It was Welland she approached first.

'You need to ask them to calm down,' she said.

'Bit late for that,' Welland said. 'What were you thinking lifting him here?' he added, laughing lightly. Lucy knew there was little point in trying to reason with him, that in fact he was right: lifting Nixon in front of the crowd had been madness. She was surprised at Tara for doing it.

Instead, she turned to Ian Nixon. 'You need to speak,' she said.

Nixon laughed. 'Yeah, right.'

'You need to calm them down. Someone could get hurt.'

'You should have thought about that first,' he said.

Lucy glanced at the space below. She could see Tara and Mickey, flanking Nixon, moving slowly through the crowd, encircled by other officers, holding back the enclosing protestors.

'Please,' she said, desperate to not have to say what she knew.

'No,' Nixon said.

Lucy hesitated a second before speaking, hating herself even as she did. 'I know you were at Paradise night club,' she muttered, just loud enough for Nixon to hear but softly enough that those nearby hopefully wouldn't. Still, Welland glanced quickly towards her, then away again as he stood talking with Nixon's wife.

'What?' Ian blushed lightly. 'I don't even know what . . . whatever that—'

'We have footage of you leaving,' Lucy said. 'You weren't alone.'

Nixon leaned close to her. 'Fuck you!' he hissed.

Lucy grimaced. 'I'm sorry. I've no choice. You need to call them off.'

He stared at her a moment, then spat drily in her face, flecks of saliva spraying her cheek. Then he turned and moved to lift the microphone.

'Please,' he said, raising his voice to be heard. 'Please. My father wouldn't want anyone to get into trouble for him. Please stand back.'

Some in the crowd had turned to see who was speaking, then resumed shoving into the police cordon inching its way towards the squad cars parked on the outer edge of the green.

Ian Nixon turned to look at Lucy helplessly, shrugging his shoulders.

'Your father could get hurt,' she said. 'Stop them. Your father could.'

Nixon's expression hardened and he turned again. 'Friends,' he said, louder now. 'Friends. Listen to me. Listen!'

The final comment was just assertive enough that it stopped most of those encircling Tara and Mickey, causing them to glance towards the stage.

'My father could get hurt!' Nixon shouted. 'He's an old man. He deserves his dignity. Let them pass through and let us deal with this properly.'

Some of the crowd peeled back a little, though those closest to the centre were too enraged to heed Nixon.

'Stop!' he shouted. 'Let my father pass. No violence! Stop!'

The comments and the vehemence with which he spoke were enough to halt the shoving of the crowd, and Lucy could see Tara and Mickey speeding the last hundred yards to the waiting car.

Once there, Nixon turned and raised his hands in acknowledgement of his supporters, smiling warmly, as if the whole thing had been preordained from the moment he arrived.

'Like Christ in Gethsemane,' Nixon's wife snapped at Lucy before turning to follow Welland off the stage.

'Then who plays Judas?' Lucy asked, as Ian Nixon passed her, his gaze not quite rising to meet hers.

Chapter Forty-Four

'WHAT WERE YOU thinking?'

Burns' voice reverberated through the incident room, the thin balsa-wood door to his office doing little to mask his words. Lucy could only imagine how Tara and Mickey would be feeling in there. Burns was already under pressure; the arrest of Nixon by some of his team was just one more thing he didn't need. Mickey and Tara had been there on Burns' behalf.

Mind you, Lucy reflected, it could have been significantly worse. They had got out of there, eventually, the crowd dissipating after Pastor Nixon had been taken. Welland had seemed happy enough to let them go: he'd wanted the people of Greenway to feel besieged and abandoned, and the arrest of Nixon had achieved both of those things.

Fleming ambled up the floor towards her. He'd been checking on whether there had been any further word on McLean. Judging by the light shake of his head as he approached, she guessed his search had been fruitless.

'Well?'

'Nothing,' Fleming said, sitting. 'Uniforms are keeping an eye on his house but he's vanished.'

'Ridiculous!'

They both started at the shout, Fleming glancing towards Burns' office door. 'Still giving them the hairdryer treatment in there?'

Lucy nodded.

'Poor sods,' he muttered. 'No doubt I'll get an earful for not preventing it. Mind you, it was a bit bloody stupid lifting Nixon like that. What was Gallagher thinking?'

Lucy had been wondering the same thing. Tara was usually so level-headed about things. And Mickey was generally so eager to please Burns. He'd clearly had to follow once Tara had engaged, but Lucy wondered if he'd tell that to Burns to cover his own back, or whether he'd stand with his partner and share responsibility.

A moment later, the door swung open and they both appeared. Tara was pale, her face downcast. Mickey held his head high, his cheeks blazing, his expression one of restrained fury. Burns followed behind, for all intents and purposes, deflated.

'Black, I heard you managed to get the son to call off the plebs in Greenway,' he muttered. 'Good.'

He glanced at Fleming and nodded curtly to indicate that he should follow him, then turned, allowing the door to swing shut.

Lucy raised her shoulder in a mild shrug at Fleming who reciprocated the gesture. 'I'll go in and update him on McLean, I suppose,' he said. 'Face the music.'

Lucy nodded, waiting until Fleming had got up to go before following Tara out of the incident room to see how she was doing.

She went down the corridor to one of the conference rooms, where the automatic ceiling light inside had just turned on, suggesting someone had entered the room. She could see Tara moving across to one of the seats.

It was only when she pushed open the door and walked in that she realised Mickey was standing at the far side of the room.

'You're a fucking moron. That was *your* fault!' he shouted. He stopped when he saw Lucy, glaring at her intrusion.

'You guys okay?' Lucy asked, glancing at him, then at Tara, who was sitting at the table now, tears running freely down her cheeks.

'What do you think?' Mickey snapped. 'Bollocked by Burns because she couldn't control herself.'

'We all make mistakes, Mickey,' Lucy said.

'Apparently *you* don't! You could dump on Burns' desk and he'd thank you for it.'

'Maybe ease off a little, eh?' Lucy suggested, moving across to Tara and putting an arm on her shoulder.

'Ease off? Fuck you! Fucking dykes running the place.'

Tara seemed to withdraw into herself.

'What did you say?' Lucy asked, rising.

Mickey stared at her, as if unsure whether to speak or not. 'You heard me,' he managed finally.

'Dykes?'

'You and your fucking girlfriend. And her,' he added, pointing at Tara. 'Everyone's afraid to turn a word in your mouths.'

'Except you, eh?' Lucy sneered.

Mickey bridled a little, straightened himself. 'Yeah. Except me.'

Lucy shook her head. 'You're a moron, Mickey. Get out.'

Mickey stood a moment, then moved to the door. 'You're not denying it, anyway,' he managed.

Lucy stared at him. 'Piss off, Mickey.'

She turned to Tara, only aware of Mickey's leaving by the swinging shut of the door.

'Are you okay?'

Tara nodded. 'I *was* bloody stupid; he's right to be annoyed.'

'He has no right to be an asshole,' Lucy said. 'Nixon had it coming.'

'I shouldn't have snapped, though,' Tara said. 'I should have just let him rant.'

Lucy nodded lightly, balling her shirt cuff into her hand and using it to dry Tara's tears.

'Your make-up's going to run,' she said, laughing.

'Like that'll matter.' Tara smiled, her face flushed, her eyes still raw with tears.

'So, what happened?'

Tara shook her head. 'I just couldn't listen to any more National Front bullshit about gypsies and paedophiles and . . .'

'Gay people?' Lucy asked softly.

Tara looked at her, held her stare a moment. 'Gay people,' she said, nodding.

'Nixon's an asshole, too,' Lucy said. 'You can't take it personally.'

Tara nodded again, lightly. 'What if it is personal?'

Lucy put her arm around Tara's shoulder, then leaning in, kissed her gently on the cheek. 'All the more reason not to let the bastards get to you, eh?'

She heard a tap on the door and turned, wondering if it might be Mickey, come back to apologise. Instead, Fleming stood in the doorway.

Lucy stood and came across to him.

'Everything okay?' he asked.

Lucy nodded. 'Fine,' she said.

'Sorry for interrupting. But Ian Nixon's downstairs to collect his father. He's insisting on speaking to you first.'

Lucy glanced back to Tara, who was standing now, blowing her nose into a wad of tissue paper. 'I'm good,' Tara said. 'Go on.'

'I'll be right there,' Lucy said.

Chapter Forty-Five

SHE LED NIXON into a free interview room on the ground floor. He'd arrived to collect his father, who was being released while a file was prepared for the PPS. Realistically, Lucy knew that this was a euphemism, a way for Burns to cover the fact that his arrest wasn't warranted. Someone in the Prosecution Service might decide to chance their luck and bring charges, but considering how other such cases had been prosecuted and lost in the recent past, the chances of a conviction were low. Still, the fact that a file was being prepared was a message to the press that Nixon wasn't being exonerated.

'I haven't long,' Ian Nixon said, refusing Lucy's offer of a seat. 'Dad will be wondering why I'm talking to you.'

'Okay,' Lucy said, sitting herself.

Nixon stood for a moment, as if realising what she had done, then reneged and sat down opposite her anyway. 'I was there for Dad,' he started. 'That club. I went to see what it was like. He asked me to go "to better know our enemy".'

Lucy nodded. 'I see,' she said neutrally.

'You don't believe me.'

'I don't care,' Lucy said. 'If you choose to go to a gay club – whether to better understand gay people or to better understand yourself – that's your choice. It's not a crime.'

'It's disgusting,' Nixon snapped.

Lucy raised both hands in a show of surrender. 'I'm not arguing with you.'

Nixon seemed somewhat deflated. 'That's fine, then. You were wrong.'

Lucy nodded slowly. 'I was wrong to use your being at the club against you,' she said. 'I apologise. It's your right to go where you like. I shouldn't have mentioned it. It had nothing to do with what was happening in Greenway.'

Nixon nodded, tapping out a light rhythm on his legs with his hands, which rested there as he sat. 'Well, if that's all.'

'*You* asked to speak to me,' Lucy said. '*Is* that all?'

'Why wouldn't it be?'

Lucy stopped herself from frowning. 'Do you want to talk to me about something, Mr Nixon? Is there something bothering you?'

Nixon stood, pushing in the chair against the desk at which they sat. 'Nothing. Just that. To tell you you were wrong.'

Lucy nodded and stood. 'That's fine, then. Though you seem to be confused. I never said you were gay. I said you had been to Paradise night club.'

'It's the same thing,' Nixon hissed.

'Clearly not,' Lucy said.

Nixon accepted the comment. He remained standing, did not speak, nor did he make an effort to leave.

'I'll not mention that you were there to your father, if that's what you're wondering,' Lucy said. 'Not if you don't want him to know.'

Nixon nodded again, though she noticed his shoulders sag a little, his grip on the back of the chair lightening, the blood returning to the whitened knuckles still gripping the top rail.

'That's fine,' Nixon said.

Lucy nodded. His excuse that his father had asked him to go there to better know his enemy held no water. She studied the man, the fineness of his nose, the high cheekbones, markedly different from the broad features of his father. He was, she guessed, in his twenties and was still hiding his sexuality from his father. She wondered if his mother knew the truth, as Martin Givens' mother claimed to have done. If they had conspired together to keep it hidden from Pastor Nixon. And, if so, for what reason? Deference to his beliefs? Or to some other aspect of his character?

'It must be difficult,' she said, the words articulating her thoughts, spoken before she realised what she was saying.

Nixon stared at her, immediately on guard again.

'What must?'

'Growing up with such strident expectations from your dad.'

'My father is a good man. A fine man,' Nixon said.

Lucy thought, unbidden, of her own father. She had always believed him to be a good man, a fine man, until she discovered about the affair with the teenage girl when Lucy was just a child. Despite the severity of the punishment meted out to the girl, neither the girl's own father nor Lucy's had done anything to help her. Lucy had found her, a few years back, living rough in Derry. She'd died not long after.

'He means well,' Nixon added, seemingly having had time to consider his response.

Lucy hesitated before she spoke. 'You know, if you had been in Paradise for your own personal reasons, then that's your choice. You know that. Your father's entitled to his views, but that doesn't mean you can't make your own choices.'

'I'm not stupid,' Nixon said.

At that, the desk sergeant knocked on the door.

'Pastor Nixon's out here now, DS Black,' he said.

'Thanks,' Lucy said, turning to Ian Nixon who noticeably blanched.

Ian Nixon may not be stupid, Lucy thought, but he was most definitely scared.

Chapter Forty-Six

LUCY STOOD IN the doorway, watching as Nixon and his son headed back out to the car park. She could see, even from here, that the older man was remonstrating with his son and Lucy guessed it was his annoyance at Ian's speaking out to the crowd, asking them to allow the PSNI officers safe passage.

Fleming came down the stairs, already putting on his coat. 'How did it go?'

Lucy shrugged. 'He says he was in Paradise doing his father's work.'

'I think, biblically, he's got that the wrong way round,' Fleming laughed. 'How did he know we'd seen him?'

'I told him in Greenway,' Lucy said, blushing. 'That was why he spoke out.'

'You threatened to out him?' Fleming asked incredulously.

'Not quite,' Lucy argued, then nodded. 'Implicitly, maybe.'

Fleming shrugged, though she could tell he was simply withholding judgement.

'We're done for the day,' he said instead. 'I chased up the background checks you'd requested on Cezar Lupei, by the way.'

'Anything useful?'

'Nothing at all.'

'So he's clean?'

'Apparently,' Fleming said. 'So, until this manhunt for Bobby McLean turns something up, we may as well get home.'

SHE DROPPED FLEMING at his house then headed down through the Waterside and out to Prehen. She'd thought of stopping with her father for a short visit, but couldn't face it. She felt bad already about what she had done to Ian Nixon; seeing her father in his current state would simply depress her further.

'Doors are wet,' Grace shouted from the kitchen as Lucy came in through the front door. Grace stood at the sink, washing the paintbrush in an old jam jar of white spirits. She wore shorts and a T-shirt both badged with paint and she had managed to get a stripe of white gloss across her right thigh.

'Finally finished,' she said, putting the jar onto the windowsill and lifting a cloth, soaked in the spirits, to begin cleaning her hands. 'That's the last of the painting.'

'Thanks,' Lucy said. 'You're a star. I'd never have got them painted otherwise.'

'S'nothing,' Grace said. 'How was work?'

Lucy rolled her eyes. 'Shit,' she said, explaining her threat to Ian Nixon.

Grace studied her as she listened to Lucy's version of events in Greenway, speaking only when Lucy had finished.

'You did what you thought best,' she said. 'The guy's a dick.'

'He's struggling with his own feelings, obviously—' Lucy began.

'He could stand up to his father. He could call him out on what he's saying. Instead, he's a part of all that spite while he's playing the other side at night. He needs to man up.'

'I was wrong,' Lucy said. 'I don't know what I was thinking. Things seem to be . . .' She moved into the kitchen, leaning against the counter. 'That guy we met in the pizza place the other night started on myself and Tara Gallagher today. Called us dykes.'

'I told you he was an arse, too,' Grace said.

'He thought you and I were a couple.'

'We *are* a couple,' Grace said. 'You're the big sister I never had. Anyone who has a problem with that can go fuck themselves, for all I care.'

Lucy smiled, despite her mood.

'Now come on, I'll get changed and we'll get something to eat.'

Lucy nodded. 'I fancy a movie,' she said.

'Let's do both, then,' Grace said. 'I'm paying.'

THEY ATE IN the Chinese in the Waterside, then headed across to the multiplex in town. It had once been the only cinema in the city until a second, larger one had opened on the outskirts of town. As a result, the city centre one tended to be fairly quiet, which suited Lucy just fine. They'd argued about what to watch, before settling on *Me Before You*. Grace paid, as she had insisted, so Lucy bought the popcorn and coke. They had just made it past the credits when Lucy felt her mobile vibrating in her pocket. It was Fleming. She declined the call, putting the phone back into her pocket. A moment later it vibrated again. This time she took it out in order to turn it off, but as she went to do so, she saw Fleming's message appear on the screen: *They've found Bobby McL. He's dead. We're wanted to ID him. Call me when you can.*

Chapter Forty-Seven

GRACE STAYED ON at the movie, telling Lucy that she would head across the street to Paradise afterwards for a drink with some of the other staff. Still, Lucy felt bad leaving her on her own.

She drove up to collect Fleming, then they both headed out to Greenway, where McLean's body had been found by his neighbour.

'She called to the house,' Fleming explained. 'She heard noises.'

'How did he die?' Lucy asked. 'Suicide?'

'Only if he beat himself up and wrote "Faggot" on his own wall,' Fleming said.

MCLEAN'S FLAT WAS a mid-terraced upper-storey red-brick affair near the outer edge of Greenway. The courtyard in front of the block was already alive with light and sound from the PSNI vehicles parked there. A cordon had been set up at the bottom of the stairway leading to the row of three flats, with a second inner cordon of tape placed across the open doorway of McLean's flat. The light shining from inside was unnaturally bright and Lucy guessed that the SOCOs had already arrived and were setting up shop inside in preparation for their evening's work.

Once they had been signed in and had pulled on their protective overalls, they waited at the doorway to the flat for Burns to come out to get them. They could hear his voice from the living room, sitting off to the left-hand side of the narrow hallway at the mouth of which they stood.

'A few hours?' they heard him ask. Occasional flashes from the SOCO photographer illuminated the room, throwing shadows of the figures inside onto the hallway wall. Lucy heard the burst of static on a radio inside, before a voice informed Burns that they were waiting.

A moment later he put his head around the side of the living-room door and called them both in.

Inside, the room was small and stuffy, a state that was not helped by the arc lights placed in the corners, nor by the presence of five figures in the room now.

Bobby lay on the floor, stripped naked from the waist down, his trousers and pants gathered at his ankles, presumably because his boots prohibited their easy removal. His groin carried significant damage, the skin purpled and bruised, both around his groin and down his legs where clearly he had been repeatedly beaten.

'Jesus,' Fleming whispered.

'Is it Bobby McLean?' Burns asked.

Lucy nodded soundlessly. Forcing herself to look away from his lower half, she studied his face, marked with bruises and a number of still raw gashes. His head was encircled by blood, which suggested to Lucy that the most severe cranial damage was to the back of his skull, because there was nothing visible to account for the pooling.

The SOCO on the ground was holding up his T-shirt so that the photographer could better capture the extent of the bruising on his torso.

'Very definite welts,' he commented to Burns. 'I'd guess baseball bats. Two assailants, coming from slightly different angles.'

'Is there a head injury we can't see?' Lucy asked Burns.

It was the SOCO who answered. 'Yep. A severe one. Probably the initial blow, which knocked him to the ground, possibly knocked him out straight away. Then the rest of the attack occurred.'

'He wasn't conscious for it?' Fleming asked, a note of hope in his voice.

The SOCO shook his head. 'There are no injuries to his arms or hands. He wasn't expecting the first blow and wasn't conscious to defend himself against the rest. The first one could well have been fatal.'

'That's something,' Fleming said.

'It suggests he knew his attackers, too,' Lucy said. 'I didn't notice any damage at the front doorway, so they didn't force their way in. Are there signs of forced entry anywhere else?'

Burns shook his head. 'No. It looks like he answered the door to them, then led them in here. No blood in the hall, so he wasn't attacked there. He brings them in; they strike him from behind, knock him out, then attack him.'

'Stripped him before they do,' Fleming said.

'Presumably to send a message,' Burns said, pointing to the wall behind Lucy and Fleming.

Lucy turned and saw now, for the first time, the word FAG-GOT scrawled on the wall. The letters were thick bodied, though the writer seemed to have lost patience towards the end of the word, the tail on the T unfinished.

'Is that blood?' Lucy asked.

The SOCO nodded again.

'It's a bit theatrical,' Fleming said. 'A bit too much?'

Burns nodded. 'You don't buy it as a hate crime?'

Lucy turned again to where McLean lay. 'It seems *too* personal,' she said. 'There was hate involved all right, but the stripping him before they attacked him, the level of damage to the genitals, it's *very* personal.'

They'd all seen plenty of punishment beating victims. Some attacked with bats or hammers, some shot in the limbs, some occasionally given a six pack, if their attackers were really sending a message. Occasionally people would be stripped completely to ensure they weren't wearing wires or surveillance equipment. But that clearly wasn't the case here, where only the trousers had been undone.

'It's someone trying too hard,' Lucy said. 'Almost like they really want us to see it as a crime motivated by his homosexuality.'

'Why now?' Burns asked.

'If they knew we were after him,' Fleming said, 'that we fairly much had him over the Martin Givens killing, maybe they were afraid he'd try to negotiate his way out of it, offer us something else instead. Some*one* else.'

'You think this is Ulster First?' Burns asked.

'It could be a drugs thing, too.'

'It could be both,' Fleming said. 'The thing is, before this week, Jackie Moss would be the person to answer those questions.'

'Maybe he still is,' Burns said. 'He is in hospital.'

Fleming shook his head. 'No; Jackie would wait until he was out. Besides, the whole faggot thing isn't Jackie. He'd want everyone to know it was him who'd ordered it. He'd not try to hide it behind something like this.'

'So who, then?'

'Charlie Dougan,' Lucy said. 'Dougan is out again; maybe he's doing some housekeeping. We know Bobby was one of his. If he didn't have him killed, he may well know who would have wanted to kill him.'

'You've dealt with Dougan already, haven't you?' Burns asked.

Fleming nodded.

'Take a run across now and have a word. See what he has to say,' Burns said. 'I'll see you back in the station later.'

Chapter Forty-Eight

THEY DROVE ROUND to Dougan's. The street beyond the cordoned courtyard was filling, word clearly having spread about the events in McLean's flat.

'No sign of the Neighbourhood Team,' Fleming said.

Lucy glanced across at him. 'Is that significant?'

He shrugged. 'I'd have thought they'd have heard about Bobby by now. I got the sense they had a soft spot for him.'

'So, do you reckon Dougan was behind this?'

Another shrug. 'If not, he might know who was. The big question will be whether he, or any of them, knew Bobby was gay.'

'Why?' Lucy asked.

'Because if they didn't – if it wasn't public knowledge – you'd have to wonder when whoever killed him found out.'

Lucy nodded. 'And from whom?'

As they pulled up outside Dougan's, two workmen were coming out of the house, carrying between them an old front door, which they threw into the back of their van. A floodlight, affixed to the corner of the house, blazed into life at their appearance.

'Looks like Charlie's fortifying,' Fleming said. 'He's scared.'

'He came to the protest this evening,' Lucy said. 'He didn't look that scared out in the middle of things.'

'No one was ever going to hit him there,' Fleming said. 'The place was coming down with us. It was an easy win for Dougan: look like he's not afraid in a place where he has no cause to be anyway. Someone hitting his house at night? That's a different prospect.'

They made their way up to the front door. Sure enough, above the entrance, two cameras, newly installed by the looks of them, pointed to left and right, covering all aspects of the approach to the house. Lucy, ignoring the door bell, lifted her fist and rapped on the door. The sound was dull, the door presumably metal lined.

'He'll never hear that,' Fleming said.

Lucy nodded towards the cameras. 'He already knows we're here.'

The click of the lock confirmed as much and a second later Dougan opened the door to them.

'Officers,' he said. 'What?'

'Can we come in, sir?' Fleming asked.

'Best not, I think,' Dougan said, glancing past them out onto the street. 'I've spoken to enough of you lot recently to do me a lifetime.'

'Fine,' Fleming said, his smile brittle. 'We wanted to let you know that one of your boys has been murdered.'

'My boys?' Dougan said unconvincingly.

'Bobby McLean,' Fleming said.

If Dougan already knew of Bobby's death, he did a remarkable job of feigning surprise. His mouth opened slightly as he stared at Fleming. 'Bobby?'

Fleming nodded. 'He was beaten to death. We think it was a hate crime.'

'A sectarian killing in Greenway? Who'd have the nerve to—'

Lucy shook her head. 'Not sectarian, sir. We think Bobby was murdered because he was gay.'

Dougan laughed out loud, then seemed to realise it was inappropriate to the situation. 'Bobby wasn't gay,' he said.

'Someone would need to tell that to whomever almost castrated him with baseball bats and scrawled "faggot" on the wall of his flat, then,' Fleming said.

Dougan stared at him again, wordlessly, as if trying to piece together what he had just heard. 'You'd better come in, so,' he managed finally, stepping back.

He led them past the lounge to the kitchen. As they passed, Lucy saw an empty box from a 42-inch TV, newly mounted on the wall, its screen displaying a number of different CCTV feeds at once, including several from the front door. There were clearly other cameras out there she'd not noticed.

'Upgrading your security, Mr Dougan?' Fleming asked.

'Not especially,' Dougan lied. 'After Jackie Moss, everyone's taking precautions.'

'You're the only one on the street with a reinforced door,' Lucy said.

'People seem to be blaming me for what happened to Jackie.'

'Have they reason to?' Fleming asked, the question greeted with a sneer from Dougan.

'Really?'

'Then why are you a suspect?'

'Lazy police work,' Dougan said.

'But you were Jackie's deputy,' Fleming said.

'Jackie *was* a friend.'

'He's still alive,' Lucy said.

'I know,' Dougan said curtly. 'So, who said Bobby was gay?'

'You didn't know?'

Dougan shook his head. 'Of course not. He never acted gay.'

Fleming laughed without humour. 'How would he have acted gay, exactly?'

'You know . . .' Dougan began, before the sentence died in his throat.

'Would any of his friends have known? McEwan? Welland?' Fleming asked.

Dougan shook his head. 'None of them said anything to me.'

'How did you get involved with Bobby, sir?' Lucy asked.

'I told you before. I worked with the young people in the area. Jackie had a lot of support from the older people in Greenway but those younger fellas, they didn't remember all that he'd done for Ulster. They wanted to push their own way. I suggested to Jackie that I could take them under my wing, get them jobs in the local community, help them get a bit of direction. Jackie was happy for me to do it; it's all for the good of the community.'

'Did you know Bobby was selling drugs?'

Dougan shrugged. 'That's more believable than him being gay.'

'So you did know?'

'I suspected some of them were tied up in antisocial stuff; that's why I got involved with them. To get them on the straight and narrow.'

'Not to control who was selling in Greenway, then?' Fleming asked. 'For Jackie?'

Another sceptical look from Dougan. 'I think I've already mentioned my views on lazy policing.'

'You don't worry that maybe someone's been playing you?' Lucy asked.

'What?'

'You get them in with Jackie, make them respectable, give them a sense of identity with Ulster First, get the community behind them, then someone takes a pot shot at Jackie. If he'd died, you'd have been the obvious suspect, you'd both have been off the board and the space would have been clear for the next generation.'

'We lived through thirty years of Troubles here. No one wants bad blood in Greenway,' Dougan said.

'They didn't live through them, though,' Fleming said. 'The younger generation. And the way Jackie talked about the past, he made it sound like they were the good old days.'

'Rubbish.'

'Some people seem to miss the fact that there used to be community-sanctioned psychopaths defending their culture for them,' Fleming said.

'That would have been handy now, when the gypsies or the queers start moving in next door,' Lucy added dryly.

'Youse can leave now,' Dougan said. 'I'm sorry to hear about Bobby. But if he was a bum bandit, he had only himself to blame,' he added, as if trying to take control of the situation, if only in his own mind.

LUCY WAITED UNTIL she got into the car before she spoke. 'How did he strike you?' she asked, staring back up at the house, the floodlight that had illuminated their departure now switched off.

'Like everything's suddenly started spiralling out of his control,' Fleming said. 'But he's obviously planning on fighting his corner.'

'If he's allowed to stay that long,' Lucy said.

'If he's left alive that long,' Fleming corrected her.

Tuesday

Chapter Forty-Nine

LUCY HAD LAIN awake for over an hour before finally deciding to get out of bed and make toast for herself. She'd sat on the sofa in the living room, a cup of hot tea balancing on the armrest as she scrolled down through Facebook, then checked the news on her phone. Grace was not yet home, and it was past three. Lucy had wondered about calling her, to check if she had money for a taxi, but decided to leave it another while.

The *Derry Journal* newsfeed was already running a story about the killing of Bobby McLean, which was being described as a 'second gay hate killing'. Lucy read through the story; whoever had written it had clearly a contact on the inside, for they had been able to link McLean as a suspect wanted in connection with the Givens murder. The fact that they had been able to claim McLean's death had been linked to his sexuality – whether it was right or wrong – suggested that someone who had been inside that room, or had seen the scene-of-crime pictures from it, had told the reporter about the word written on the wall. Either way, Burns wouldn't be happy.

Just then, she heard the key turning in the door.

'Hey you,' Lucy called out. 'Good night?'

Grace appeared in the doorway sheepishly. 'I didn't think you'd be up,' she said. 'I've brought . . . I've a friend with me. Is that okay?'

Lucy smiled a little uncertainly, then glanced around Grace to where a youth, perhaps in his early twenties, stood, a blue bag of beer cans in his hand. He was slim, neat, his hair quiffed, a beard, checked shirt.

'All right,' he managed, catching her eye, then looking away.

Lucy felt exposed for the first time in her own house, despite the fact she wore a T-shirt and pyjama bottoms. Grace clearly sensed it, for she turned.

'Sure, maybe you should head on, Ciaran,' she said.

'No, it's fine; I'm heading to bed,' Lucy said, standing. 'I've an early start in the morning.'

Grace smiled, though Lucy could tell she was embarrassed. The idea of her bringing someone home had never been an issue before. Grace had been turning tricks when she'd lived rough and had shown little interest in men after moving in with Lucy; Lucy had always assumed that it was because of her previous experience with them. In a way, her bringing someone back showed progression, that she was feeling more like a normal nineteen-year-old again.

But if Lucy was being honest, it had suited her. Since breaking up with Robbie, she'd not been with anyone. A few of the uniforms had chatted her up at nights out; she'd shared a messy, drunken kiss with one of them at the Christmas party, but that was it. Robbie had wanted her to commit, to move in. And she hadn't been ready to do that. She'd also never really considered why. Robbie had been a good man, even when he'd been injured in an attack intended for her. Perhaps that had been it; perhaps if he'd been angrier, she'd have understood it, accepted it more. Instead, he was a good man, just like her father had been. And she couldn't help but remember how that had turned out.

Sorry, Grace mouthed as she passed her.

'It's fine,' Lucy said, her smile brittle on her lips.

'We'll tidy up, don't worry,' Grace said. 'I didn't think you'd mind. I should have texted.'

Ciaran shuffled embarrassedly in the hallway, swinging the bag of cans from side to side.

'It's fine,' Lucy said. 'Goodnight.'

But as she lay in bed, she could not ignore the gnawing loneliness that she felt in her stomach, nor the extent of the space around her in the bed.

SHE DIDN'T KNOW whether Ciaran had stayed the night when she got up next morning, but, as Grace had promised, the kitchen was clean, the empty cans in the recycling bin in the kitchen. Lucy had a quick breakfast, then headed out, despite being a little too early for work.

She stopped at the shop on the way down to the Strand Road – she knew they would have a briefing there first with Burns before she would have to go down to Maydown to the PPU. The local papers were each running the story of McLean's killing on their front page. One had managed to get a photograph of McLean and it was clear that the 'gay killing' angle was the one that all the media had decided to pursue. Lucy bought one of the papers and a sandwich and Diet Coke for her lunch, then drove on down to the Strand.

The incident room was already fairly busy when she arrived, just short of 7.30 a.m. Coffee was being brewed in the corner and she headed across and poured herself a cup, more to join some of the others who had gathered there than because she wanted it.

One of them, a sergeant called Jacqueline Doherty, asked her how Tara had been doing since.

Lucy hesitated. 'Since what?'

'The whole thing with Burns yesterday,' Jacqueline said. 'She seemed gutted after it. He was just blowing off steam; I told her that.'

'She took it to heart,' Lucy said. Tara clearly hadn't told them about the aftermath with Mickey.

'Sinclair seemed pretty worked up about it, too.'

Lucy nodded. 'I noticed,' she said.

'Tell her not to sweat it. Burns is getting it tight from the ACC.'

Lucy nodded.

'Did you get your parcel?' Jacqueline said, topping up her cup.

'What parcel?'

Jacqueline shrugged. 'The desk sergeant sent it up; internal mail. It's sitting on Tara's desk.'

Lucy moved across and saw the package. Whatever it was, it had been placed inside an internal post envelope meaning it had come from a colleague.

She lifted it and opened the envelope. She pulled out the contents: a box about one foot long and six inches wide. The lid had been taped shut. Had it not been an internally posted item, she'd have left it down and called for someone in the Bomb Squad to check it. Instead, she flicked the lid open. Inside was an object, half hidden among a bed of polystyrene beads. She made to lift it out, only realising as she gripped it what it actually was.

Thankfully, she managed to replace it in the box before anyone else saw it.

Closing the box, she looked up quickly, aware she was blushing, glancing around. Over at the coffee, Mickey Sinclair stood with the other team members, studiously not looking in her direction.

'Is it your birthday?'

Lucy turned to where Fleming stood, having just arrived. He nodded at the box she held.

'No. Someone's idea of a joke.'

She opened the lid a little to show Fleming the large black vibrator inside.

'And I think I can guess who,' she added, catching Mickey's eye for the first time.

He turned away quickly from her stare, but every so often his glance would slip back towards where she and Fleming stood, as if waiting for her response.

Chapter Fifty

BURNS CAME IN just after 8.15 a.m. He'd clearly been awake most of the night, his jawline rough with stubble, his hair greasy and uncombed.

'Right, people,' he began, 'as you'll have heard by now, our main suspect in the Martin Givens killing was murdered last night. I've spoken with Martin's parents this morning and updated them on progress. Sadly, it looks like they won't get their day in court so, while we can only hope that identifying Bobby McLean as Martin's killer will have brought them some relief – and God knows his death might bring them some, too – they won't have a chance to see him answer for what he did.'

'So that's that, then,' Fleming muttered. 'Givens' murder is being pinned on Bobby.'

'The dead have no defence,' Lucy said.

'What we now have to do is turn our attention to the Bobby McLean killing,' Burns said. 'You've heard the details, I'm sure. Forensics have managed to recover several sets of prints from the house. Our priority is looking for the murder weapons and

canvassing the neighbourhood. We'll be working with our colleagues who've been investigating the attack on Jackie Moss,' he
added. 'They've been interviewing in Greenway already and will
have some insight into the factions operating there at the moment.
Many of you will know of Jackie Moss, but the new faces there
might not be so well known. Our partners in the PPU visited one
of the suspects in the Moss shooting last night and DI Fleming
will say a few words about that now.'

Fleming seemed caught off guard by the introduction for it
took him a moment to stand up, and Lucy knew him well enough
to tell he was buying time while he considered his words.

'DS Black and I spoke with Charles Dougan last night, at CS
Burns' request. Dougan is a leading force behind a group calling
themselves Ulster First. Dougan's version of events is that Jackie
Moss lost control of the youth element of Greenway a year or two
back: drugs and that. Dougan was instructed by Moss to take the
youths under his wing, get them settled into apprenticeships and
the like, which he claims he did. Bobby McLean was one such
figure.'

'He did a bang-up job,' Mickey commented, glancing around.
Beyond the odd forced smirk, no one responded.

'Bobby was selling legal highs last year in the local school.
We know he was still at it recently in the clubs and that, but had
progressed from seller to supplier if Gareth McGonigle is to be
believed. We can only assume that Dougan and Moss's concern
about the youth of Greenway was actually because they wanted to
take control of the drugs trade in the estate.'

Lucy glanced across and realised that at some stage in proceedings, her mother had come into the room and was standing just
inside the doorway, listening to Fleming.

'There are a number of youths connected with McLean. One is a guy named Stephen Welland whose family own the pub in Greenway and who organised the protest at which Nixon spoke yesterday. Dougan would have us believe that he took control of these troublesome kids. Myself and DS Black suspect the opposite. Our impression is that Dougan has been played. He was sympathetic to the xenophobic tripe Ulster First were spouting, so he backed them on that. They've got their feet under the table in Greenway now and maybe feel they don't need either Dougan or Moss any more. Based on the shooting of Moss, and the fortifying of security at Dougan's, we can assume that Dougan has decided to bunker in for a fight, which shows that he knows it, too.'

'So maybe he hit McLean to teach the young lads a lesson?' Jacqueline asked.

Fleming shook his head. 'Perhaps. But both Lucy and I agreed that Dougan seemed shocked to hear that McLean was gay: it hadn't registered with him at all.'

'Could it have been a simple gay hate crime?' Mickey asked. 'Maybe we're looking for hidden depths where there are none.'

'Bobby came home,' Lucy said, the thought only just dawning on her.

She saw her mother smirk almost as she said it and realised that she had already wondered the same thing.

'I don't follow,' Burns said.

'Bobby was in the wind because he knew we were looking for him,' Lucy said. 'So why did he come home? Why did he open the door to someone?'

Fleming nodded. 'Someone told him he was safe.'

'Someone he trusted,' Lucy said. 'Someone who, he must have thought, would have first-hand knowledge of the state of our investigation.'

'You think someone on our team is—' Burns began.

Lucy shook her head. 'Of course not, sir,' she said. 'But we mentioned that McLean was wanted in connection with the Givens case and suddenly he's killed for being gay, even though Dougan, who knew him well, had no idea about his sexuality.'

'People hide being queer,' Mickey piped up. 'Even from their colleagues. No big surprise that he didn't tell his boss he was a poof.'

'I'll not tolerate that type of language here, DS Sinclair,' ACC Wilson said suddenly, stepping in from the doorway.

Lucy glanced at Mickey who had visibly reddened, having clearly not realised Wilson was in the room. 'Sorry, ma'am,' he said. 'It was a slip of the tongue.'

'Don't let it happen again,' Wilson added. 'Sorry, Tom; I interrupted you.'

'I'm done, thanks, ma'am,' Fleming said, sitting down.

'Right, folks—' Burns began.

'Sorry,' Wilson said, 'can I borrow DS Black for a moment?'

Lucy stood and glanced at Fleming who shrugged lightly. She lifted the package with her lest someone might take a look into it if she left it behind.

'Excuse me, sir,' she said, passing Burns. As she did so, she could smell the freshly sprayed deodorant he'd applied over his shirt to cover the fact that he hadn't gone home to change.

Her mother held the door open so it was not until she was outside the room that she saw Tara standing, her eyes red, her face drawn and pale.

Chapter Fifty-One

'LET'S FIND A room, shall we?' Wilson said. 'DS Gallagher, maybe take a few minutes to get yourself sorted, eh?' she added softly.

Tara nodded, then mouthed a silent apology to Lucy as she passed.

Wilson had already set off down the corridor, her pace quick, her back erect. She peered into a few of the rooms she passed until she found an empty one and opened the door, waiting for Lucy.

'How are you?' she asked, closing the door after Lucy once she'd come in and indicating that she should sit.

'Fine,' Lucy said, then added, 'How are you?'

'I could complain, but who'd listen?' her mother joked. 'Have you seen your father recently?'

'A few nights ago,' Lucy said. 'He doesn't know me most of the time.'

Wilson nodded. 'I called in,' she said. 'He was sleeping so I didn't wake him.'

Time was, Lucy would have made some petty comment to hurt her mother. She surprised herself when she realised she had no wish to offend the woman now.

'Maybe some day we'll even have more to talk about than your father,' Wilson added.

'We're talking now,' Lucy said.

Wilson nodded. 'Do you know why?'

Lucy hesitated before answering. 'Something to do with Tara, I'm guessing. DS Gallagher.'

Wilson nodded. 'And DS Sinclair.'

'I see.'

'Is it true?'

Another hesitation. 'That depends on what you're asking about.'

'After that mess with Nixon yesterday, CS Burns read them both the riot act. Afterwards, DS Gallagher claims, DS Sinclair verbally abused her and then you. He referred to you both as 'dykes'. Is that right?'

Lucy didn't speak for a moment. 'Are you asking as my mother or my superior officer?'

Wilson smiled lightly. 'Let's say as your mother?'

'That's right,' Lucy said. 'That's pretty much what happened.'

Wilson nodded, her mouth tightening. 'Now, as your superior officer, I have to tell you that DS Gallagher is making a formal complaint about what happened. She will be naming you as a witness and, I suspect, counting on you to corroborate her statement.'

Lucy looked down at the box in her hands.

'Now, I would have to advise you that DS Sinclair will have to be informed of the complaint and witness statements against him. As your mother, I would suggest you take a little time to think about the repercussions of making that statement. It will, if proven, almost certainly result in a redeployment for DS Sinclair. How other people on the team feel about that, and how they express those feelings towards those they consider responsible for that move, is anyone's guess. Even if they think Mickey's an ass, they might not take kindly to someone turning on one of their own.'

'I understand that,' Lucy said.

'The other side to it is, if it goes unchecked now, this division will become a very cold house for LGBT officers, of which there are several. If this is happening – and I have no doubt that it is – it needs to be stopped. Tara is prepared to take that risk. Are you?'

Lucy looked to her lap, weighed the box she held in her hands. 'I . . .'

'You would be considered to be ratting on a fellow officer.'

'Or defending one.'

Wilson nodded. 'You know which way it will be seen.'

Lucy felt no love for Mickey, and had, in some ways, simply turned a blind eye to the locker-room banter of the male officers. She'd heard stories of female officers being stripped from the waist down by their male colleagues and having the station stamp inked all over their buttocks. She'd been lucky. Institutional sexism was endemic by its nature but of all people, her own mother had challenged it: a female ACC who had remained hands on, remained fair, remained respected.

'What would you have done?' Lucy asked. 'If it was you? Would you grass another officer? Stick up for a friend?'

'I'd take some time to think,' Wilson said. 'Now? I'd probably back my friend, if I'm honest. But when I was your age; at your stage in my career? I'm not sure I'd have had the backbone to do it then. And I'm not sure I'd have made it to the point where I am now if I had done.'

Lucy nodded. 'Tara's my friend.'

'Friends come and go,' Wilson said. 'Her complaint will still stand, I'd imagine. But a corroborating statement would seal it for her. Of course, the other issue is that the content of his comments will become general knowledge, no matter how confidential the process. This nonsense about you being a lesbian will make its way around the station.'

'I'd imagine it already has,' Lucy said.

Wilson nodded. 'Is it true?'

Lucy looked at her mother but didn't answer. Despite herself, she felt her face flush.

'That was me being your mother again,' Wilson said. 'I'm sorry. It doesn't matter.'

'I know,' Lucy said, shifting the box in her grip. 'I'm not gay.'

Wilson nodded, standing, businesslike again. 'I shouldn't have asked anyway. Think about your statement,' she said. 'Let me know what you plan to do. You have my mobile number.'

Lucy nodded. 'By the way, what happened with the SPED form for the Lupei family? Did you sign it?'

Wilson shook her head. 'Not with what's happening in Greenway. If there is a power play, I can't legitimise this Ulster First crowd. As soon as I do, the media will be all over it, making them into something they're not. They may be big in Greenway, but we can't give them wider credibility.'

'And what about the Lupeis? Do they wait for someone to burn them out?'

Wilson frowned. 'The father is getting out of hospital today. I spoke with them last night. I've spoken to a friend in the Housing Executive who will get them relocated until we can get their house sorted.'

Lucy's expression softened. For all her indignation, she'd not been in contact with the Lupei family in a few days and yet her mother had been.

'You're not the only one with a soft spot for the underdog, Lu,' Wilson said.

'Lu' was a pet name her mother had called her when she was a child and which she had taken to calling her again more recently, almost as if testing the limits of their relationship. Lucy smiled despite herself, hefting the box in her hand.

'A gift from an admirer?' Wilson indicated the box with a light nod.

Lucy wrapped both hands around the box instinctively. 'Not quite,' she said. 'I'll see you later.'

Chapter Fifty-Two

FLEMING WAS WAITING for her in the incident room when she returned.

'Everything good?'

Lucy laughed mirthlessly. 'Not sure I'd say good.'

'Did you show her your special gift?'

'Not yet.'

'Are you going to?'

Lucy said nothing.

'You should. Don't tolerate that for a second.'

'The rest of his team will hate me if I make a complaint.'

'It's good to be hated,' Fleming said. 'It means you stood up for something.'

'That's one way of looking at it,' Lucy said.

As they spoke, a uniform came across. 'DS Black? There's a call for you.'

Lucy moved across to the desk the uniform indicated where the phone sat off the hook. She recognised the number on the display as being the switchboard.

'DS Black here.'

'We have a Mr McEwan on the line for you.'

'Put it through,' Lucy said. She waited for the call to transfer, heard the click as it did so. 'This is DS Black. Mr McEwan?'

As soon as he spoke, Lucy realised by the timbre of the voice that it was the father and not the son speaking. 'Yes. You spoke to me last week.'

'That's right, sir. You broke your leg, I hear. I hope you're doing okay?'

'I'm . . . it's not that. It's my son, Frankie. I'm afraid he's in trouble.'

'What kind of trouble?' Lucy asked, sitting up suddenly.

'He's at work now but he's not . . . he didn't sleep last night. I heard him up.'

'And . . .?'

'He put clothes in the wash,' McEwan said suddenly, the words tumbling out lest he think twice and stop himself talking. 'And his trainers. They had blood all over them. I think he's done a bad thing.'

'Can I get your address, sir?' Lucy asked. 'We'll be right up with you.'

McEwan was sitting on a stool just inside the door when they arrived, evidently having struggled his way out to the hallway in preparation for their arrival. He wore baggy football shorts to accommodate the plaster cast encasing his leg.

He looked like he had not slept much either, his features haggard, his hair unkempt. He held a cigarette tightly in one hand as he thudded his way back up the hall and into the kitchen, his free hand pressed against the wall for support.

A mug of tea sat on the counter, a skin forming on it. He lifted it and took a mouthful, seemingly not noticing the fact that it was cold.

'They're over there,' he said, gesturing to where a pair of trainers nested among a pair of jeans.

Lucy moved across and, squatting down, examined the shoes without touching them. The material was stained brown with dried blood.

'Have you touched these?'

McEwan shook his head, but said, 'Just to put them there. They were in the washing machine, inside his jeans. There was too much packed in, so I pulled some stuff out and they fell out too.'

'Did you ask him about it?'

'No. He'd gone to work by that stage. He's covering for me being out and that.'

'And without Bobby . . .' Fleming began, letting the sentence hang.

'And without Bobby,' McEwan echoed, his voice dry. 'Do you know what happened to him? They're saying it was because he was gay. That wasn't true, was it?'

'You didn't know?'

A shake of the head. 'He'd hardly tell me about it.'

'He wouldn't have told Frankie?'

McEwan shrugged. 'I don't know. Those fellas, they're all about looking hard, you know. I'm not sure that Bobby would've wanted it going round that he was a poof.'

Lucy ignored the comment. 'Why did you assume this was blood?'

'Because of Bobby,' McEwan admitted.

'Do you think Frankie was involved?'

The man's expression was drawn, his gaze sliding from Lucy to the shoes on the ground. 'I hope not. But it's gone too far. This whole thing. I need to get Frankie away from that.'

'From what?'

'This Ulster First nonsense. It started out all right: looking after the community, sticking together. But it's gone mental now. The attacks on that Roma family; they weren't welcome in Greenway, but . . . I never wanted Frankie involved in that kind of thing.'

'Is Frankie's mother still with him?' Lucy asked.

McEwan shook his head. 'She had her problems, God rest her. She didn't . . .' He seemed to choke a little on the word, then cleared his throat, straightening in his chair. 'She killed herself when he was a baby. That post-partum thing got too much for her. She'd be heartbroken if she knew he was involved in anything like this now.'

Fleming, who had remained quiet throughout the visit, coughed lightly before speaking. 'You do know, Mr McEwan, that if Frankie was involved in Bobby's death, he'll go to prison for it?'

'I know *that*,' McEwan said. 'But if that's what it takes to get him away from the likes of Dougan and Welland and his bullshit, so be it.'

Fleming smiled encouragingly, though Lucy could tell that he, like her, was reflecting on the fact that in prison, Frankie would probably end up involved with much worse.

'Your own injury,' Lucy said. 'You fell down the stairs.'

McEwan nodded, but without conviction.

'In a bungalow?'

He managed a bitter laugh. 'I thought it would keep Frankie safer if I said nothing.'

'Do you know who did this to you?' Fleming asked.

'No,' McEwan said, turning to Fleming, shifting the cast on his leg as he did so. 'There were two of them. They came into the office with balaclavas on, and baseball bats. I guessed it was because they found out that you'd got Dougan's name off me.'

'Was Dougan one of them?'

'I don't think so,' McEwan said. 'He doesn't get his hands dirty. Even that nonsense lifting him for the Moss shooting. Dougan doesn't have the balls for that. He's an armchair general; likes the intrigue and the politics, likes to think he's important. Signing forms and organising groups. Jackie has blood on his hands; Dougan only ever managed ink.'

He laughed without humour at the irony of the comment. 'No, Stephen Welland is the true believer,' he said. 'Dougan's a stepping stone for him, nothing else.'

'Why do you think that?' Fleming asked.

'Look at all this immigrants shit. That never bothered Dougan before. He couldn't care less about that; he hired some of the outsiders that came into Greenway as drivers because they were cheap. Then Welland started spouting all this pure Ulster crap and Dougan jumped on the bandwagon. I think he fancied himself as a mentor to them. A chance to step out of Jackie's shadow.' He shrugged again. 'That's what I think, for what it's worth.'

'We'll need to bag these,' Lucy said. 'And we'll need to send someone out here to do a forensics sweep in Frankie's room. Okay?'

McEwan nodded. 'I'm not going anywhere,' he said. 'Not any more.'

Fleming nodded to Lucy and moved out of the kitchen to call for a team to come to McEwan's.

'One of them had a scar on his arm,' McEwan said. 'Not a scar, but like a burn.'

'Who was this?'

'The two who did this,' he said, tapping his plaster cast. 'One of them pulled up his sleeve before he hit me, like he was getting ready to do a day's work or something. He had scarring on his forearm, like he'd been burned.'

Lucy nodded. 'Thank you, Mr McEwan. This can't have been easy.'

McEwan smiled bitterly. 'It's easy now. It's done.'

Chapter Fifty-Three

FRANKIE MCEWAN WAS standing outside the printing works in the industrial estate when they arrived. He was chatting on his mobile to someone while he smoked. Either he couldn't get a signal inside or he was so used to having to go out to smoke that even when he was the only one there, he continued to do so.

He ended the call when Lucy pulled into the bay next to where he stood. Pocketing the phone, he dragged on his cigarette, watching them.

'Dad's not here.'

Fleming nodded. 'We're here to speak to you, Frankie. We've a few questions, if you don't mind.'

McEwan flicked his cigarette butt over towards the bushes to their left, bordering the roadway they had driven up to get to the industrial units.

'Ask away.'

Fleming grimaced. 'I have to caution you, Frankie, that you don't have to say anything, but if you do, anything you say . . .'

Lucy saw the spark of recognition in Frankie's face as he realised the purpose and significance of the caution.

'What—'

'Do you understand what I've said to you?' Fleming asked.

McEwan looked at him, then to Lucy. 'I didn't . . .'

For a moment she thought he was going to make a run for it. His gaze darted across towards the bushes, as if attempting to gauge the chances of his escaping them. But there was nowhere to go: six-foot wire fencing surrounded the industrial estate, the only entrance or exit the main gates through which they had driven. Both Lucy and Fleming stood between him and the gate.

'What do you want?'

'You heard about Bobby?'

Frankie nodded.

'You're not upset?'

'Fuck you,' he said.

'When did you learn he had died?'

'Last night,' Frankie said, taking out his cigarette packet and pulling out a fresh smoke.

'From whom?'

'The word went round the pub,' Frankie said, bowing his head to light the cigarette.

'What word?'

'That he was dead,' Frankie said with a shrug. 'That he'd been killed.'

'Do you know why he was killed?'

'For being gay, weren't it?'

'Was he gay?'

Frankie looked at Fleming directly. 'I don't know.'

'You were friends, though? He never told you? Never confided in his friend?'

'We worked together,' Frankie said.

'Can you think of anyone who would want to kill Bobby?'

Frankie shook his head. 'He was a dose sometimes, but he was solid, you know?'

'And you didn't kill him?'

'Fuck no,' Frankie said, seemingly relaxing a little. He'd obviously been expecting something more intensive and Fleming appeared to be bringing the questions to a close.

'So, you were in Greenway last night? When you heard?'

Frankie nodded. 'I was at the pub with some of the lads, after that rally yesterday.'

'Is Stephen Welland one of the lads?'

Frankie was on his guard again at the mention of Welland's name. 'He's a mate,' Frankie said.

'Was he there last night? In the pub?'

He nodded.

'The whole time?'

'Yeah; he owns it.'

'So, who told you about Bobby?'

Frankie shrugged. 'I don't remember. Someone came into the bar.'

'And that was it? The first you heard about him being dead, the first you knew about it, was when someone came into the pub and told you about it.'

Frankie nodded, once, with conviction. 'That sounds about right.'

'So, if we had evidence linking you to the crime scene, we'd be what? Wrong?'

'What are you on about?' Frankie said. 'What evidence?'

'Say we had your trainers?' Fleming said. 'And your clothes from yesterday. Covered in blood. That wouldn't be Bobby's blood? That wouldn't place you at the scene of his death?'

Frankie nipped the head off his smoke. 'My trainers is dirty. They're in the wash—'

Fleming shook his head. 'No, they're in an evidence bag being tested by some of our forensic technicians as we speak to see if we can match the blood on them to Bobby McLean.'

Frankie paled. 'I don't know what . . . that's not . . .'

Lucy could tell that, this time, he'd decided to take his chances. He shifted suddenly to their left, sprinting for the fence, clearly hoping that, with enough momentum, he'd be able to propel himself up and pull himself over the top.

Lucy went after him, catching up with him as he tried to scale the fence, his boots struggling to get a grip in the small chain links. She grabbed at his belt to pull him back down, but in doing so, set herself immediately behind him. Suddenly, he kicked out, backwards, to shake her off, the kick connecting with her jaw and knocking her sideways.

Fleming was behind her, a little out of breath, but McEwan was already pulling himself over the top of the fence and dropping down the other side. He'd misjudged the drop, though, and rather than landing on his feet, he skidded and fell down the embankment on the other side.

Lucy shook off the knock and, glancing up to see how far away the entrance was, decided instead to scale the fence. 'Give me a foot up,' she said.

Fleming cupped his hands together and squatted a little to give Lucy a boost. She reached the top of the fence with ease and, pulling herself up and over, dropped to the other side. She could hear a ringing in her right ear, near where Frankie's boot had connected, a high-pitched whine that was audible even against the noise of the traffic on the road beyond.

She took the embankment at a run, aware that she'd have to pull herself to a sharp stop at the bottom, lest momentum carry her out into the road. Frankie was hauling himself off the ground and was making for the pavement beyond the undergrowth and trees bordering the industrial estate.

Lucy hit the pavement, grinding to a halt, just at the kerb. Frankie had already set off across the road, a dual carriageway, dodging traffic as he did so. Several drivers hooted their horns at him as he tried to manoeuvre his way across. One, a taxi man, shouted a mouthful at him from his open window.

Lucy stepped out into the roadway, her hand held up in an attempt to stop the oncoming traffic. The road was busy, the section they were crossing on the approach to traffic lights at the top of the incline. Lucy could only hope that, if the lights changed, the line of cars would come to a halt.

Frankie, though, had given up on the slow approach and was racing into the left-hand lane at full tilt, clearly hoping to brazen his way through. He'd almost made it when a driver coming down the road, distracted by Lucy's progress across towards him, swerved a little and, in so doing, clipped McEwan with the bumper of his car.

The impact spun the youth sideways, bringing him down in the path of a bus on the inside lane.

Lucy's view was blocked by the car which had struck him, which now stopped, but she saw the bus shudder to a sudden halt, heard the surge of the hydraulics hiss as the driver braked.

She ran the rest of the way, sliding across the bonnet of the car blocking her view. McEwan lay on the ground, blood marking his face where he had grazed himself in the fall. He cupped his right knee in his hands.

'Wanker!' he shouted at the driver who had hit him.

'Can you stand?' Lucy asked.

'I think,' Frankie muttered, taking her proffered hand and pulling himself to his feet.

'Good. You're under arrest.'

Chapter Fifty-Four

THEY WERE DRIVING across the bridge on their way back to the Strand Road when the call came through to confirm that the blood type taken from McEwan's shoes matched that of Bobby McLean. Fleming passed on this information to Lucy, loudly enough that Frankie, sitting in the back nursing his knee, could hear.

'I didn't kill him,' Frankie said sullenly. 'I'd not do that to Bobby. He was a mate.'

'But you *were* there?' Lucy said, glancing at him in the rearview mirror.

Frankie paused a moment, as if contemplating his choices, and then nodded. 'He was already dead.'

Lucy shook her head. She'd not understood how Gareth McGonigle could have found Marty Givens and not called for help. Here, for the second time, was a mate who'd let his friend lie without calling for help.

Fleming was clearly thinking along the same lines for he said, 'And you didn't call for an ambulance?'

'His neighbour was at the door,' Frankie said. 'She said she'd heard a racket and came in to see. She phoned for help. I arrived just before her; Bobby and me were to meet up for drinks. When he didn't show, I went looking for him. The door was open and I'd gone in. I told her that; she'd promised she'd not say I was there. Bitch.'

'She didn't,' Lucy said, too quick to defend the unknown neighbour to realise the implication of what she said.

'Then . . .?' Frankie began, then sat quiet. After a moment he exploded in anger.

'Fucker!' he snapped, punching the door with his bound fists. 'Fucking prick!'

'Easy, Frankie,' Fleming said, turning in his seat.

'It was my da, wasn't it?'

'Just take it easy, Frankie,' Fleming repeated.

'Bastard!' Frankie spat.

He settled into sullen silence while Lucy quietly cursed herself for having spoken. Frankie had been talking, telling them what had happened. She'd distracted him, given him reason to stop.

'Bobby was dead when you got there?' she prompted, glancing in the mirror again. This time, Frankie wasn't biting.

'Did you see who'd done it?'

'Do you not think I'd have fucking mentioned it if I had?'

'That depends,' Lucy said non-committally, keen to keep him chatting. 'Did he mention being afraid?'

'Bobby wasn't the type.'

'No one after him over anything?'

Frankie said nothing. Perhaps the list was too long to start.

'Drugs?'

'Bobby wasn't like that.'

Lucy cocked an eyebrow. 'We know he was, Frankie. We know he was dealing legal highs. We know he was supplying to sellers. We've got all that already.'

Frankie shrugged. 'That's nothing to do with me.'

'But you're the one cuffed in the back of a cop car,' Fleming said. 'How'd that happen?'

'It was just a bit of craic,' Frankie snapped. 'The Romas and that. It was a bit of a laugh. No one wants gypos living next to them. You can sit there, all judging me and that, but if they moved next door to you, you'd not be smiling about it.'

'Is that all it was about?'

Frankie nodded.

'But they weren't living next door to you,' Fleming said.

'You know what I mean.'

'What about Bobby? Was it a laugh for him too?'

Another nod, less certain this time.

'I think Bobby was just getting his kicks where he could,' Lucy offered, watching McEwan in the mirror. 'Like the drugs and that. Was he the same with the Roma?'

'He'd a run-in with them,' Frankie said.

'A run-in? With the Lupeis?'

'I don't know,' Frankie said. 'He said one of them from Greenway was hassling him.'

'When?'

Frankie nodded. 'He said the guy was at that gay night club at the weekend when he arrived to sell. They got into it on the stairs. The guy followed him out and broke his car window. He said that was why he was hiding that car you were asking about.'

Fleming looked across at Lucy.

'In Paradise?'

'I dunno,' Frankie said. 'He said the guy got in his face on the stairs. Bobby smacked him one, he said. The gypo followed him out and smashed his window.'

'Why?'

Frankie shrugged.

They were on the Strand Road now, but Lucy didn't want to reach the station just yet, aware that parking the car would create a natural break in the conversation. Instead, she turned up Princes Street and looped back around.

'Whose idea was it to attack the house?'

'Don't remember,' Frankie said, lying.

'And attacking the man on his way from work?'

'I don't know anything about that.'

Another lie.

'Was that payback for Bobby's car?'

Frankie nodded. 'It were nothing to do with me. None of this were.'

'Then why are you telling us?' Lucy asked, already knowing the answer.

'Bobby's death. You lot should be looking at the gypos. Bobby weren't queer. I'd bet that gypo saw him in the club and thought he was one of them just cos he was there. That's why "faggot" was wrote up on the wall.'

He sat back in his seat, his job done. He'd managed, he thought, to explain the presence of blood on his shoes whilst implicating the Roma community in Bobby's murder and not having to mention his own friends.

Lucy thought again about the story of the Roma attacking Bobby and his car. The car window wasn't broken on the way into Bay Road Park. They could check the CCTV to see if there had been something on the stairs in Paradise. If there had been, it would have happened in the hour after Lucy had visited the Lupeis' house for the first time.

Chapter Fifty-Five

WHILE FRANKIE MCEWAN was being processed, Fleming asked Tara to check the CCTV footage again for proof of the alleged altercation Bobby McLean had had with a Roma on the stairs. Lucy volunteered to likewise check McEwan's claim that he'd been in the Greenway Arms during the time Bobby had been murdered. Burns had asked to be informed once Frankie was transferred to the interview room and his brief had arrived.

Lucy phoned Frankie's father to tell him that they had his son in custody. He'd been expecting it, waiting for her to let him know in which station he was being held.

Fifteen minutes later, McEwan senior struggled in through the front door, asking to see his son. Frankie, standing at the booking desk with Lucy and Fleming, cursed when he came in.

'Fuck off!' he shouted, kicking out at his father as he approached.

'Frankie, son—' his father began.

'I'm not your son,' Frankie spat. 'Fuck off!'

'Frankie,' McEwan pleaded, his eyes brimming.

'Fucking die, would ya!' Frankie shouted.

'Let's go,' Fleming said, pulling Frankie by the arm to get him into the interview room.

Lucy, for her part, went to the father.

'He's raw,' she said. 'He'll come round.'

McEwan shook his head, freeing a tear in so doing, which ran down his cheek unhindered.

'No,' he said, 'he won't.'

'He'll see that you were protecting him, Mr McEwan,' Lucy said. 'You did the right thing,' she added, though without the conviction the statement required.

'I'd rather him locked up than dead,' McEwan said simply. 'Tell him that for me, will you?'

Lucy nodded. 'Let me arrange to have someone take you home,' she said.

BURNS CAME DOWN a few moments later to officially interview Frankie. Lucy could tell, though, by the youth's set as he sat in the chair that he'd said as much as he would. The appearance of his father at the station had cornered him, caused him to take sides. As a result, once his solicitor arrived, Lucy wasn't surprised to hear his responses to the first few questions asked were a constant 'No comment'.

Before she left for Greenway, Lucy headed up to the incident room to find Tara. Lucy'd not spoken to her since her mother had asked whether she'd corroborate the complaint against Mickey.

Tara was sitting in the room they'd used to watch the footage the previous day. She smiled as Lucy came in. 'A friendly face,' she said. 'I've been abandoned in here.'

'Mickey still huffing?' Lucy asked.

'I don't care if he is. I spoke to your mum.'

Lucy nodded. 'She told me.' Tara had seen Lucy being called out by the ACC, so bringing it up now was simply a way to lead to the inevitable question.

'She says it'll be my word against his, unless you can confirm what I've said.'

'And what have you said?'

'The truth,' Tara said. 'Even at that, it'll be his word against ours.'

Lucy nodded lightly.

'You are going to back me up, aren't you?' Tara asked, smiling uncertainly. 'He called you a dyke, too.'

'It doesn't bother me what he says,' Lucy said, avoiding the question. 'It's not true, so it's water off a duck's back to me.'

'And what if it was true?' Tara asked quickly. 'What then? Would that be different?'

She stared at Lucy, her eyes bright and shiny in the glare from the screen in front of which she sat.

'Is it true?' Lucy asked.

'Should it matter?'

'Of course not.'

'Then why ask?'

Lucy nodded. 'Because I'd want to think you trusted me enough to tell me and know it wouldn't change anything.'

'Like you not telling me the ACC is your mother until I worked it out?'

'Exactly like that,' Lucy said.

Tara nodded. She swallowed, glancing at the TV screen. 'It's true,' she said.

Lucy thought of Frankie McEwan's father, risking losing his own son to do what was right by him, risking in fact his own position in Greenway if word leaked that he'd handed over his own boy. And word would get out. Word always got out.

'I'm to see my mum later,' Lucy said.

Tara nodded, although Lucy couldn't tell whether she had realised that Lucy had still not committed to backing her. And for that, Lucy felt herself blushing with shame.

'Fair enough,' Tara said. 'I've got your picture.' She'd paused the footage on a single image of the stairwell. The image was grainy, and, while Lucy recognised Bobby McLean, she couldn't make out who the other figure was. He was taller than Bobby, for though he stood on the step below him, their heads were almost at the same level.

'It's clear of Bobby,' Tara said, 'but not the other guy. I can't get enough detail from the images to even look for him in other footage; I need one good shot to be able to compare it.' She was completely businesslike now, her tone clipped.

'What about when they leave? If he followed Bobby out, would you not have him then?'

'A crowd came out after Bobby did,' Tara said. 'If he was part of that, I'd have no way to pick him out.'

Lucy nodded. 'Thanks anyway.'

'Maybe ask Gareth McGonigle? Someone who was there might have seen them row on the stairs.'

'Maybe,' Lucy agreed. She knew whom she could ask, and, on the way there, she could also check McEwan's claim that he'd been in the pub when McLean was killed.

Chapter Fifty-Six

THE GREENWAY ARMS was already open when Lucy arrived. Stephen Welland was standing on the pavement outside, perched on a stool, watering the hanging baskets with water from a pint glass. The overspill splattered on the pavement beneath him.

'Officer,' he said as he watched Lucy get out of her car.

'Mr Welland, have you got a moment?'

Welland smiled. 'For the forces of law and order, anything. Come in.'

He stepped down and, lifting the stool, headed into the bar. Inside, the place appeared to have been recently renovated. The wood panelling along the bar was light pine, the tables and chairs likewise. Framed prints of footballers hung on the walls except in one alcove where the whole wall held a tattered pipe band banner.

'The boys were caught in a bomb attack,' Welland said, having noticed the banner had caught Lucy's attention. 'Thirty years back. Three killed. That was recovered from the wreckage. The banner has been in the Greenway Arms ever since. Lest we forget.'

'You heard about Bobby McLean, I assume,' Lucy said.

'Of course. Bad business. Bobby was a good lad.'

'He was a friend?'

Welland shrugged. 'Everyone knows everyone in Greenway.'

'I need to check if Frank McEwan was here last night just before eight p.m.'

'Frankie?' Welland said. 'Why?'

'Can you confirm he was here, please?'

'He might have been. I'll check the CCTV for you. Eight o'clock, you say?'

'Just before,' Lucy said. Bobby's death had been reported at 8.05 p.m. If McEwan had been in the Greenway Arms until just before 8, it was unlikely he'd have been involved in the killing.

Welland led her through to a small back office, which housed a desk and a monitor. He sat at the desk and brought up the feed from the previous evening. He typed in '8 p.m.'.

'Make it seven forty-five and scroll on towards eight,' Lucy said. 'Please.'

Sure enough, McEwan was sitting at the bar at 7.45. Lucy watched as he chatted with the barman in double time, his small movements exaggerated by the speed of the tape. At 7.51 p.m. he stood and vanished, his coat still hanging on his stool. He appeared in one of the other feeds, entering the toilet. At 7.53 p.m. he returned to his seat and finished his drink. At 7.55 p.m. he stood and, pulling on his coat, waved his goodbyes to the barman and left.

'How long does it take to get to Bobby's from here?'

Welland thought for a moment. 'Walking, about five minutes. Frankie would have been walking.'

He'd have reached Bobby's just after 8. It was unlikely he'd have had time to inflict the injuries they had witnessed on McLean and get away before the neighbour reported the death at 8.05 p.m.

Lucy heard the outer door opening and a voice calling, 'Hello? Mr Welland?'

Welland stood and smiled at Lucy. 'My fifteen minutes,' he explained. 'Do you need anything else?'

Lucy shook her head, glancing out to see two men standing in the bar now. One she recognised as a local reporter, dressed in suit and tie. The other was a cameraman, holding his camera by his side.

'Are you being interviewed?' Lucy asked.

Welland nodded. 'They're doing a piece about the pros and cons of Brexit ahead of the vote on Thursday. They've asked me to speak as a local businessman and community representative.'

Not Jackie Moss. Or Charlie Dougan, Lucy reflected.

'Where do you want to set up?' Welland said, moving across to the reporter.

'Just one thing,' Lucy asked, the thought suddenly striking her. 'Did *you* not remember Frankie being here last night? He was sitting at the bar.'

Welland shrugged. 'I wasn't here last night.'

Lucy nodded, wondering both where he had been and why Frankie had lied about Welland having been in the pub the whole time he was.

Chapter Fifty-Seven

McGONIGLE WAS SITTING up in his hospital bed when Lucy went in. A table was pulled up in front of him and he was spooning soup into his mouth.

'Sergeant,' he said, when Lucy came in.

'Mr McGonigle,' Lucy said. 'I hope I'm not disturbing your lunch. I've a few follow-up questions, if you don't mind.'

'Do I need my lawyer?' McGonigle asked.

Lucy shook her head. 'I'm not here about you. I've a few questions about Paradise night club.'

McGonigle put down his spoon, interested now. 'Right,' he said a little uncertainly.

'We've been told that Bobby McLean got into a row with someone on the stairs of the club,' Lucy said. She handed McGonigle the picture they'd pulled from the CCTV. 'Do you know who this is?'

McGonigle studied the picture. 'I'm guessing you know Bobby. I don't know the other one.'

'You didn't see a row? Bobby didn't mention it?'

McGonigle shook his head.

'Why didn't he stay?' Lucy asked. 'After he arrived, you said he left again. Why didn't he stay and leave with you?'

McGonigle slumped back lightly against the pillows behind him. 'There was another seller there,' he said. 'He spooked when he saw him.'

'Why? Bobby wasn't selling; you were.'

McGonigle nodded. 'He knew him. Bobby said he used to sell for him. But I didn't see them getting into anything.'

Lucy paused, piecing together what he had said. McEwan told her that one of the Lupeis had got into a fight with Bobby in the club. What had Mulholland, the SIO on the Moss shooting, told her? A Roma gang had been selling in Derry, using local muscle to shift their stuff in the estates. And the woman in Greenway had claimed she'd heard Roma were selling into the school, when in fact it had been Bobby McLean. Hours after the Lupei family home had been attacked, a Roma started a fight with Bobby McLean in Paradise. Now McGonigle was suggesting that Bobby had once sold for the Roma who attacked him. One of the Lupeis had to be involved in some way.

'This other seller,' Lucy asked. 'Was he local?'

McGonigle shrugged. 'I don't know. Bobby never gave me a name.'

'Would you know him if you saw him again?'

Another shrug. 'Maybe. I didn't really pay him any attention. He was normal looking, hair, clothes, nothing special.'

'Was this him?' Lucy asked, holding up the CCTV image again.

'That could be anyone,' McGonigle said. 'I wasn't really paying attention to the people there,' he added. 'I had my mind on other things. Maybe someone else who was there that night might be able to help. Or if you had a better picture.'

Lucy reflected that the only other person she could think of was Ian Nixon, and he was unlikely to help. She knew there were no file images of either Andre or Cezar Lupei or his family. She could think of no other way to get a picture of them except to go directly to the source.

Chapter Fifty-Eight

ADRIAN AND CEZAR Lupei were helping the removal team carry kitchen chairs out to the large white van that was parked on the pavement outside their house. Across the street, a few neighbours had come out to watch, though none had offered to help with the moving of the furniture.

The two looked across at Lucy as she got out of the car, then turned their attention back to their work.

Lucy passed them and went up to the open front door. Constanta Lupei appeared, carrying a box of ornaments, which she seemed about to hand to Lucy, having presumably mistaken her for one of the removal team.

'I'm sorry,' she said. 'Come in.' She had been crying, her eyes still raw and bright with tears.

'How are you, Mrs Lupei?' Lucy asked.

Constanta shook her head, saying something in her own language. 'Fine. Sad. Sad.'

Lucy nodded her understanding. 'And how is Mr Lupei now?'

Andre Lupei sat on the sofa, his face still badly bruised, the injuries yellowing now around the edges. His arm was in a cast, which explained his sitting out the furniture movement. He was trying to wrap picture frames in newspaper, one-handed, balancing the picture on his knee as he attempted to fold the excess paper around it.

'How are you feeling, sir?' Lucy asked.

Andre glared at her. 'I didn't ask for this,' he said, indicating the van outside with a nod. 'I didn't want it.'

'I understand, sir,' Lucy said. 'But for your own safety—'

'I never asked.'

'Your wife did, sir,' Lucy said. 'We told her we would try to get you relocated.'

'She shouldn't have!' he snapped. 'That was not her place.'

'With respect, sir,' Lucy said, 'she was dealing with a very difficult situation.'

'You should have waited to discuss it with me,' he said, lifting the picture frame from his knee and flinging it across to the chair opposite.

'I understand your anger,' Lucy said. 'I do. But we can't guarantee your safety in the estate at the moment. Nor your wife's and son's.'

'Things are different now,' Andre said.

'How?'

'That one was killed. Last night. We saw it in the news,' he added, nodding at the set playing soundlessly in the corner, the volume muted.

'Bobby McLean?'

Lupei nodded. 'He was one.'

Lucy thought back to the night she first met the family. They had told her the number of men in the car, but they had said they didn't recognise any of them.

'How did you know?'

Andre stared at her, his expression drawn scornfully. 'I know a face. I hope he suffered.'

Lucy stopped herself from telling Lupei how he had died. For a moment, she wondered if he had been involved in some way, but his plaster cast seemed to preclude that. 'Was he one of the ones who beat you?'

'Probably,' he said.

'But you can't be sure?'

Lupei shrugged.

'If you knew anything about the others who attacked you, you should tell us, Mr Lupei,' Lucy said.

'Why? What good would it do? *They* attack us but *we* lose our home. This is your answer? Punish the people who did nothing.'

'Because . . .' Lucy said, struggling to find a flaw in his argument. Finally she said, 'Because they'll just get to keep doing it to the next family and the next one after that if you don't.'

Lupei stared at her. His right pupil was still encircled with blood.

'I don't care,' he said.

'Where were you last night, sir?'

Lupei glared at her. 'Here. Where else?'

'And Adrian?'

Lupei nodded defiantly.

'And what about Cezar?'

'We were all here. With that protest, we locked ourselves in. My brother spent the night.'

Lucy took out her phone. 'Would you mind if I took a picture of your injuries for my own report,' she asked. 'It would be useful to use in my investigation into the events in Greenway.'

She'd kept it deliberately vague so that Lupei could not claim he'd not consented to the image being used to show to Gareth McGonigle, even though she felt certain that he was not involved.

She took two shots, then wished Andre Lupei luck with the move and, excusing herself, went back outside.

Adrian was climbing back down from the back of the van in which his uncle still stood, shifting pieces of furniture around to make more room.

'You heard about the man who was killed in Greenway last night?'

Adrian nodded.

'Did you know him?'

Adrian glanced past her, towards the house, as if looking to his father for guidance.

'I'm not . . . I don't know what—'

'Was he one of the men who attacked your home?'

'I didn't see them clearly.'

'You're sure?'

Adrian swallowed drily. 'Yes,' he said, 'I'm sure.'

'I see. I'm sorry you've had to move,' Lucy said. 'It's not right. But it is for the best.'

Another nod.

'Can I get a picture?' Lucy asked lightly. 'For the paperwork for the move. It's nothing important. Just to have evidence that you'd had to leave? Your dad agreed inside.'

Adrian shrugged good-naturedly and Lucy immediately felt bad about the lie.

'Maybe your dad could . . .' Lucy began. 'No, your uncle will be fine. Mr Lupei?'

Cezar dropped down from the back of the van and moved across to them. 'What?'

Adrian spoke to him in Romanian, presumably explaining what Lucy wanted. Cezar stared at her sceptically, but finally stood uncomfortably by his nephew's side, the two of them cupping their groins in their hands, as if taking their place in a defensive wall on a soccer pitch.

Lucy took two pictures with her phone which she showed to Adrian and Cezar as evidence of her purpose. Cezar cast a cursory glance at it, then tapped his nephew's arm, indicating they had more work to do.

'I have to go,' Adrian said.

As Lucy turned to leave, she noticed a woman who'd been part of the group of neighbours from across the street step down off the kerb, at the encouragement of the others, and move across towards the house.

'Is she there?' she asked Lucy, presumably referring to Constanta.

'I'll get her,' Lucy said, immediately wary.

She moved up the pathway again and, knocking lightly on the door, leaned in and called for Mrs Lupei. The woman appeared a moment later, a T-shirt clasped in her hand.

The neighbour coughed embarrassedly, before handing Constanta Lupei an envelope.

'We took a quick whip-round,' she said. 'The neighbours, like.'

Lucy watched as Constanta opened the envelope and pulled out a ragged wad of notes.

'It's not much,' the woman said. 'But it might help you get settled. In your new home.'

Constanta's face crumpled into tears and she moved out suddenly and embraced the woman.

'Thank you,' she said, hugging her tightly. 'Thank you.'

The woman smiled nervously at Lucy, her own eyes brimming. 'It's just to say . . . we don't agree with what's happened. It's nothing to do with us.'

'Thank you,' Constanta said again, straightening, her face bright. She raised the notes above her head to indicate them to the neighbours opposite and raised her voice. 'Thank you. Thank you for your kindness.'

She turned to go back inside. 'Andre,' she called, her words, in Romanian, tumbling as freely as her tears.

'That was very good of you,' Lucy said to the neighbour who was now stemming her own tears with her index finger.

'We should have said something sooner,' the woman said simply. 'Before it was too late.'

Chapter Fifty-Nine

LUCY COULD NOT help but reflect on the woman's words as she drove through Greenway and down to the hall where Nixon was preaching. The protestors from the last time she had visited were long gone; all that remained of their presence was a few strands of twine tethered to the fence posts, the posters of protest long since pulled down.

Norman Friel was outside the hall, brushing the pavement that led to the main doors. A washing basin of soapy water steamed on the ground next to him. Every few strokes he would dip the head of the yard brush he was using into the mix and scrub at the pavement once more.

He looked up at Lucy's approach, smiling a little uncertainly at her as he tried to place her. Evidently, he couldn't, for he straightened and extended his hand, still smiling. 'You're very welcome to Greenway Gospel Hall.'

'We've met before, Mr Friel,' Lucy said, earning a nod and a wag of his finger in response.

'I never forget a face,' he said.

'I'm DS Black. I'm a friend of Tom—'

'Tom Fleming,' Friel said, as if in an attempt to belatedly prove his claim.

'That's right,' Lucy said.

'Tom's not here,' Friel said.

'No. I'm here to see Mr Nixon.'

Friel stiffened slightly. 'The pastor asked not to be disturbed. He's at prayer.'

'That's fine,' Lucy said. 'It's the younger Mr Nixon that I'd like to see.'

Friel looked to the ground ruefully, as if the prospect of Lucy walking on his newly washed path discomforted him.

'You may come in,' he said finally, the warm welcome to Greenway Gospel Hall now gone.

Ian Nixon was sitting in the lounge area of the hall, watching an *Inspector Morse* repeat on ITV3. He looked across at Lucy when she came in and stood, but did not come over to her.

'Can I get you something?' Friel offered, the hope that she would say no clear in his tone. This was further evidenced by his smile of relief when that was her response.

Lucy waited for the door to close before she spoke.

'I'm sorry to bother you, Mr Nixon,' she said. 'But I need your help.'

Nixon stared at her scornfully. 'My help?'

Lucy nodded. 'When you were at the club . . .' she began.

Nixon exhaled exasperatedly, rolling his eyes. 'I've told you already—'

Lucy raised her hand lightly. 'That's not what I'm interested in. I'm guessing you heard about the killing last night, in the estate.'

Nixon nodded, suspicious now and clearly on guard. 'The gay thing.'

Lucy didn't answer him. 'The victim was at the club on Friday night.'

Nixon folded his arms. 'This has nothing to do with me.'

Lucy nodded. 'I know that, sir. But we've been told he got into a row with someone on the staircase as he was leaving. You had left the building in the moments before him, which makes me think that you might have passed them on the stairs.'

Nixon shrugged, though Lucy could tell he was thinking, trying to remember his own exit from the club. 'I doubt I'd remember.'

Lucy pulled out her phone and opening the BBC News app, scrolled to the story of Bobby McLean's murder, at the top of which was placed a picture of Bobby.

'This is the man who was killed,' she said. 'Do you recognise him?'

She handed the phone to Nixon. For a moment she thought he was going to refuse to take it from her but eventually he relented and, unfolding his arms, took the handset and looked at it.

He considered the picture for a moment. 'I know his face,' he said finally. 'I'm not completely sure. I might have seen him somewhere else. Maybe at the rally?'

'He wasn't there,' Lucy said. McLean had gone to ground by that stage.

'Would he have been at some of our services?'

Lucy shrugged. 'Maybe,' she said. 'I don't know if he would support your father's views on some issues.'

Nixon accepted the comment with a curt nod. 'Is that all?'

'Can I show you some other pictures?' Lucy asked, taking the phone from him and scrolling through her pictures until she came to the images of the Lupeis.

'Were any of these man at Paradise?'

Nixon glanced at the pictures, scrolling from one to the next. Lucy thought she saw a flicker of recognition in his expression, but he quickly shook his head. 'I'm sorry. I don't recognise them.'

'You're sure?'

Nixon looked at her. 'I said I don't recognise any of them.'

Lucy took the phone again and, pocketing it, thanked Nixon for his help.

'I've not been any,' he said.

They both turned at the sound of the door opening and Pastor Nixon strode into the room, his prayer period presumably finished.

'What are you talking about?' he asked.

Lucy smiled. 'Police business, sir,' she said. 'Nothing to concern you.'

'You're talking to my boy.'

'I'm talking to your son,' Lucy said.

'Then I have a right to know.'

'Once your son turned eighteen, Pastor, he became entitled to his privacy. And his independence.'

Nixon took a step closer to Lucy, the girth of his chest almost pressing against her. She resisted the urge both to shudder and to move.

'Listen,' he began, 'if you're here about that other pederast's killing—'

'I respect this building, Pastor Nixon. But if you don't step back from me, I'll arrest you again for assaulting a police officer.'

Nixon stared at her. 'Is that right?'

'I guarantee it.'

Nixon held her stare a moment before glancing up at his son. 'Ian, I need you in here. Now.'

'I'm coming, Dad,' Nixon said. 'Excuse me,' he added to Lucy, moving past her. His father smiled at Lucy, then turned and overtook his son, striding back out of the room.

'Pastor Nixon,' Lucy called.

Both Nixon and his son turned to look at her.

She struggled to find something to say that fully reflected her feelings about the man and the cost his behaviour must surely be having on his own son. But it was not her place to comment on it. In the end, she simply shrugged. 'It doesn't matter.'

Nixon smirked and walked through the door, Ian following behind.

Chapter Sixty

LUCY WAS MAKING her way back to the car when her mobile rang. It was Fleming.

'Where are you?' he asked. 'We're done with McEwan. I'm heading back to the office.'

'I spoke to McGonigle again. He confirmed that someone had been in Paradise, another seller. I think one of the Lupeis was part of the crew that were trying to sell MD here last year and got burned by the locals. McGonigle confirmed it was another seller that Bobby got into it with, but couldn't give me any physical details. He said he might be able to ID if we had a clearer picture.'

'Do we?'

'We do now,' Lucy said. 'I called at the Lupeis' myself and got one of Cezar, Andre and the son, Adrian. They're moving out. On a hunch I took it to Ian Nixon, showed him the picture.'

'Lucy . . .'

'I know,' she said. 'He couldn't help anyway.'

'Couldn't or wouldn't?'

'Either. Both.'

'What about DCI Mulholland?' Fleming said. 'He was working that drugs gang last year.'

'I'll call him,' Lucy said.

'By the way, the bloods are back from Bobby's car. The DNA on the samples taken will be a few weeks, but they have a blood type match for Marty Givens on the passenger side of the car and they've matched pubic hair samples from Bobby that were found in the footwell.'

'So Bobby and Marty were together in the car?'

'Seems so. The thing is, they've found a third blood sample on the side of the car that doesn't match either of them or McGonigle's.'

'Someone else was there?'

'Outside the car,' Fleming said.

LUCY DROVE ACROSS to Lisnagelvin, the station only being a few minutes from Greenway. Mulholland was just finishing a briefing when she reached his office.

'I dug out those notes for you,' he said, clearly assuming that's why she was there. 'I meant to get them to you sooner. Sorry. The Moss case has tied me up a bit.' He lifted a lilac folder from his desk and handed it to her. 'Bobby was one of the kids we'd heard mention of, but there's not much on him. Having heard the news from Greenway, I suspect it's too little too late anyway.' He grimaced apologetically.

'That's fine, sir. Thanks,' Lucy said. 'That's not why I'm here, though. The Roma gang you were investigating last year? Were either of these men involved with it?'

Lucy offered him her phone with the pictures of the three men. He scrolled through them.

'I don't remember faces.'

'They're called Lupei,' Lucy said.

Mulholland nodded. 'Let me see,' he said, taking back the folder and flicking through it. He selected one of the sheets and handed it to her; it was a photocopy of the page from his notebook. Various names were scribbled in pencil on the page, amongst them, C. Lupei.

'C. Lupei. Cezar?'

Mulholland shrugged. 'I don't remember. They were names a CI provided to one of the team about who was running a stash house in Tullyally. The gang went quiet soon after.'

'Why?'

'The stash house was raided, emptied and the place burned to the ground, with a Roma still inside. One of our own men tried to save him, but couldn't. He ended up getting injured himself: the Roma died.'

Lucy vaguely remembered hearing about the fire. 'Who raided it?'

Mulholland shrugged. 'The Romanians got into bed with the loyalist paramilitaries, thinking it would give them protection from the Provos. After the fire, our thinking was that the loyalists double-crossed them, hit their stash, took their stuff, and then let the Provos know so they could hit them harder on the city side while they were down. The head shops attacks happened just after that.'

'So what happened to their stash?'

Mulholland shrugged. 'Presumably whoever stole it sold it themselves.'

'Why didn't the Romanians retaliate?'

'They were outnumbered and outgunned, essentially,' Mulholland said. 'I heard they did a bit of internal housekeeping afterwards. Look, to be honest, the man you'd be best talking to was the one who got the names off a CI. He's based here actually. Jason Lloyd.'

'The community officer?' Lucy asked.

Mulholland nodded. 'He was the one got injured trying to get the Roma out; he burnt his arm.'

Chapter Sixty-One

DESPITE HER INITIAL impulse to confront Lloyd, Lucy needed to speak to Fleming first. As she drove down to Maydown, she heard the familiar jingle of the news on the radio and turned it up. The first report was on the killing of Bobby McLean, which in turn led to a second piece on the outbreaks of violence in Greenway. The piece ended with a snippet of the interview with Stephen Welland, introduced by the reporter as a community activist. Lucy assumed they had appended the question to the Brexit discussion.

'The people of Greenway are sick and tired of this. Good people, people who have lived their lives here, are suffering with drugs and antisocial behaviour. And it's not the people from here causing it; these are outsiders, coming in and destroying our estate. The people of Greenway feel under siege, from outsiders and from the police.'

The newscaster was promising that listeners could hear more about the story on the extended evening bulletin just as Lucy switched off the radio.

FLEMING WAS SITTING in his office when Lucy arrived. He listened as she explained all that she had been told about the Romanian gang and about Lloyd.

'So Lloyd got information on a stash house from a CI and the stash house was later raided and emptied. Now, that same product is being sold in the city and Bobby McLean is the supplier?' Fleming said.

Lucy nodded. 'McLean, whose drugs offences were never recorded by Constables Lloyd or Huey.'

'So are Lloyd and Huey members of Ulster First?'

Lucy shrugged. 'There were three attackers on the Lupeis' house, then Lloyd and Huey appeared on duty, so they can't have been part of those three. But both McEwan and Lupei mentioned someone with burn scars on their arm being involved in their beatings. I'd bet Lloyd, at least, was involved in that.'

'We know two people were involved in the beating of Bobby McLean. If your timings from the Greenway Arms are right, Frankie McEwan can't have been one of them. That leaves Lloyd and . . .?'

'Huey, Charlie Dougan or Stephen Welland,' Lucy said. 'McEwan reckoned he and Bobby got involved with Ulster First for the craic. I'd say Welland is the true believer. I might be wrong.'

'I think we can discount Dougan, too,' Fleming said. 'His house has been attacked with a pipe bomb. It didn't explode, though. His wife was bringing in the shopping and found it lying on the path.'

'Any indications of who targeted him?'

'Burns claims the intelligence in the area is saying Jackie Moss.'

'You're not convinced?'

Fleming shook his head. 'I've known Jackie a long time. He may be older now, but he's not mellowed any. If he was hitting back at Dougan, especially over the gun attack on him, he'd not waste time with a pipe bomb.'

'Maybe he didn't know about the reinforced door.'

'Everyone in Greenway will know about it,' Fleming said. 'Having it put in so publicly will be more effective than the door itself ever will be. It suggested Dougan was digging in for the long war.'

'And a pipe bomb couldn't be an opening salvo?'

'That's not Moss's style,' Fleming said. 'He's more of a shock and awe type of fighter.'

'Then who? Welland? Huey and Lloyd?'

Fleming shrugged. 'Maybe. It's not McEwan or Bobby, obviously. Maybe it's in retaliation for Bobby. Maybe they think Dougan was behind it.'

'So, what now?' Lucy asked.

'We go and speak to the good constables,' Fleming said.

CONSTABLE HUEY WAS already in the station when they reached Lisnagelvin. Lucy asked if Lloyd was about, too.

'He went home early,' she explained when they asked for him. 'He said he must have picked up a stomach bug. Why?'

'We need to speak to him,' Fleming said.

'You could try his mobile,' Huey said. 'Or call at the house.'

Fleming took the address from her. While he jotted it down, Huey looked at Lucy. 'Is something wrong?'

Lucy shook her head. 'We'd just like to speak to him.'

'Can I help you with whatever it is?'

'Why didn't you put on Bobby McLean's record about the legal highs he was selling last year?'

Huey blushed. 'Honestly? Lloyd told me not to. He said it would help to have some of the young people in the area on our side rather than being antagonistic.'

'Your partner was involved in a drugs case last year: you weren't part of that, too?'

Huey shook her head. 'That was before I graduated from training. I became his partner after he returned from illness. He burned his arm pretty badly; he's still scarred. Look, has he done something he shouldn't have?'

'Why would you ask that?'

'He's my partner. If he's done something wrong, people will . . . people will tar me with the same brush.'

'Where were you last night at eight p.m.?' Fleming asked.

'Putting my son to bed,' Huey said. 'My mum and dad can tell you. I live at home with them so they can help me with the wee man.'

Lucy regarded her, the earnestness with which she had answered the question. Somehow, she found it hard to imagine this woman beating someone to death.

'Thank you,' Fleming said. They both turned to leave, before he thought of a final question.

'Just out of interest, was there anyone else looking for Lloyd today?'

'That new DCI, Mulholland, phoned down to ask him about some case just before he went home. Why?'

AS THEY RETURNED to the car, Lucy realised she had left her phone lying on the dash. She had three missed calls from the same number. When she redialled, it was Constanta Lupei who answered.

'Mrs Lupei. How did the move go?'

'We're not . . . It's my son, Adrian. He's missing.'

Chapter Sixty-Two

THE LUPEI HOUSE was almost completely empty of furnishings when they got there. Andre still sat in the living room, his wife pacing the floor next to him.

'When did you last see him?' Lucy asked.

'Earlier. He helped Cezar move all the furniture. We had lunch, then he . . . he went somewhere.' She glanced at her husband.

'Where did he go?'

Constanta shrugged, but once again she glanced at Andre.

'Mrs Lupei, if you have some idea of where your son might have gone, you need to tell us. Greenway's not the safest place for him to be out.'

It was Andre who answered, his mind seemingly made up. 'He saw one of them on TV at lunch,' he said.

'One of who?' Lucy said, suppressing a shiver.

'The ones who attacked the house. He saw one on the TV. Being interviewed at the pub.'

Welland. Lucy looked at Fleming who nodded.

'Why would he have gone after him?'

'Over me,' Andre said bitterly. 'He's angry at what they did to me.'

'How could he be sure that it was even him?'

Constanta lowered her head and Lucy could see the blush rising on her neck. 'He took pictures of them the night it happened. From his room.'

'You said they wore scarves,' Lucy said.

Her face reddened. 'That wasn't true.'

'Why would you lie?'

Andre thumped the arm of his seat. 'Adrian called the police. He shouldn't have. We told him not to.'

'Where's his phone now?'

'He has it with him,' Constanta said. 'He saw the man on TV at lunch. He was furious. Andre's brother had him fired up; a real man doesn't lie down to these people, he'd said.'

'Adrian has gone after the man he saw on TV?'

Constanta nodded. 'He's a soft boy. He's not like his uncle.'

The comment earned a scowl from Andre, but no comment. Cezar's insult had clearly been aimed at him.

'What does Cezar do?'

Constanta snorted. 'Who knows?'

'That's enough,' Andre said.

'He's caused nothing but trouble,' Constanta said. 'Nothing.'

'He's my brother.'

'He's an embarrassment. Even his friends turned on him. His leg, his limp? That wasn't a motorcycle accident. His friends stabbed him, on the *buca*. Stabbed him.'

'That's enough,' Andre snapped, slamming his palm against the arm of the chair.

'The *buca*?' Lucy asked.

'The *buca*,' she repeated, pointing to her buttocks.

'We'll look for Adrian,' Fleming said.

THEY DROVE THROUGH Greenway, heading towards the Green-way Arms, Fleming glancing from left to right, checking down each alleyway that they passed.

'Turkish revenge,' he said. 'Stabbing someone on the backside. It's the ultimate mark of dishonour. Shame.'

'They cut Cezar loose after the stash house got hit,' Lucy said.

'And marked him for his failure,' Fleming said. 'He was lucky they didn't kill him.'

When they arrived at the Greenway Arms, the place was alive with sound, the noise and lights from inside spilling out onto the pavement. A straggle of smokers stood at the open doors, half inside, half out, in a lazy compliance with the smoking ban.

Lucy parked up on the double yellow lines outside and got out. She pushed her way into the pub, one or two of those standing in the doorway doing little to move out of her way. A crowd was inside, the mood raucous. Welland was behind the bar.

Lucy scanned the place, though she knew instinctively that Adrian Lupei would not be here; she assumed that the current crowd would not tolerate a Roma youth sitting in their local.

She moved her way towards the bar. 'Big crowd,' she said.

Welland smiled. 'The beauty of free advertising,' he said. 'We're celebrating Bobby's life. An Ulster wake.'

'The teenager from the Roma family is missing. He wouldn't have been here, would he?'

Welland laughed. 'Seriously?'

'Seriously.'

He shook his head. 'If he'd been in here, we'd be marking two wakes, not one.'

'That's not helpful,' Lucy said.

'If he's smarter than his parents, he'll have fucked off back to Romania.'

'Not Rome?'

Welland frowned. 'What?'

'Never mind,' Lucy said, turning as Welland hefted a crate of empties and moved out towards the rear of the building.

When Lucy had managed, gratefully, to get back outside, Fleming was standing just off to the left, away from the smokers.

'Anything?'

Lucy shook her head. 'He'd not be mad enough to go inside,' she said.

Fleming nodded towards the edge of the block where Lucy could see the entranceway to an alley running along the back of the building.

'Maybe take a look there before we go,' he suggested, leading the way.

They walked up to the end of the block and turned down the darkened alley, along which were already stacked empty kegs and crates of empty bottles. A fire-exit light above the emergency exit of the pub cast a spectral greenish light. Looking up, Lucy could see, towards the end of the alley, two large metal dumpsters.

Just then, the exit doors opened and Welland backed out, the crate in his hands, having used his rump to push open the bar on the door. He looked up, surprised to see Lucy standing there, when a second figure suddenly appeared from behind one of the dumpsters and grabbed Welland.

Adrian Lupei had a small kitchen knife in his hand which he jabbed sharply against the right-hand side of Welland's neck, though not hard enough to break skin. It was only then that Adrian, who had clearly been sitting in wait for Welland to appear, realised that they were not alone in the alleyway, for on seeing Lucy, he shifted suddenly behind Welland, using the other man's body to shield him from Lucy's view. He must have gripped Welland's top in his other hand, for Lucy could see the material of the garment stretching as he did so.

Lucy resisted the urge to move forward. She was aware of Welland watching her, trying to gauge from *her* reaction the severity of the threat behind him.

'Adrian, it's DS Black. You need to put down the knife and let Mr Welland go.'

In response, Adrian must have increased his pressure on the knife, for Welland winced lightly.

'Adrian. This isn't going to solve anything. Let Mr Welland go. Your father doesn't want this.'

'He hurt my father,' Adrian said, his voice barely more than a whisper.

'I'll fucking kill you,' Welland snapped, twisting as much as he could before the point of the knife stopped him.

'Shut up,' Lucy snapped. 'Adrian, ignore him. Your dad told us about the phone, about the pictures. We have enough to help you.'

'Lucy,' Fleming said, his tone ominous. 'Company's coming. The smokers.'

Lucy glanced around, to see Fleming, at the mouth of the alley, watching down towards the entrance to the bar. The smokers who'd been standing outside must have realised something was happening and were coming to investigate.

'Adrian, now!' Lucy said, trying to keep her voice quiet, her tone calm. 'You've got to let him go, now. Before things escalate.'

'Am I in trouble?' the boy asked.

'You are now,' Welland laughed, just as Lucy heard Fleming behind her.

'Back inside, men,' he said.

Lucy turned and saw that a group of six men had appeared now. A few of them were squinting into the darkness of the alley, trying to see what was going on.

'You all right, Stephen?' one called.

'Adrian, give me the knife now,' Lucy hissed. Once the smokers worked out what was happening, there would be nothing she or Fleming could do to stop them. 'Please.'

Slowly, she saw the tautness of the material on Welland's top loosen in the greenish glow of the exit light and the youth stepped back from the older man.

'Can you step aside, Mr Welland?' Lucy said, moving forward.

'What's the problem?' a voice called from the street beyond. Lucy risked a cautious glance to where they stood.

'Lost and found,' Fleming said. 'Go back inside, gentlemen.'

'We will, like fuck,' one man said, his face in the shadows.

Lucy moved towards Adrian, but Welland stood his ground, smiling, waiting for her to make her next move.

'Call them off and step back, Mr Welland,' Lucy said.

He shrugged. 'They've had a few. I'm not the boss of them. Cops haven't done us any favours here the past few days.'

Lucy moved closer to Welland. 'The Lupeis took photographs of the people who attacked their house. Your picture is among them.' As she spoke, she held out her left arm, indicating to Adrian that he should move around Welland to where she stood.

Welland straightened. 'And?'

'Call them off and we'll forget we saw your picture.'

Welland spotted, too late, that Adrian had already made it past him and the crate he still held made it impossible for him to further impede the youth's progress.

'Who's that in there with you, Stephen?' one of the men called from the street.

'This is your only chance,' Lucy said to Welland. 'Call them off.'

Lucy could see Welland's expression crease. Like Adrian, he'd put himself in a hopeless position. Realistically, he and his friends couldn't do anything to Lucy and Fleming and he knew it. But, to save face, he'd want to feel he'd gained something from backing down. The offer was a shrewd one.

'Let them past,' Welland said finally to the men. 'Get rid of the stink of gypsies from here.'

Lucy moved up the alleyway, her hand gripping Adrian's arm. She drew alongside Fleming who positioned himself to the other side of Adrian, effectively sandwiching him between them for his own safety.

The smokers stood a moment, in a last show of bravado, before reluctantly moving back and allowing the three figures passage out towards Lucy's car.

'And don't come back to Greenway,' Welland shouted after them.

Lucy couldn't be sure whether the comment was intended for Adrian or for herself and Fleming.

THEY DROVE BACK towards the Lupeis'. Adrian sat in the back, his head bowed, his hands clasped in his lap, as if in shame.

'You did the right thing,' Lucy said, glancing at him in the rearview mirror.

He nodded, but did not speak.

'Why did you not tell us that night that you had pictures? It could have helped us prevent a lot of what happened since,' Fleming said. He didn't mention the beating of Adrian's father, but Lucy knew the boy was smart enough to have worked it out for himself.

'I phoned the police,' Adrian said. 'Mum phoned Cezar. When he arrived I showed him the pictures. He told me not to say anything when the police came. That he'd take care of it.'

'How was he going to take care of it?'

Adrian looked out the window. 'He said he knew one of them. He knew where he lived. He went just before the police came. I only did what he told me to do.'

Lucy reflected on the night she'd first gone to the Lupeis'. There had been no sign of Cezar.

'Did he say anything afterwards?'

Adrian shook his head. 'Nothing.'

'Can I see the pictures?' Fleming asked.

Reluctantly, Adrian drew his phone from his pocket and flicked through his images until he found what he wanted. Then he handed it to Fleming.

Lucy glanced across at him, his face illuminated by the screen. He stopped on one image.

'Was this who Cezar knew?' he asked the youth, holding the phone so that Adrian could see it.

The youth nodded.

Fleming held it up now for Lucy to see. The image was grainy, though at least illuminated as the figure in it was pictured beneath the street lamp outside the Lupeis' house. Even with the quality of the image, she could still clearly identify Bobby McLean.

Chapter Sixty-Three

AFTER DELIVERING ADRIAN safely to his parents, Lucy and Fleming drove to Lloyd's house, on the off chance that he was there. The house was in darkness when they arrived, his car not in the driveway.

'You'd think if he had a stomach bug, he'd be in his bed,' Fleming said. 'Or at least answering his mobile,' he added, turning on the speaker on his own phone so Lucy could hear Lloyd's voicemail message.

As he did so, Lucy's own phone rang. It was the Strand Road. 'DS Black. There's an Ian Nixon here to speak to you. He looks like he's taken a beating. He'll only speak with you, he says.'

IAN NIXON SAT in the reception area waiting for them. When he looked up at Lucy on her appearance at the desk, she saw straight away the bruising around his eye. He had a second, small gash on his cheek, bedded on the lividity of another bruise. His lip had been split and curled slightly with the swelling.

'Mr Nixon,' Lucy said. 'Do you want to come through?'

She led him into one of the free interview rooms, offering him tea, which he accepted. She left him while she went and got two cups, one for each of them, and carried them back in. He was sitting behind the desk, biting at his thumbnail as he waited for her.

'Was this an accident?' Lucy asked, nodding at his injuries.

'My father,' he said simply.

'Your father did that?'

Nixon nodded.

'Why?'

'After your visit, he kept pushing at me, wanting to know why you were there.'

'I'm sorry,' Lucy said. 'I didn't mean to—'

Nixon waved away her apology. 'Don't. I told him the truth,' he said. 'About me.'

Lucy nodded, sitting down opposite him. 'Why?'

'The picture you showed me,' Nixon said. 'I did know one of them. The older guy with the limp. He was at the club.'

Cezar Lupei, Lucy thought. 'You're sure?'

Nixon nodded. The gash on his cheek must have irritated him for he pressed at it gingerly.

'How can you be certain?'

'I bought off him once or twice before,' Nixon said. 'He sells legal highs there. I've seen him a few times. He was there that night.'

'Selling?'

He shrugged. 'I don't know.'

'And you couldn't admit that the other day because if you said you recognised him . . .'

'I'd have had to tell you that.'

'So, what changed?'

Nixon shrugged. 'We were watching TV last night and there was a whole spiel on about the gay fella that was killed in his flat. Dad was ecstatic, like this was the best news ever. All he could talk about was the numbers that would be at his service next weekend.'

Lucy nodded.

'That could have been me,' Nixon said. 'The guy that died; he was at the club. The fella that was found in Bay Road was the same. And Dad was happy about it. I don't know why I'm even surprised; I know what he's like, but today, something just . . . just . . .'

'Snapped?' Lucy offered softly.

Nixon nodded.

'I'm sorry,' Lucy said again, realising the paucity of the comment.

'I'm not. I asked him how he'd feel if his child was gay. "I'd disown him," he said. "I'd beat the queerness out of him and if that didn't work I'd disown him."'

Lucy shook her head.

'So, I told him,' Nixon said. His hands were shaking, the tea spilling over the edge of the polystyrene cup. 'I don't know why – I just . . . I told him.'

'And he did this?'

Nixon nodded. 'He thought I was joking. He got kind of angry about that, even. That I would make a joke of it. I told him I wasn't, but he didn't believe me. He lost it and hit me a slap. I just . . . that made me dig in my heels and I just told him outright.'

'Has he ever hit you before?'

'When I was a kid,' Nixon said. 'He's Old Testament,' he added, as if this was explanation enough.

'What about your mother?'

'He hits her, too, sometimes.'

Lucy shook her head, put down her tea. 'That's not . . . not what I meant. What did your mother do when you said this?'

Nixon didn't speak for a second, as if trying to remember, but Lucy guessed that the memory of it was still close to the surface.

'She sat there, looking at her hands, as if it had nothing to do with her, like it was between me and him. The men.'

'Do they know you're here?'

'No. They'll not care. He'd be too ashamed after all that's happened to admit his own son is gay. And she won't want to rock the boat too much with him, in case he takes it out on her.'

'Have you somewhere to stay?'

'I've friends in town.'

'But you came here first?'

Nixon nodded.

'Why?'

'It's the right thing to do,' he said. 'That's one thing he taught me,' he added, tears filling in his eyes. 'He always taught me to do what was right.' He looked at Lucy a moment. 'It's just that his idea of right seems wrong.'

Lucy reached across and laid her hand on Nixon's. 'Thank you for doing the right thing,' she said.

Nixon raised his head a little. 'I'd love to say it feels good, but . . . it feels like shit.'

'Do you want to press charges?' Lucy asked. 'Against him?'

Nixon shook his head. 'What's the point?'

'To punish him. To make sure that he won't do it again,' Lucy said.

'He only has the one son,' Nixon said, then corrected himself. 'Had one. Besides, he's punishing himself. He's losing me.'

'That's true,' Lucy said, offering him a smile. 'He's sacrificed that.'

'God let Abraham keep his son,' Nixon said. 'Maybe someday, Dad will realise that *he* wasn't allowed that much.'

'I hope so,' Lucy said.

Chapter Sixty-Four

'It's Nurses' Night in Paradise,' Lucy said.

The Major Incident Team had gathered in the room. Fleming had updated Burns on what they had learned: Nixon's account of Cezar being at Paradise confirmed the identity of the man Bobby had argued with on the stairs.

'If Cezar has started selling again, that's where he might be,' she concluded.

'We know he rowed with McLean in the club,' Burns said. 'It doesn't follow that he would have followed him to Bay Park.'

'There was a blood sample on both the rock used to kill Martin Givens and the car,' Fleming said. 'We should at least eliminate him from our inquiries.'

'If he's selling in Paradise, we can lift him,' Lucy said. 'That'll give us justifiable reason to take a DNA sample and bloods, to check if he's using. We can compare them.'

'He got slashed on the arse for messing up a drugs deal with loyalists in Greenway,' Fleming said. 'We know Bobby sold for him back then; then Bobby started selling the same product but for himself. And, to rub salt in the wounds, he attacked Lupei's family. That sounds like grounds for him to want to hurt Bobby back. Either in Bay Park or in Bobby's own flat.'

'But it wasn't Bobby who was attacked in Bay Park; it was Martin Givens,' Burns said.

Wilson, who had been sitting in with them, nodded. 'Is there any way we can confirm if Cezar Lupei's even in Paradise before we send in the cavalry?'

Lucy pulled out her phone and, opening the image she'd taken of Cezar, texted it to Grace: *Have u seen this man in Pdise this pm?*

'My friend's working there tonight,' Lucy explained, earning a glance of recognition from Mickey.

A few minutes later, her phone pinged.

He's here, the message read.

THE UPPER FLOOR of Paradise was heaving when they arrived. Despite it being Nurses' Night, Lucy guessed by the ages of some of those who passed her that they were more likely secondary-school pupils than nurses.

Those gathered on the dance floor shifted with the pounding of the music, which shivered through the wood beneath them. Lucy wondered how Grace could stick working in it, night after night.

The rest of the team spread out, moving through the crowd, the uniforms who had accompanied them already earning glances from some of those dancing. Lucy moved across to the bar. It took her a second to place the barman.

'Ciaran?'

He nodded, frowning lightly to indicate that he hadn't recognised her.

'Lucy Black. Grace's friend. Is she here?'

He angled his head, cupping his hand behind his ear, flipping the glass he held as he did so.

Lucy leaned forward, pulling him towards her. 'Where's Grace?'

His expression changed as he realised who she was. 'She's on her break. Wait a minute.'

He headed in through the door to the rear of the bar, reappearing a moment later with Grace.

'Hey,' she smiled. 'What's up?'

'Is he still about?'

Grace nodded. 'He's been over near the toilets for the past half-hour,' she said. 'He's dealing, I take it?'

Lucy nodded. 'See you in a bit.'

She began moving across to the toilet area. Ahead of her, she could see two uniforms being led by one of the doormen from downstairs, obviously heading in the same direction.

As she rounded the corner, she spotted Lupei. He had been standing with two girls, but the uniforms moving through the crowd towards him now caught his attention. Lucy watched as he lowered his arms to his side and dropped the small packets he'd been holding. His right hand went quickly to his trouser pocket and another batch tumbled to the ground around his feet.

Still keeping an eye on the uniforms, who were across to the right, he began backing away, moving towards Lucy though angled away from her, his attention focused on the two men.

One of the uniforms pointed to him, perhaps for the benefit of the doorman, and Cezar knew he was trapped. Instinctively, he reached across and grabbed a pint bottle of cider off the nearest table to him. He cracked the bottom of it against the table edge and held it low, ready to defend himself, the bottle hidden from sight of the two men.

Just as Lucy made to call to Cezar, to distract him, one of the uniforms began lunging through the revellers, aiming to get to him. Cezar twisted, pulling up the bottle with one hand while, with the other, he grabbed a girl standing next to him, pulling her against him. He held her in front of him, his arm across her throat as he moved backwards, away from the uniforms, towards Lucy.

At the sight of the broken bottle, the girl screamed, causing those around her to stop. The uniforms stopped too, both suddenly aware that any movement could prompt Cezar into action. He moved back, towards Lucy, his eyes on the uniforms, the broken bottle held aloft, nearly touching the girl's neck in a manner that reminded Lucy of how his nephew, Adrian, had done the same thing hours earlier with Stephen Welland.

Lucy pulled out the telescopic baton she'd brought, strapped to her leg, in case Cezar proved difficult. She flicked it open. Those around her moved back suddenly, aware of what was happening. She had, she realised, one attempt to disarm Lupei. She didn't want to risk hitting his arm, lest in so doing he jabbed at the girl. Then she remembered Fleming's comment on Turkish revenge.

As Cezar backed towards her, glancing around him now, his desperation evident, she angled herself. With a deft swish, she struck him full force across the top of the back of his legs. Instantly, his back arched, the bottle falling as his right hand shot to his rump.

The movement was enough for the girl to shift suddenly away from him. Exposed, only for a second, Cezar had barely time to register as the uniforms lunged for him, bringing him to the ground.

Lucy stepped quickly forward, kicking the broken bottle away from his reach. She caught the snarl of hatred as one of the uniforms knelt on his back, pulling his arms around to cuff him.

'Thanks, Sergeant,' the man said, acknowledging Lucy for the first time. 'That was a low blow,' he added.

Chapter Sixty-Five

THEY SAT IN the same interview room where, hours earlier, Ian Nixon had identified Cezar Lupei as having been in Paradise. Now Lupei was slouched in his seat, the duty solicitor sitting next to him. Burns had asked that Lucy lead the interview. Following his arrest, Lupei's fury seemed more focused on the fact that a woman had incapacitated him than on his actual apprehension. She suspected that he thought he was being lifted for selling legal highs. He'd already admitted selling them as the interview started, assuming it was a straightforward issue.

Now, Lucy opened the folder in front of her and presented Lupei with a picture of Bobby McLean.

'Do you know this man?'

Lupei regarded the picture coldly, shifting slightly in his seat, as if to get more comfortable.

'No. Why?'

'You're sure you don't recognise him?'

A shake of the head.

'How about in this picture?' This time she handed him a copy of the picture Adrian had taken where Bobby stood near his car outside the Lupeis' family home.

Lupei looked from the picture to her and smirked.

'I never seen him before,' he said.

'You don't recognise this picture? The one your nephew showed you following the attack on their house?'

Cezar shrugged. 'He might have shown me something. I don't remember. The quality is not very good.'

Next Lucy presented him with the CCTV image of Bobby and him. 'Is this you?' she asked.

'It could be anyone, Sergeant,' the solicitor commented. 'The quality of *that* image is atrocious.'

'I agree,' Lucy said. 'Though we also have one eyewitness who places you in Paradise the night this was taken and a second who witnessed this altercation.'

Lupei shrugged. 'No comment.'

'Do you recognise this vehicle?' Lucy asked, handing him the picture of Bobby's car.

Another cursory glance, another shake of the head.

'So you can't account for how we found blood matching your blood type on the bodywork of this car?'

Lupei shook his head slowly, wary about where this was going.

Lucy handed him the picture of the bloody rock. 'And that same blood, matching your blood type, was also found on this rock, which was used to beat a young man to death in Bay Park in the early hours of last Saturday morning.'

Lupei tried to hold his nerve, though Lucy could see his eyes flicking back to the picture every so often.

'No comment.'

'What happened to your buttocks, Mr Lupei?'

The change in questioning threw him. 'What?'

'You have injuries to your buttocks and legs. What happened?'

'A bike accident.'

'Not a razor attack. Not Turkish revenge for allowing a stash house in Tullyally to be raided and torched?'

Lupei licked his lips drily.

'I'm not sure where you're going with this,' the solicitor commented.

'We know that you were supplying legal highs to youths to sell in the Waterside last year. We know the stash was being held in a house in Tullyally, which was raided. We believe that you were held to account for that by your former gang members. We know that the youths you paid to sell Magic Dragon last year have started selling that same product themselves this year, presumably shifting what they took from the stash house. We know that one of those youths attacked your brother's house and was photographed by your nephew. We know your nephew showed you those pictures and you told him not to show them to us, that you would take care of it.'

Lupei shifted again in his seat, but did not speak.

'We know you were in Paradise night club. We know you got into an altercation with Bobby McLean there, on the staircase. We can place you at the car in Bay Park, and with the rock that killed Martin Givens. This youth.'

At that, she handed him another picture: Martin Givens lying on the grass in Bay Road Park, his broken skull cushioned by his own congealed blood. It was this picture that Lupei studied most closely.

'There was hatred in the killing of this young man,' Lucy said. 'Almost as much as in the killing of Bobby McLean himself.' She laid the final shot now on the table: Bobby lying dead, the word 'faggot' written in blood on the wall.

'I didn't do that,' Cezar said softly. 'I wish I had, but that wasn't me.' He pushed the picture back across the table.

'You didn't kill Bobby McLean?'

Cezar shook his head. 'But thank you for showing me the picture.'

'I don't believe you,' Lucy said. 'You've lied about killing Martin Givens: I don't believe you about Bobby.'

Cezar shrugged.

'We have you,' Lucy said. 'Comment or no comment, your blood is on the rock, mixed with Martin Givens' blood. You can't deny that.'

Another shrug.

'Family is important to you, isn't it, Cezar?'

He looked at her. 'It was,' he said.

'Martin Givens' family deserves to know the truth. They deserve to know why you killed him. Why not give them that answer now?'

Cezar looked to his solicitor, who had not spoken, clearly having been surprised at how a legal high arrest had ballooned into a murder inquiry so quickly.

'We've placed you at the scene,' Lucy said. 'Why not put them out of their misery?'

He looked down at the picture again, then to where his hands were folded on the desk in front of him. 'It was an accident,' he said softly.

'An accident?' Lucy repeated.

He nodded. 'I followed Bobby on my motorcycle into the park. I parked a distance away so he wouldn't hear the engine and I walked up. As I came near the car I saw a figure sitting. I went to the wrong side by mistake: in Romania the steering wheel is on the other side. I thought it was the driver, that it was Bobby. Only when I had pulled him out of the car did I realise it wasn't.'

'But it was too late,' Lucy said.

'After I hit him, he still walked away. Bobby sat up, started the car, drove off. I ran after him, but by the time I reached my bike again, he was far gone.'

'Did you go back to check on the boy?'

'I got on my bike and left. Went to check on my brother. I thought the boy was okay. He walked away,' he repeated.

'He made it a few hundred yards and collapsed,' Lucy said. 'He died in the park during the night.'

Cezar nodded. 'So that is what you tell them, his parents. You tell them it was an accident. Tell them that I'm sorry.'

He held her gaze, his expression empty.

'Do you think that will help them?' he asked.

Chapter Sixty-Six

SHE HAD EXPECTED that Grace would be in by the time she got home, but the house was in darkness. She felt the draught when she went in, and moving through to the kitchen, found that one of the small windows lay open. The room still smelt of paint and, she guessed, Grace had left the window open to air the room. Lucy left the window ajar and headed upstairs to shower.

Afterwards, she towel dried her hair, then padded into the bedroom to change into her pyjamas. She called downstairs, lest Grace had arrived back, but the house was still quiet. She dropped the wet towel on the floor, and rifling through her bedside-cabinet drawer, pulled on a pair of pants. She grabbed her pyjamas from beneath her pillow, turned the T-shirt top the right side out, and pulled it on.

It was at this moment, her vision momentarily obscured by her T-shirt, that the first blow struck her.

The impact knocked her off the bed, her head striking the side of the still-open cabinet drawer.

She felt hands grip her legs, and, instinctively thrashed out, her foot connecting with soft tissue. She knew she had to pull the T-shirt away from her face, to at least gain her sight again. As she did so, the hands gripped her once more, this time around the ankles. She felt weight press on her feet, guessed her assailant was kneeling on her legs.

She managed to get the T-shirt pulled down and saw, for the first time, the figure sitting on her. Her stomach twisted; it was a man. She had guessed as much from the ferocity of the attack and the breadth of the hands holding her, but to have it confirmed made sweat pop on her skin. She was suddenly aware of her vulnerability, wearing only pants and a T-shirt.

He wore black jeans and a padded bomber jacket, open to reveal a neat frame. His face was covered by a balaclava, but something in the expression registered with her. His mouth was firm set, no joy in his conquest, efficient, businesslike.

Lucy reached back towards the upper drawer of her cabinet, in which she kept her service revolver. It was usually locked but she knew that it wasn't now, the bottom drawer still being open. She twisted, clawing for purchase against the exposed edge of the gap where the drawer had been pulled out.

The man holding her stood again, tugging at her feet, pulling her away from the cabinet, out towards the hallway opposite. Rather than flailing, she jerked both legs simultaneously, causing him to lose his grip on one as he shifted his hold to contain the right foot. In so doing, she was able to aim a kick directly at his face with her left foot. It was weak, no doubt, and he, standing, was almost out of range, but it connected enough with his jaw to jar him a little and she felt the right foot's hold loosen. She grabbed the leg of the bed next to her and gave another sharp thrash of the right foot, dislodging it from his grip now.

It was enough for her to gather herself, try to stand, using the bed to push herself up off the ground.

He was on her again now, though, grabbing at her hair, aiming to use that to pull her backwards, out of the room. But the shortness and dampness of her hair, coupled with the lack of grip on the gloves he wore, meant his hold was not as strong as he must have wished and, with a twist of her head, Lucy was free of him again, leaving him with a handful of her hair.

She turned on him, as he raised his fist to swing a punch. She dipped slightly and aimed a sharp jab at his throat, connecting with the windpipe. He jerked back quickly, both hands going to his throat. Lucy aimed a kick now, for his crotch, but he shifted and she connected instead with his hip, the kick hurting her bare foot more than it would his hipbone, she knew.

He came at her suddenly, this time grabbing her and flinging her across the room, away from the cabinet holding her gun. She landed on her side, banging her foot off the bed frame. He was lurching towards her again, his hands outstretched. In that instant, she saw, on the exposed skin of his forearm, the puckered edge of scarring.

'Lloyd!' she shouted. 'I know it's—'

The use of his name seemed to enrage him. He was on her, punching her once. She felt the crack of bone in her nose, felt the heat of blood burst over her mouth and chin. Then he was on top of her, using his weight to try to pin her down while she tried to buck him off.

Desperately, she looked around for anything near at hand to use. On top of the chest of drawers in the corner stood a brass bedside lamp. If she could just reach the electric cable, hanging down the side of the unit, she might be able to pull it to the ground and grab it.

Lloyd leaned one hand heavily on her left shoulder while, with the other hand, she could feel him tugging at her pants, as if to tear them off. She felt, for the first time, the rising bile in her mouth, the cold realisation that she was trapped and there was nothing she could do. In that moment, her powerlessness terrified her and infuriated her. She thrashed as hard as she could, determined to fight until the end.

'Lloyd!' someone shouted and, for a moment, he looked at Lucy, confused as to from where the voice had come.

He twisted and Lucy saw, behind him, Huey standing, in uniform, in the doorway, her gun aimed at the man.

Lucy could feel the tensing of his muscles as if he was considering lurching for his own partner.

'Get up!' Huey said.

Lloyd pushed himself up roughly, standing in front of Lucy, his hands raised slightly, as if unconvinced as to the seriousness of his partner's intentions.

'Take off the mask,' Huey said.

Lucy scrambled back from him, her body shuddering involuntarily. She felt the coldness of the wall against her back, reached up and used the windowsill to help steady her as she stood.

Lloyd pulled off the balaclava, his face flushed from the fight, his attention focused on his partner. 'This isn't—' he began.

Lucy turned suddenly and gripped the brass lampstand in her right hand. She swung it, the heavy base forwards, striking Lloyd on the side of the head.

'Fucker!' she screamed.

Lloyd staggered sideways with the blow, holding onto the end of her bed for stability. Lucy raised the lamp and struck again, harder this time, and he fell to the floor.

Moving across she stood over him, raising the lampstand and striking him, over and over, his head, his back, his arms. She tore at the padded jacket, which was cushioning the blows.

'It's done,' she heard Huey say and she gradually became aware again of the woman's presence in her room. Huey stood next to her, her hands on Lucy's arm, though Lucy couldn't tell quite when she had placed it there.

'He's done,' she said.

Lloyd lay on the ground, immobile, the first welts already vivid on his face and temple, blood gathering in the hollow of his cheek from the wounds, then overflowing and slowly tracing a path along the line of his neck.

Chapter Sixty-Seven

HUEY CUFFED LLOYD's hands, though he showed no signs of gaining consciousness. He was lying on his side, in a form of the recovery position, and they left him there while they sat, side by side on the bed, waiting for the response team that Huey had called.

Lucy wore a jacket and her pyjama bottoms now, but despite this, she could not control the shivers that coursed through her body in intermittent electric bursts. Huey put her arm around her shoulders and hugged her close, just as Lucy had done so many times before to other women in such circumstances. She knew, in fact, that she was the lucky one; that Huey's intervention had saved her.

'I can't . . .' she tried to say, but she seemed unable to control her jaw muscles, couldn't formulate the words.

'It's okay,' Huey said. 'I thought there was something screwy about his saying he was sick. I spotted his car in Greenway and followed him to see where he was going. He came here. I saw him going round the back of your house so I followed him in.'

'Tha . . . thanks . . .' Lucy said.

Huey hugged her a little tighter. 'I knew he was up to some-thing; all that stuff in Greenway. I just didn't think he'd do some-thing like . . . I'm so sorry.'

Lucy shook her head. 'It's not your fa . . . fault. He was your partner.'

'Exactly,' Huey said. 'If he was dirty, everyone will think that I was dirty, too. They still will, probably.'

'Not now,' Lucy said, grateful for the warmth of her embrace.

Huey shrugged. 'No matter,' she said.

Lucy looked at Lloyd where he lay, his breathing laboured. She could hear now, in the distance, the keening of sirens. She was suddenly aware of his injuries, of the fact she had attacked him when he was no longer threatening her.

'I need to help him—' she started, but Huey held her close.

'Fuck him,' she said. 'By the time I arrived, you'd managed to overpower him, defending yourself. He got everything he deserved.'

'He'll say different.'

'Then it'll be his word against ours,' Huey said.

'You'll get into trouble. If they find out you lied.'

'It's not a lie,' Huey said. 'You defended yourself. I'd have done exactly the same.'

Lucy leaned her weight against her, feeling suddenly sick, the bile burning her throat, the room seeming to spin around her.

Chapter Sixty-Eight

THE AMBULANCE CREW had patched her up and insisted on taking her to hospital to be checked over. She made it clear that nothing sexual had happened, though the doctor with whom she met still offered her the phone number of the Rape Crisis Line.

'It's normal to feel disempowered,' she said, 'after things like this. Even if it didn't end with—'

'I'm okay,' Lucy said. 'Honestly.'

'I heard you left him in quite a state,' the woman said, standing.

Lucy nodded.

'Good for you,' she said, offering her a brief smile. 'We'll get you a bed for the night.'

Lucy stood. 'I'm okay,' she said. 'I'd rather go home.'

The doctor looked at her sceptically. 'Well, with the painkillers you've been given, you can't drive.'

It wasn't a problem in the end, for her mother was waiting outside. She came across, as Lucy was brought out of the examination room, and embraced her, her hand cradling Lucy's head, holding her tight.

'Are you okay?'

Lucy smiled, a little embarrassed by her mother's presence.

'Where's Lloyd?'

'In surgery,' her mother said. 'He has a fractured skull from where you hit him with the lamp.'

Lucy felt the ground shifting a little, her balance suddenly unsteady. She told herself it would be the painkillers, knew that it was not.

'Is he going to pull through?'

Wilson shrugged. 'I don't really care,' she said.

Lucy nodded, and in doing so, again felt the corridor seem to slide a little to the left. She put out her hand to steady herself, grasping her mother's, instinctively.

'You're staying with me tonight,' her mother said.

'I need to get home,' Lucy said. 'Grace will be wondering where I am.'

'SOCO are in your house, Lucy,' her mother said. 'You're not fit to be on your own.'

'I'm fine,' Lucy said.

'You're staying with me and that's the end of it. We'll get word to Grace that she'll need to find somewhere else to stay tonight.'

LUCY LAY IN the bed in her mother's spare room. The décor was bland, functional. There was a bookcase with an assortment of paperbacks, mostly crime, which were well read, the spines broken. Lucy recognised some of the titles, some of the author names.

Atop the bookcase sat a small crab, made from shells. At first, in the dimness, Lucy thought it might be a souvenir, but something of it seemed familiar. She got out of bed and walked across to the bookcase, lifted the crab. It was made of two shells, stuck together, with eyes and a nose glued on. The eyes were slightly offset, the globules of glue thick. Lucy turned it over and felt her breath catch when she saw her own name, the C written backwards, pencilled on the bottom.

'You made it for me in P1.'

Her mother was standing in the doorway.

'You still have it,' Lucy said, replacing it gently on the shelf. 'In your spare room, too.'

Her mother took the dig, smiled mildly. 'You should sleep.'

'My mind's buzzing,' Lucy said. 'I might read.' She lifted one of the titles, vaguely recognised it as the name of a Tom Waits album she'd once bought.

'That's a good one,' her mother said.

'How do you find time to read?' Lucy asked.

'What else would I be doing?'

'Working,' Lucy said. 'Socialising.'

'At my age?'

Lucy smiled. 'You're not that old.'

'I'm past socialising,' she said.

'No men.'

Her mother shook her head. 'No men.'

'Why not?'

'The authority thing doesn't always work,' she said simply. 'Some people find it a bit . . .'

'Intimidating?'

Wilson smiled. 'Intimidating.'

'Dad didn't,' Lucy said.

'Yes, he did.'

Lucy considered the comment. Her mother was right, she guessed.

'Don't leave yourself alone, Lucy,' she said suddenly. 'You're not built to be on your own.'

'I have Grace.'

'Until she meets someone and moves out.'

'I'm not going to date someone just to have a roommate.'

'I'm not saying that,' Wilson said. 'But don't have it that the only person who comes to collect you from the hospital is your mother.'

'I'm not alone,' Lucy said, suddenly defensive.

'I know,' Wilson said, her tone conciliatory. 'Just . . . I'm just concerned about you.'

'I'm fine,' Lucy said. 'I might leave the book and just sleep.'

Her mother nodded. 'Goodnight, then.' She turned to leave, then came back quickly and embraced her daughter. Lucy was surprised, and a little saddened, by how thin her mother felt in her arms, how sharply her bones protruded through her skin, just as her father's had.

'Goodnight, Mum,' she said, her voice lost in the embrace.

Friday

Chapter Sixty-Nine

LUCY HAD WOKEN early the next morning. Her sleep had been solid, as a result of the painkillers, though, perhaps equally due to them, it had been rife with dreams that, even now, she could not quite recall if they hadn't actually happened.

She got up and stretched, testing the limits of her muscles, and was surprised to find herself aching from head to foot, more perhaps from tension than from the exertion of the fight.

She showered, twice, once with hot water and then with cold, scrubbing at her legs where Lloyd's grip had, in a few spots, left bruising. By the time she appeared out from the bathroom, her mother was up and had left out some clothes, clearly her own, which she guessed would fit Lucy.

They breakfasted together. Wilson was dressed for work, though told Lucy she would take the morning meeting and come back home.

'I'm coming with you,' Lucy said.

'No you're not.'

Lucy stared at her defiantly. 'If you don't take me in, I'll order a taxi.'

'You need time off.'

'And I'll take it when *I* choose,' Lucy said. 'Not today. Not because of this. I'm not giving him that.'

Her mother nodded lightly, seemingly realising there was nothing further she could say.

THE INCIDENT ROOM was different that morning, both because they had arrested one of their own in Lloyd and because of what had happened to Lucy. Some of the female officers swamped her when she came in, Tara among them, though on the periphery, to see how she was. The men kept their distance, but offered her sympathetic looks as they passed her.

Fleming came across to her when he came in.

'Don't,' Lucy said, before he could speak.

He smiled. 'I wasn't even going to try. Your mother filled me in.'

'What's the latest?'

'Lloyd made it through the surgery,' he said. 'He'll be charged this morning when he wakes. If he wakes.'

Lucy nodded, felt a knot tighten in her gut.

The door opened and Burns entered. He looked tired, his default state these days, Lucy thought. She remembered when he'd started in the District: he'd a full head of sandy hair, bright sharp eyes. Now he looked dull and faded and lifeless, like the picture of Mary Quigg Lucy had pinned to her wall. It no longer held the essence of the child, her life, her ferocious love for her brother. Burns, too, seemed bereft of the spark that had characterised his early days in Foyle.

'Morning all,' he said, scanning the room, his gaze settling briefly on Lucy. 'You've heard, no doubt, about last night's events. I've nothing to add except to offer all our good wishes to DS Black. It's good to see you up and about, Lucy.'

A few glances in Lucy's direction, a few whispered updates for colleagues late to the briefing. She nodded lightly in acknowledgement of Burns' comments.

'I interviewed Frankie McEwan again last night. I'd hoped that, with Lloyd in custody, he might be prepared to talk, take advantage of one of the Ulster First crowd being caught red-handed. But he's staying shtum. Which makes me think that Lloyd isn't the one he's afraid of. We have, however, been able to tie Lloyd to two other assaults in Greenway over the past week – Frankie's father and a Romanian man named Andre Lupei. But this doesn't help us with the killing of Bobby McLean.'

'Do you think Lloyd was involved in that, too?'

The voice came from across the room. Burns looked over and nodded. 'I do. Lloyd was involved in raids of drugs shipments last year. Several were robbed before our colleagues in the Drugs Squad were planning on intercepting them. We think Lloyd was feeding information to Ulster First who then used the drugs to start selling in Greenway and make a name for themselves. The ACC and I are of like mind in thinking that with Bobby wanted for the killing of Martin Givens and already implicated in the sale of legal highs, Lloyd panicked that he'd talk, offer up Lloyd in return for a reduced sentence. So Lloyd, or those with whom he's involved, killed Bobby and used the gay slogan as a way of hiding their involvement.'

'Can forensics tie Lloyd to McLean's flat?'

Burns nodded. 'We know they were friends; he can explain the presence of his hair and prints there very easily if he wants to. That doesn't prove he killed Bobby. Our main hope was that Frankie would implicate Lloyd in it; but he's refusing to comment now.'

Fleming leaned close to Lucy. 'If he saves himself, he's back with his father. If he doesn't, he's going to jail.'

'And he's choosing jail?'

Fleming nodded. 'How much can one kid hate their father?'

LUCY HAD TAKEN Wednesday afternoon off work. She and Grace spent it cleaning her room. In the end, the stains of Lloyd's blood on the carpet had bedded so deeply that they tore the whole lot up and ordered new flooring. Grace slept in the room with her on both Wednesday and Thursday nights.

FRIDAY MORNING BROKE in a mist of rain, which draped itself across the city. Lucy and Grace sat in silence as the TV news reported on the Brexit result that had seen the Leave campaign win a slim majority.

'It's like the world's changed in some way,' Grace offered. 'But I don't know how.'

Lucy nodded, wondering how the Lupeis, and many families like them, would feel this morning, wakening to the news that the country had voted to cut ties with the rest of the European Union.

Fleming called her just after 8.30 a.m., as she was getting ready to leave the house and head down to the PPU in Maydown.

'Meet me at Jackie Moss's place for breakfast,' he said.

Lucy drove up through Greenway. She passed the Lupeis' old house, the windows boarded up, the shadow of *Romans Out* still visible on the brickwork even though the paint had been removed.

Posters promising £350 million per week to be returned to the NHS remained hanging on the lamp-posts, even as the lie was already being retracted by a politician on the radio news.

Fleming was sitting at the usual table when she went into the Bluebell Café. He was already tucking into a fry, a mug of tea steaming on the table next to his plate. Lucy had barely sat down when Annie set down a second fry for her.

'For your kindness when Jackie had his wee accident,' she said.

Lucy smiled and thanked her, looking at Fleming who had scrupulously not reacted to the shooting being referred to now as a 'wee accident'.

'How is he?'

'He's on the throne,' Annie said. 'He'll be over in a minute.' She laid her hand lightly on Lucy's shoulder, a brief contact, and then returned to the counter.

'He's back at work?'

'An unstoppable force,' Fleming said, forking a piece of sausage.

'So, what's the occasion?' Lucy asked.

'Charles Dougan has vanished,' Fleming said.

'Vanished?'

'Vanished,' he repeated. 'Literally.'

'What happened to him?'

'That's what we're here to find out,' Fleming said.

At that, the door to the kitchen opened and Jackie Moss struggled out. He looked to have shed a few pounds since last Lucy had seen him. As he moved down towards them, a second figure appeared behind him, holding his arm to offer him support. Lucy recognised him instantly as Stephen Welland.

'Officers,' Jackie said, his forehead gleaming with the sheen of sweat the exertion of his movement had elicited.

'How are you, Jackie?' Fleming asked.

'Never been better,' Jackie said, the comment punctuated with a wracking cough. Welland pulled him over a chair, helped him to sit.

'Bad news about Charles Dougan,' Fleming said.

Jackie feigned ignorance. 'What's happened to him?'

'That's the big question,' Fleming said. 'He's just disappeared.'

'Like Jimmy Hoffa,' Moss said. 'Do people still know about Hoffa?' He glanced at Welland who pantomimed a shrug. Moss laughed, slapping his knee with one hand. Again, the laugh dissolved into a cough.

'You wouldn't know anything about it, would you?'

Jackie turned to Welland, again in shock. Welland reciprocated. A real double act, Lucy thought.

'I know nothing about him,' Moss said.

'The rumour was he ordered the hit on you,' Fleming said. 'So the thinking goes that—'

'I finished what he started?' Moss asked. 'I've no interest in that kind of thing. I'm just glad that things have settled back into the way they were.'

'Not quite,' Fleming said. 'There's a new order in Greenway.'

Moss inclined his head towards Welland. 'There's always a need for new blood once the bad blood's been let. The old guard can't go on for ever.'

'And poor Charlie Dougan peaked too soon?'

'You know me,' Moss said, smiling, 'I always like to cut out the middle man.' He turned to Welland. 'Get me a few of those bangers in a sandwich, son, would you?'

Welland nodded and cut across to the counter.

'Good to see someone has benefited from Dougan's misfortunes,' Lucy said.

'What? Stephen? He's a bright lad. Got mixed up with the wrong crowd, but that's all over now.'

'Ulster First? I thought that was his brainchild.'

'Some people are easy led,' Moss said, then quietened down as Welland approached again.

Lucy studied the younger man's face, the sharpness in his glance. He was playing Moss just as he had played Dougan, and used Lloyd and McLean and McEwan. He laid the plate of sausages and bread in front of Jackie, then moved back to the counter and stood, watching him as he ate, a man biding his time.

THAT EVENING, HAVING left Grace at the cinema where she was meeting Ciaran, Lucy went to her mother's house. They sat together in the kitchen, drinking tea and eating biscuits. Lucy talked about Brexit, about the bloody carpet, about Grace, about the redecorating of the house. Her mother listened, as if waiting to learn the ulterior purpose of her visit. She struggled to hide her pleasure when she realised that there was none.

'What's the latest with Lloyd?' Lucy asked as they walked out to the hallway, having announced that she had to go home.

'He's recovered enough to talk,' her mother said. 'And enough to be charged,' she added. 'We're still trying to link him to Bobby McLean. Even if we don't find that, he'll be done for what he tried to do to you.'

'Good.'

Her mother winced lightly. 'You'll have to give evidence. You know that.'

Lucy nodded. 'I know.' She took out her keys. 'That reminds me,' she added, 'I've something for you.'

She returned from the car with the box that had been left for her on Tara's desk. Her mother opened it and peered inside, smiling quizzically. Her expression changed when she saw the toy inside. She looked up at Lucy uncertainly.

'I know I said I was lonely but this is a little strange,' she said, trying to force a laugh in the hope it was some ill-conceived joke.

'That was left for me in the Strand Road,' Lucy said. 'The day after Tara and Mickey's incident.'

'Mickey?' her mother asked, indicating the box.

'I'd guess so,' Lucy said. 'It was sent by internal mail.'

Her mother shook her head. 'The bloody moron.'

'I'll be in to make a statement,' Lucy said. 'It'll back up what Tara said. Every word.'

Her mother put the box down on the hall table, straightened up. 'You're sure, Lucy? You know how the rest will react to it.'

Lucy nodded. 'I'm sure. It's the right thing to do.'

Her mother nodded. 'It's *a* right thing to do at the very least,' she said.

Lucy smiled. 'I'd best be off. Grace is out so I'm going to have a drink and watch rubbish on TV.'

'You could stay here tonight,' her mother offered, the comment so off hand as almost to go unnoticed.

'Maybe next time,' Lucy said, and realised that she actually meant it. 'I need an hour to myself in the house, I think. Alone. To get used to it again.'

'You know you're welcome anytime,' her mother said. 'I don't . . . I don't want there to be any more bad blood between us, Lucy.'

'There's no bad blood,' Lucy said, but her mother interrupted her.

'I know I hurt you. When you were young. I'm sorry. I shouldn't have left you. But, please, don't be angry with me,' she said. 'Please.'

Lucy looked at her, fully aware of the fragility in her features. She smiled. 'I'm not, Mum,' she said.

She opened the door and stepped out into the freshness of the evening air. The summer stretched before her, the coming months uncertain but rich with promise.

Acknowledgements

As EVER, I am indebted to a number of people who are instrumental in helping each book come to life, not least my friends, colleagues and students, past and present, for their support over the past decade.

Thanks to Jody Kirby, Susan McGilloway and Stephen Birkett for their advice on various aspects of this book. Any mistakes are entirely my own.

I'm hugely grateful to the teams in Corsair in the UK – especially Hayley, Olivia and my editor James Gurbutt – and Witness Impulse in the US – particularly Dan, Emily and Margaux.

This book is dedicated with thanks to Jenny Hewson of RCW and Emily Hickman of The Agency who have been both good friends and wise counsellors throughout my writing career.

Thanks as always to my family – the McGilloways, Dohertys, O'Neills and Kerlins – and most especially Carmel, Joe and Dermot, and my parents, Laurence and Katrina, for all that they have done and continue to do for me.

Finally, my love and thanks to Tanya and our kids, Ben, Tom, David and Lucy.

About the Author

BRIAN McGILLOWAY is the *New York Times* bestselling author of *Little Girl Lost, Someone You Know,* and *The Forgotten Ones.* He lives near the Irish borderlands with his wife and their four children.

Discover great authors, exclusive offers, and more at hc.com.